LOVE PROOF

ROBIN BRANDE

RYER PUBLISHING

LOVE PROOF
By Robin Brande

Published by Ryer Publishing
www.ryerpublishing.com
Original Copyright 2012 by Robin Brande (writing as Elizabeth Ruston)
Revised Edition 2014 by Robin Brande
www.robinbrande.com
All rights reserved.
Cover photos Dreamstime.com
Cover design by Robin Ludwig Design, Inc.
www.gobookcoverdesign.com
ISBN: 978-1-952383-32-8

❀ Created with Vellum

ALSO BY ROBIN BRANDE

Romance

Love Proof

Freefall

Heart of Ice

Fire and Ice

Winnie Parsons Mysteries

The Genius Track

A Man of Appetites

A Drop of Sweat

The Long Gray Hook

The Slip of a Rib

Dove Season Series

Dove Season

Finder

Seeker

Believer

Bradamante Saga

Book of Earth

Book of Water

LOVE PROOF

"You're the hired gun?" Joe asked.

Sarah made two pistols with her fingers and shot Joe Burke in the gut. It felt remarkably satisfying.

She had been looking forward to the look of shock on his face when she showed up at her first deposition, the one in San Diego, but instead Joe had the bad judgment to smile.

"Well, welcome to it, Red," he said. "Nice to have you along."

"Red, huh?" said the other lawyer, a man named Paul Chapman. "You two know each other?"

"No," they both answered at once. Joe shot her an amused glance.

They took their seats around the hotel conference table, Joe and his client on one side, Sarah and Paul Chapman across from them, the court reporter at the end of the table between them.

"This ought to be interesting," Joe said, looking Sarah in the eye.

She had learned that sometimes the best strategy when dealing with other lawyers was to say nothing at all. Let her opponents talk and talk, let them bluster and threaten and boast, until finally they realized they sounded more idiotic and less effective with each passing moment. That was when Sarah would quietly enter back into the conversation with one simple statement—"The judge won't see it that way," or "You can try that, although the jury in my last trial gave the plaintiff absolutely nothing for the same argument"—then she would quietly wait again while the lawyer blustered and threatened some more.

In the end, Sarah usually got what she wanted, whether it was a favorable settlement for her client or a ruling from a judge on a key motion. Her opponents had learned over the last five years never to underestimate her. Not to be fooled by the package she came in. The petite, feminine redhead in front of them could be as lethal at trial as any silver-haired, seasoned litigator or one of those tough-talking women Sarah used to look up to until she actually had to try cases against them and saw them for what they were.

What Sarah realized was that nearly everyone in the law business was insecure. Some of them tried to cover it with fancy offices and expensive cars and other proof that they were successful and unafraid. Others drank. Some believed the more they bullied people, the less likely anyone would notice their own weaknesses.

But Sarah noticed. She'd been noticing her whole life. And finally she reached a point in her own career where she could use that knowledge to bring her the kind of success she had worked so hard for since high school.

Until one single moment six months ago had brought it all crashing down around her. And now she found herself in this cramped conference room, sitting as calmly and as casually as she could across from the man who had hurt her almost as much as losing everything six months ago.

But he never needed to see that on her face. So when Joe spoke directly to her—*"This ought to be interesting"*—Sarah practiced what she'd perfected since the last time they saw each other. She simply gazed at him in return, saying nothing, keeping her face as neutral as possible.

While Joe made absolutely no effort at all to hide a wicked smile.

HE'D FILLED out since she last saw him, Sarah thought. Not fattened up—far from it—but become broader in the chest and shoulders, as if he put on more muscle. He even looked taller than the six-foot-two she remembered, although she doubted he kept growing between the ages of twenty-five and thirty-one. Maybe he'd just grown into a man, period. Better late than never.

He wore his dark hair shorter now, clipped closer to his head, and his face was clean-shaven instead of scruffed up with that constant stubble she had gotten used to. He looked good—better than she expected, better than she had hoped—dressed in his navy suit, striped shirt, and tie. She wanted to find him hollow-eyed and haunted, with the look of a man who knew his best years were already behind him. Instead he looked fit, strong, and, worst of all, content.

Joe glanced up just then, and Sarah quickly started typing again on her laptop. That was all she needed, for him to catch her studying him.

Maybe it wasn't so surprising that he looked better, she thought. They had all been so unhealthy and malnourished in law school, living off of fast food, caffeine, and beer. Sarah kept up with the first two, unfortunately, for another several years before finally seeing the light, but obviously Joe had taken good care of himself. The results were...impressive. She couldn't deny it, even if she would never admit it to Burke's face.

But she was glad she wore her best suit today: the slim black skirt and perfectly-tailored jacket, with a white silk shell underneath. Her hair had behaved, looking smooth and under control and curling only at the ends the way she wanted. Normally it fought her—hard. She had taken special care with her makeup, too, giving her eyes more drama than she normally would for a daytime work event, and making sure the color on her lips would last for several hours.

It had been a long time since she had a reason to put on her full lawyer uniform and war paint. She'd gotten a little too used to spending her days bare-faced and in workout clothes. But she was back now, ready to do battle. And she knew she looked the part.

Joe wasn't the only one who had grown up over the past six years, Sarah thought. She couldn't help wondering if he noticed.

. . .

"I THINK I have something for you," Sarah's friend Mickey said when he called her the week before. "Get off the couch and come down here this afternoon."

"I'm not on the couch," she said, panting into the phone.

"Then get off of whoever you're doing right now and get down here," Mickey said before hanging up.

Sarah ended the call and her music kicked back on. She had both ear buds in and had already run two miles on the treadmill. Now Neko Case sang to her while she sweated through the next quarter mile. She already had her lineup of music to carry her through the last three miles, but glancing at the clock, she knew she had to cut it short or she'd never get the weight-lifting in, too. As much as she hated short-changing any workout—and what a laugh that was, considering how she felt about exercise as little as a year ago—she knew she needed the time to go home and shower and change and make herself look like a lawyer again. A working lawyer. An employed one. God, she hoped so.

Whatever the job was, she'd take it. If Mickey really had come through for her, she owed him something big. Just not the thing he pretended he wanted.

Sarah slowed to a walk, then hit the stop button a few minutes later. She signaled her trainer, Angie, who had her own ear buds in as she worked through a weight-lifting session of her own. Sarah's time didn't start for another half hour, but she hoped Angie wouldn't mind taking her early. This could be it. This could be Sarah's salvation.

Even, as she found out a few hours later, with Joe Burke on the other side.

· · ·

"It's just a contract job," Mickey's boss, Calvin, told her. "We decided to bring in someone from the outside instead of using manpower from in here."

Mickey handed Sarah an expandable file that was expanded to its full capacity. "Here are the pleadings so far. It'll probably take you the weekend to read through them."

"Are you saying I have the job?" Sarah asked both him and Calvin.

"Mickey says you're a killer," Calvin answered, rising to his feet and signaling the interview was over. "Check in with HR and they'll get all your paperwork."

"We haven't discussed the pay yet," Sarah said, and even though Mickey gave her a look that said, *Not now*, Sarah persisted. She was doing this for the money, not for the prestige. Especially since there was absolutely no prestige in being the traveling lawyer who would take depositions all around the country for the next five months or so while the real attorneys on the case would sit comfortably in their plush Los Angeles offices waiting for her to report back in.

Calvin mentioned a number, and Sarah shook her head. As desperate as she was for the job, she guessed Mickey's firm needed her, too. It was hard to find a lawyer with her experience and reputation—or at least her former reputation—who would be willing to fly to four or five different cities each week and sit through hours of testimony about how the firm's client had ruined the plaintiffs' lives.

And if Sarah could actually make something of the case, she thought, come up with some defense none of the other attorneys had considered, maybe this would be her ticket to a full-time job.

But she held all that in check as she haggled over her price. It amused her how no one sat down again—the three of them stood clustered in front of Calvin's door, just where they'd been when he rose to see her out. Sitting down, accepting a lower elevation than the others, might signal a loss of status. Sarah always liked to notice the different methods her fellow attorneys used to try to hold on to their power.

Finally they reached a deal. If the job really was going to last only five months, Sarah knew she would need every single penny of that salary to dig herself out of the debts she'd incurred since April. She might even be able to rebuild some of her savings, to protect against the next dry spell if this job didn't turn into something more permanent.

But she couldn't think that far ahead. She had work now, and that was what she needed.

She offered her hand first to Calvin, then to Mickey.

"She's a killer, all right," Calvin said to Mickey.

Mickey held Sarah's hand a little too long. "Told you."

Sarah gave her former law school classmate a wry look and a raised eyebrow until Mickey chuckled and released his grasp.

"Sorry to hear about that whole mess," Calvin said in parting.

Sarah nodded. "Unfortunate," was all she said.

The worst experience of my life, was what she thought.

· · ·

The first series of depositions would begin in San Diego, then continue to Pasadena, San Jose, and Fresno. But Sarah knew this first one would set the tone for all the others.

Set the tone between her and Joe.

Unfortunately, two full hours passed before she got to ask a single question.

Paul Chapman was one of those lawyers who didn't understand the crux of a case. He had his standard deposition questions—ones he'd probably learned in his first year as a lawyer, twenty or however many years ago—and Sarah assumed he never deviated from them since, no matter how irrelevant they were to the particular case before him.

"Where were you born? ... What are your parents' names? ... Where did you go to high school? ... Do you have any degrees? ... Describe your work experience ... When were you married? ... How many children? ... Their ages?"

Sarah could barely contain her irritation. The deposition could be over in one hour, two at most—even with her questions as well as Chapman's—if only he'd get to the real issue at hand:

When did you buy your hair iron? Where? How many times per week did you use it? When did it catch on fire? What happened then? What injuries, if any, did you sustain? What expenses, if any, did you incur?

Out, deposition over, on to the airport.

At one point, when Chapman actually had the idiocy to ask the woman whether she tried to call the toll-free number on the Atheena Hair Glory website to ask them what to do in case her hair caught on fire, Sarah looked up and caught Joe smiling at her. She narrowed her eyes, and just for something to do, said, "Objection."

Chapman turned to her, obviously out of sorts. It was the first time either Sarah or Joe had said anything to interrupt his brilliant line of questioning.

"On what basis?" Chapman asked.

"Sustained," Joe said, even though only a judge had the power to do that. "Are you almost done, Paul? I think we could all use a break."

Chapman flipped through his notes. *Notes*, Sarah thought, as if he couldn't ask those useless questions from memory. How did a guy like that get to be a partner in one of the largest insurance defense firms in L.A.? But Sarah knew very well the inequities of a climb up the ladder of a firm. She had been a partner once, too. Briefly, for what it was worth.

And that turned out to be not much at all.

"Have you done anything to try to restore the damaged hair?" Chapman asked the woman.

"Like what?" she shot back. "Get a damn wig?"

"Yes," Chapman answered, undeterred by the woman's tone, "something like that."

"Hats," the woman said. "Lots of ugly-ass hats."

"Okay, thank you, Darlene," Joe said, gently touching the woman's arm. "I think we need a break here. Back in fifteen?"

Sarah stood up and stretched, then turned over her legal pad and closed the lid to her laptop before heading out into the hallway. The court reporter joined her as they both went in search of a restroom.

"I'm Marcela," the court reporter said, offering her hand.

"Sarah Henley—but you already know that," Sarah added with a smile. The court reporter would have listed the names of all the attorneys present at the beginning of her deposition transcript.

Unlike some lawyers she had met over the years, Sarah always made a point of being nice to the support staff, whether they were court reporters, bailiffs, legal assistants, law clerks—anyone and everyone who did the behind-the-scenes work that she knew made the machinery hum. Having spent years as a secretary herself, she understood the value of a good assistant.

"Hope you don't mind me saying this," Marcela said, "but it's nice to see a woman in there for a change."

"Thanks," Sarah said, pushing open the door to the bathroom. "It's nice having you in there, too. Balances out the macho."

"That poor woman," Marcela said, shaking her head.

Sarah smiled politely. "I'm sorry, I'm not allowed to talk to you about that."

"Oh! Of course," Marcela said, clearly embarrassed. She disappeared into one of the stalls. "I'm sorry," she continued from inside. "I shouldn't have said anything."

The bathroom door swung open again, and Joe Burke's client entered. She frowned when she saw Sarah, and quickly went to one of the empty stalls. Sarah was used to opposing parties hating her—of course she was the enemy, the evil lawyer, all of that. It went with the territory. She rarely took it personally.

But she'd also stopped trying to make sure everyone

liked her. If people thought she was evil, so be it. If they thought she was a bitch, oh well. Like her mother always said, "You're not a bite of candy. Not everybody's going to love you."

Sarah checked her hair, her makeup, her suit, and satisfied that she still looked put together, quickly moved to the last empty stall before the other two women could emerge. She stayed where she was until she heard them both leave. Then she came out and spent a few extra minutes washing her hands and looking herself in the eye in the mirror.

He's just a man. He's no one special. He was six years ago.

No, Sarah corrected herself, *five years, ten months, and three days.*

She gave herself a mean, steely gaze in the mirror.

"Go show him," she whispered to herself.

Although she knew what she really meant was, *Make him suffer.*

2

"Hello, Mrs. Franklin, thank you for coming in today," Sarah began. "My name is Sarah Henley. I'm the attorney for Mason Manufacturing. They provided the heating element for the Atheena hair iron you purchased."

Darlene Franklin folded her arms over her chest and glared at Sarah.

"Speaking personally," Sarah continued, "I'm very sorry for what you went through. I'm sure that had to be horrible."

She could see the woman soften. Just a little.

"Is that official?" Joe asked.

"As I said," Sarah repeated without looking at him, "I was speaking personally, woman to woman. Now, Mrs. Franklin," she went on before Joe could make any more of that statement—which really was just a tactic to make his client feel more comfortable and hopefully less hostile—"I only have a few questions for you, then we can let you be on your way."

She smiled, but Mrs. Franklin did not smile back. That was fine.

Sarah asked her few simple questions—fewer than ten of them—then smiled again at Joe's client and thanked her for her time.

The court reporter waited for Joe, to see if he had any questions of his own.

"We're done," he said. "Thank you." He took a few minutes to escort his client from the room, then returned, checking his watch. "Next one's at one o'clock, then I assume we're all on the same five-thirty flight. Think you can condense some of your questions, Paul, so we can make it?"

"I'll take as much time as I need," Chapman answered.

"Of course." Joe looked at Sarah, obviously expecting her to signal in some way that she, too, thought Chapman was an idiot. Instead she resumed typing her notes from the deposition.

"How about you, Sarah?" Joe asked. "Are you on the five-thirty?"

"I don't know," she said without looking up, "probably." Although she knew very well she had chosen that flight instead of the one two hours later. She hoped to have a light dinner somewhere cheap, then go to bed at a decent hour so she could wake up early enough to work out before the next morning's deposition. But none of that was Joe's business.

The court reporter finished putting away her equipment. Sarah looked up and smiled. "Thank you, Marcela. We appreciate your work."

"You'll see me again," Marcela said. "Our company got

the contract for all of the west coast depositions. I'll be at some of them next week."

"See you then," Sarah said. She accidentally caught Joe's eye, and quickly looked back at her laptop screen.

"Sarah, can I talk to you for a minute?" Joe asked.

"Not right now," she said. She typed a few more lines, just as cover.

"Sarah?"

"What?" she answered, not bothering to hide her annoyance.

"Can I interest you in lunch?"

"No, thank you."

"You buying?" Paul Chapman asked him.

"No," Joe said. "I was going to make Sarah pay."

Funny, she thought, looking him straight in the eye, *I was thinking the same thing about you.*

3

———

The woman at the afternoon deposition had hair not that different from Sarah's. It was that same dark auburn, not the lighter shade of red Sarah always thought was so pretty. It had the same thick texture, and even though the woman had obviously blown it straight, Sarah could imagine the thousand crazy, mini spirals just waiting to pop out again the minute her hair was wet.

"It used to be long," the woman told Chapman after he finished an hour's worth of irrelevant questions and finally got around to asking about her hair. "Even longer than hers," she said, pointing at Sarah. "I was growing it out since high school. People said it was my nicest feature. Then that iron thing of yours caught it on fire and now all I've got left is this..."

She held up a hank of the shortened ends, but Chapman couldn't be bothered to look.

"Did you call the toll-free number on the Atheena website?" he asked.

"Did I what?"

"The toll-free number," he said. "It's there for a reason. It's under Customer Service."

"No, I didn't call some *number*," the woman snapped, her anger practically steaming out through her pores. "A friend of mine had to rush me to Urgent Care. My scalp was *burned*. You could smell the hair—it was disgusting. They had to cut a whole bunch of it off—even the part that was okay—so they could put bandages all over my head. And then I still had scabs all over for weeks—"

"Mm-hm, mm-hm," Chapman answered, sounding bored and still not looking up from his notes.

Sarah saw the woman turn to Joe and give him a look that asked, *Am I allowed to punch him?*

As soon as Chapman finished, Sarah jumped right in. "Ms. McIntyre, I'm sorry we didn't get to hear your whole story before. Please start at the beginning again and walk us through it, moment by moment. You said you felt the unit getting hotter..."

Sarah enjoyed the psychology of law as much as she enjoyed law itself. She liked trying to understand what people wanted and needed in every situation so she could mold a case to her advantage.

And just as Sarah expected she would, Joe's client seemed to calm down—to sound less hostile—the more Sarah let her talk. She had seen it before with people involved in law suits: this desperate and angry need to make someone listen, to feel like they'd finally been heard.

It was why some parties refused to settle until they had their "day in court." Sometimes all it took was that one day. They just wanted the formality of sitting at a table next to their lawyer, with their opponent at a table nearby, and a judge sitting behind the raised bench in front of them. They wanted to see the faces of a jury looking at them sympathetically. They wanted to see all the trappings of law they'd grown up watching on TV: the *Hear ye, hear ye, all rise, the Honorable So-and-So presiding,* even though that wasn't how it was in the real world.

And more times than not, just that one day was enough. Litigation was nerve-wracking. People didn't realize how stressful it was to actually be part of the pageantry of court. To have to sit there silent and unemotional while people told lies about you.

That was how it always sounded, Sarah knew: like lies. It was the nature of law to pit one person's story against another person's completely different one, but lay people didn't understand how brutal that would feel while they had to be on their best behavior in front of a judge and jury.

So even though many lawyers gave up trying to settle a case once they began their opening statements, Sarah always scheduled time at the end of that first day of trial to meet again with her opponent to see if the client had changed his or her mind. If not that day, then Sarah would try again once the client had had a chance to testify. *Just listen to me!* their whole attitudes seemed to scream. *I want someone to hear my story!* So Sarah listened, and it had been one of the secrets of her success.

When Ms. McIntyre finally finished taking Sarah

through the events, step by step, Sarah asked her a few more questions about where she purchased the product and when.

"Thank you," Sarah said. "No further questions." She saved the work on her laptop and immediately began packing it away along with her files. She could catch up on her notes at the airport.

She purposely didn't look over at Joe. She had felt his eyes on her the entire time she questioned his client, and she felt tempted to check for his reaction: did he approve of the way she was handling it? Did he think she was good? Did he still think she was smart?

Don't care, don't care, don't care...

She knew the secret to remaining immune to him was to keep her defenses on high alert every second the two of them were together. Sarah had no intention of melting into a little puddle at his feet, desperate for any sort of acknowledgment or compliment.

He could tell her she had the most brilliant legal mind of the twenty-first century—that she was beautiful, gorgeous, that he couldn't believe he had lived without her all this time —and it wouldn't make up for one minute of the anguish he'd put her through. He could think whatever he wanted to about her. Sarah was there to do a job.

And if she could somehow figure out a way to win this case against him as part of the bargain, then bonus.

She retrieved her carry-on bag from where she had stored it in the corner of the room, thanked Marcela for her work, then nodded to Chapman and Burke. "Gentlemen." Then she strode through the door and headed for the hotel lobby.

She could see taxis lined up outside. She wanted to get to one before either of the other lawyers could catch up with her and suggest they share a ride to the airport.

She needed the time alone. This was only her first day, and already she felt drained. Not from the two depositions —those were nothing. It was Joe. Being in the same room with him. Hearing his voice again. Seeing the way his body had changed, improved, and wondering what new muscles and contours hid beneath those expensive lawyer clothes. Looking into that face again and realizing it had only grown more handsome and masculine over time.

Damn him.

Her friend Mickey had asked her, point blank, once they were alone again in his boss's office and Sarah had just accepted the job, "Are you going to be able to handle spending all that time with Burke?"

She pretended it was a stupid question. "Of course."

"I mean without killing him?"

"We were children back then," she said.

"I don't know," Mickey said. "I seem to recall I had a kid of my own by then, so we all must have been at least out of puberty."

"Barely, in his case," Sarah said.

"This could go one of two ways," Mickey said. "Either you're going to be the best lawyer our client could ever have for this case because you'll pummel Burke to the ground. Or..."

Sarah waited, but Mickey was having too much fun.

"Or?" she prompted, knowing she was playing into his hands.

"Or Burke is going to steal you away from me for the second time."

"You and I were never together, Mickey."

"In my dreams we were."

"How's Julie doing?"

"Julie who?" he asked.

SARAH SAT in the gate area eating a teriyaki vegetable and rice bowl from the food court and checking her e-mail on her phone. She saw Joe out of the corner of her eye, but continued staring at the small screen. Even though she could almost feel him as he came within the last ten feet of her.

Without asking, he took the seat next to her.

Sarah couldn't help but turn her head just the slightest and glance at him, but then she went back to appearing busy.

"How are you, Sarah?"

"Fantastic." She could feel the heat from his nearest leg and arm, even though both were at least four inches away.

"No," Joe said, his voice serious, "I mean how are you really?"

Sarah forced herself to turn to him and smile. "What, are we going to talk about our hopes and feelings now, Burke? I don't think so."

He studied her face for one long moment, then nodded. He stood and grasped the handle on his bag and found another seat far away.

Sarah looked down at her phone again, pretending to be absorbed. But she couldn't help swallowing the bitter taste in her mouth. She had planned to say something exactly like that to Burke, but it felt much better in her imagination. He looked hurt, and she should have been glad. She'd rehearsed it that way.

She sat up straighter and crossed a different leg. She still wore her suit. She could have changed into something more comfortable in one of the airport bathrooms, but Sarah preferred keeping her armor on until she was safely away from Joe for the night.

She had dressed very carefully that morning, all the way down to the black bra and panties that reminded her she was a warrior, a black belt in this game. She had no intention of ruining the effect by packing her outfit away and putting on the only other outfit she'd brought: loose workout pants, a T-shirt, and running shoes. She noticed Joe had taken off his coat and tie, but he still wore the suit pants and shirt.

Everything was power, Sarah knew, clothes in particular. She had known that since childhood, when her own generic jeans and off-brand shoes had marked her as poorer than most of the kids at her school, even though none of them would have qualified as rich.

There were so many nuances to how people saw you, Sarah thought: whether they assumed you were better than they were or worse. And she intended to capture and hold every single advantage she might gain now in her adult life, no matter how small that advantage might seem to someone else.

If wearing a tight skirt and high heels for a few more

hours might make her appear more powerful than she felt at the moment, then they were worth it.

She took another bite of vegetables and rice, no longer enjoying the taste. But she needed the energy. It was the same reason she decided to make sure she got at least seven hours of sleep every night while she was on the road. And she wouldn't have a drop of alcohol, even if a day spent with both Paul Chapman and Joe Burke would drive any woman to drink. Each of them for different reasons.

Sarah understood the rules of engagement: stay alert, always be watching for opportunities, and never let your guard down.

Check, check, and check.

She stole a glance at Joe, who now sat reading his own phone. Keeping his own gravitational force to himself, way on the other side of the room.

She felt it, and it bothered her. That familiar, comfortable pull of a body she used to know so well. A body she used to claim with as much right as if it had been her own. And a body that treated hers the same way.

Sarah sighed and stopped trying to read the irritating little screen. Her eyes naturally wandered in search of something more interesting.

And found Joe's in return.

Sarah didn't look away this time. She needed to be fiercer than that. The key was to have absolutely no expression on her face.

Joe obviously played by the same rule book. When he was done looking at her, a few long moments later, he calmly returned to his own work.

But Sarah knew: no matter how he acted now, she had gotten to him, if only just a little. How did she know? Because he was the one to make the first move.

And she was the one who shut it down.

Victory would taste a lot sweeter if only her chest would unclench. She'd have to work on that.

That, and the way all the cells in her body seemed to pull her in one direction whenever the man came too near.

But that was easy to fix: just stay as far away as possible.

4

Paul Chapman lumbered past her up the aisle of the airplane.

"I'm in back," he said unnecessarily. Sarah nodded as if she cared.

Joe had already boarded and sat a few rows ahead of her. Close enough that she had a view of him sitting in his aisle seat.

What was it, she wondered, that made him look so different? It wasn't just his filled-out frame. It was the way he carried himself now, no longer slouching with that easygoing gait. Like the difference between a loose-jointed puppy and a full-grown dog.

And his hair looked good cropped close like that. Not unruly the way she remembered. Everything about him looked better, unfortunately.

Sarah closed her eyes and leaned back.

"Here on business?" the man next to her asked.

"Mm," she answered, hoping to discourage any conversation.

"What are you, one of those women stockbrokers?" he asked.

Good guess, Sarah thought, for a guy obviously using it as a line. He must think a woman would appreciate being taken for a stockbroker instead of someone's assistant or a salesgirl or whatever else he really thought she was.

Sarah turned and opened her eyes just a slit. "Surgeon," she said. "I took out a brain today. I'm really exhausted. So if you don't mind..." She closed her eyes and leaned back again.

"Surgeon?" the man said loudly enough that when Sarah opened her eyes again she could see Joe looking back at her with a smile playing on his lips.

"Yep," she answered just as loudly. "Today brains, tomorrow intestines. We do it all."

"Are you shittin' me?" the man asked.

"No, I am not shitting you," she said with perfect enunciation. "Now if you don't want me to kill my next patient in the morning, you'd better let me get some sleep."

"You're shittin' me," the guy muttered.

Sarah risked one more quick check on Joe. He'd obviously been waiting for her to meet his eye, because as soon as she did, he turned his fingers into scissors and cut at a downward angle.

"Big vasectomy tomorrow afternoon," Sarah added. "Wouldn't want me to make a mistake there, would you?"

Joe nodded, satisfied. Then he turned back around.

And Sarah immediately regretted what she had done.

Why was she playing with Burke? They weren't friends.

They weren't anything. If she could take back that last statement, she would.

"Now I know you're shittin' me," the man said with renewed confidence. "Nobody does all that."

Sarah shrugged. "I'm the best. And we're done here, sport. No more talking." She popped in her ear buds, even though she wouldn't be able to turn on her music until the plane leveled off.

She wished she had never let herself get drawn into the conversation. She could tell herself it was because she couldn't resist making her seatmate look like a fool, but she knew the real reason: she was showing off for Burke. As soon as she knew he was listening, she just had to remind him how clever and smart-mouthed she could be.

Why? she scolded herself. *Why do you have to prove anything to that man?*

Because, she answered honestly, *it would be worse to think he forgot.*

5

As soon as the plane landed at LAX, Sarah prepared to make a fast exit. Joe's row emptied before hers, so there was nothing she could do about that, but she could certainly beat Paul Chapman out of the airport before he felt compelled to ask for or offer her a ride.

Sarah had the feeling he didn't understand the boundaries of co-defense attorneys who worked for different clients. Yes, Chapman was technically on her same side against all of Joe's plaintiffs, but Chapman's client was the main manufacturer, whereas Sarah's was just the subcontractor. If she had any chance at all to heap all the blame on Chapman's client and get hers released from the case entirely, she would take that victory any day. There was no chumminess on the defense side of the table as far as she was concerned.

She also had the feeling Chapman undervalued her because of her looks. And, no doubt, her age. It wasn't so much any particular thing he had said, but just this overall demeanor toward her of *All right there, little lady, you go ahead, but try not to hurt yourself asking all your big girl questions.*

Maybe it was her imagination, but she didn't think so. She could usually smell a jerk.

Too bad she had missed the scent on Joe.

Although he never seemed to underestimate her intelligence, so maybe that wasn't a fair comparison. If she was worried about being fair.

She saw him up ahead, reading his phone while he made his way toward the baggage area and ground transportation. She had no idea where he lived, but assumed it had to be somewhere in the Los Angeles area, since he worked in the city. Her place was in Culver City, close enough to tomorrow's deposition in Pasadena that she decided not to stay at the hotel, but to spend the night in her own apartment instead. She would have to leave with plenty of time to spare in the morning in case of traffic, but it was worth rushing a little in exchange for sleeping in her own bed.

As they neared the doors to go outside, Sarah saw the line of black-jacketed drivers holding up signs with their passengers' names. Sarah saw one that read "Burke."

Joe approached the driver, said something, then the two of them continued on. At the last moment Joe turned around and saw Sarah just a few paces behind him.

He's going to ask me, she thought. He was going to offer her a ride. Then she would tell him no, and finally their first day together would come to a close. She liked it ending on another no.

But Joe simply noted her presence, then turned around and kept walking. Leaving Sarah to fend for herself.

She fished for her keys in the pocket of her laptop case and slipped them into her suit jacket while she headed for the parking garage. Joe had done her a favor. He'd spared her one more conversation with him.

But nice move, gentleman, she thought, *not offering the lady a ride in your fancy chauffeured car.*

Even after her ill-advised attempt to amuse him on the plane.

The game was on. She knew it and he knew it. They were obviously going to see which of them would bend before they broke.

Sarah had grown stronger in the past six years, not weaker. If he thought he was still dealing with the young woman she used to be, now was his time to learn.

She had been through a lot since their last year of law school, as anyone reading the newspapers would know. Even before then, she had to scrap her way through one trial after another, and through the competitive hierarchy of one of the most prestigious—at one time—law firms in L.A. The girl Joe had known in law school couldn't have handled that pressure—look how easily she fell apart just because a guy like him dumped her.

But Sarah wasn't that girl anymore. And she knew she would handle the Joe situation completely differently now if she had a second chance.

Sarah unlocked the door to the car her father found for her back in April. It was old, but it ran well, thanks to his skills as a mechanic, and Sarah wasn't too proud to drive a twenty-year-old car. It suited her lifestyle now.

When the firm imploded, all of her perks instantly disappeared. Gone were the leased Mercedes and the generous gas allowance; gone was her expense account that she sometimes had trouble spending by the end of each month; gone was the free gym membership that had finally introduced her to the wonders of exercise; and gone was the salary that made her secure enough financially that her parents finally let her start helping them with money. Gone, all gone in the space of a single day.

Sarah flipped on the radio to one of the talk stations that regularly gave traffic news. She slowly made her way out of the airport gridlock into the gridlock that would take her home. Finally she unlocked her front door and returned to the sanctuary of her one-bedroom apartment.

She liked her little apartment. Every time she walked into it, she appreciated how clean and friendly it seemed—especially after a particularly hard day spent fighting with people from morning until night. It all washed off of her, it seemed, the minute she walked through her door.

She spent her first week in the place painting everything white. From the walls, to the wooden paneling on one side of the living room, to the built-in cabinets and the wooden frames on all of her windows. She painted red accents here and there, but mostly she just wanted to see the clean. To know that everything in there was nice and new and something she bought just for her.

When she first started making money—real money—Sarah sat down and made a list. She called it her *Flourish* list:

anything and everything she had ever wanted, but didn't really need.

It included things like a pillow-top mattress. Plush towels. High thread-count sheets. Red velvet pillows and a beautiful, white faux-fur throw she saw in a catalog draped over a white upholstered couch. She made a point to buy all three of those, including the exact couch. Triple-wicked, scented candles. Sweet-smelling bath salts. A long list that she felt a little foolish making, yet at the same time it made her feel deliciously pampered even to sit there and think about it.

She had held off for so many years buying herself the kinds of things she dreamed about: even something as simple as pretty, lacy underwear, bought at full retail price instead of from a discount store. Every time she checked off another item on the list, she felt more prosperous. And what was most shocking, by the time she got to the end of it, was that the entire spree cost her less than three thousand dollars. Somehow she thought it would cost closer to ten thousand—maybe even more. She had built it up so much in her mind, it seemed an unreachable goal back when she had practically nothing.

She still remembered too vividly that day in college when she looked at her bank statement and saw a balance of $4.32. Back then, spending three thousand dollars on luxuries might as well have been ten thousand—fifty thousand, for how impossible it seemed. But these were different times, she told herself with joy. She had finally made it. And furnishing her perfect apartment was one of the happiest experiences of her life.

She didn't regret any of it now—not a single purchase. Even though she could have used those thousands of dollars over the past six months. But she had to believe she would find her feet again one day. And when she did, she didn't want to have to start over, pulling herself up from the kind of impoverished life she had grown so accustomed to since her childhood. She accepted that her rapid rise was over—there was no other way to see it. What she didn't want to accept was the idea that she might start sliding backward to where she came from in the first place.

The food she ate at the airport wasn't sitting well in her belly. Sarah pulled out the ingredients for a smoothie—organic orange juice, a frozen banana, frozen strawberries and raspberries and blueberries—and whirled them all in her blender. Then she took sips here and there as she changed out of her battle suit and wiped off all her makeup. She pulled a shower cap over her still-behaving hair and stepped into her bathtub shower. And replayed portions of the day as the warm water washed it all away.

SARAH SET her alarm for four o'clock the next morning to give herself time to exercise. She never used to be that way. She'd roll out of bed, drink a huge mug of coffee, and answer her e-mails before she even started to dress.

But becoming a partner had reformed her. Her immediate boss, Richard, sat her down the day he made the offer and told her she needed to make some changes.

"We're making you a team leader," he said. "Elevating you to partner. Not an equity partner," Richard had continued before Sarah could even register the news. "So you won't receive any of the firm's profits, but we consider this level of partnership an important step to full status, once you've proven yourself."

He assigned her a team of five younger litigators. From then on, Sarah would be responsible for all of their files, all of their cases, and for making sure they turned in time sheets for every minute of their time by the end of every day.

"If you don't write down the time, it never happened," Richard said. "We only get paid for what we bill." Sarah had heard that speech many times. She always had more billable hours than any of the other associates. It was one of the factors, Richard said, they'd considered when promoting her. "We know you understand money, Sarah."

She agreed that she did.

And then she proved it by negotiating an even higher salary than the last team leader had been given.

"We have one concern," Richard told her. "We need our team leaders to be in top form. The job comes with a lot of stress—you already know that. But being partner is going to double, triple that stress. You understand?"

"Of course."

"You're not much for working out, I take it."

Sarah tried not to feel insulted. She thought she looked pretty good: same slim body she had maintained since high school, always turned out in professional-looking clothes and hairstyle.

"Our insurance premiums go down if all the key employees have gym memberships," Richard told her. "So that's included in your package. We have a list of different ones you can go to—you can find one close to the office or close to your house. But we'd like to see you meeting with a personal trainer at least twice a week."

"I'd rather work," Sarah said, assuming that was the right answer.

Richard shook his head. "You need to stay focused. Even-keeled. We've heard a few complaints that you're sometimes too hard on people. Hard is good—don't get me wrong," he said before she could defend herself. "We wouldn't put you in charge if you couldn't lead. But it's good for everybody if those of us in power take a little time to sweat off some of the pressure, you understand?"

Sarah had no desire to waste time at some gym when she could be billing, but she wasn't going to argue. If the firm thought it would make her a better leader, so be it. She would put in the minimum time with a trainer in case anyone checked up on her, then she'd work extra hours to make up for it.

Because nothing was going to interfere with this promotion. It had come much sooner than she ever could have hoped: right before her twenty-ninth birthday.

Sarah loved responsibility—always had. Not so much bossing people around, but instead being the problem-solver in any group. Figuring things out. Some people worked for praise, she noticed over the years, but she took much more value out of being proud of herself. She liked knowing she was the most reliable person she knew—except for her parents, who had given her that training in the first place. But as far as any other lawyer she'd ever met—and before that, any other student she met—Sarah felt comfortable believing she worked harder and smarter than any of them.

Her five months as partner in the firm she had been working for since law school was one of the favorite periods of her life. She would wake up sometimes at three-thirty in the morning because she was so excited to get to work. It meant she often passed out dead tired by nine o'clock at night, but she loved knowing she was up before anyone else, working long before dawn.

On April 6, she arrived at seven AM and began working on a Motion to Dismiss. She had already checked the status reports from her team members before she even came in, and knew she would have a few hours to herself now to work on her own cases.

The agents swarmed the building. One minute the only people she noticed outside the glass wall of her office were the attorneys and staff she saw every day, and the next there were navy blue uniformed men and women everywhere, seizing papers and files, emptying cabinets, and ordering people away from the shredders that stood conveniently beside every desk.

Sarah rose slowly, her legs unsteady. She was tempted at first to stay in her office, hidden behind the wooden door, but she realized that wasn't her way. No matter how horrible things would be once she confronted what was happening, she was a partner, she was a team leader, she was Sarah Henley. And Sarah Henley *stepped up.*

She could see now the bright yellow lettering on the agents' uniforms: FBI.

As one of the female agents moved toward Sarah's office, sweeping the contents of one of the secretaries' desks into a sturdy cardboard box, Sarah asked, "Would you please tell me what's going on?"

"Who are you?" the agent asked.

Sarah gave her name and position.

The agent pulled a list from her pants pocket and quickly scanned it. "Henley, you're to go to the fourth floor."

"What's on the fourth floor?" Sarah asked, fighting hard to sound calm.

"Command post," the agent answered. "We have to interview you before we can release you."

"Interview me about what? What is all this?"

"Ma'am, if you'll just proceed to the fourth floor—"

"Please," Sarah said, her voice finally betraying her fear. "Just tell me what's going on. Why are you here?"

The agent studied her for a moment, then answered, "Allegations of securities fraud, tax fraud, conspiracy, and money laundering."

"Money laun...oh my God." Sarah's legs started to fail her. She braced herself against the edge of her desk. "Wh-who?"

"They'll give you more information downstairs, Miss Henley. Now I'm going to have to ask you to vacate this office," the agent said, already angling past Sarah.

"Can I—" Sarah cleared her throat. She saw one of the young lawyers on her team staring at her wide-eyed from beyond the door, her face as white as Sarah's.

Sarah forced herself to remain calm. "What can I bring with me?"

"Just your personal effects, ma'am," the agent answered. She was already disconnecting Sarah's computer.

Sarah wanted to throw up. A group of her litigators and staff now stood clustered in her doorway, watching.

The agent pointed to Sarah's purse. "Anything related to this firm's cases in there?"

Sarah shook her head.

"How about in there?" the agent asked, pointing to Sarah's laptop case.

This time Sarah nodded.

"You'll have to leave those," the agent said. "Let's go through them."

Sarah's hands shook as she pulled out the files she had been working on the night before. The notes she'd made about the Motion to Dismiss she was going to work on all morning. Time sheets she had printed out for the past week to check her team members' progress.

"Thank you, ma'am," the agent said. "I'll have to ask you to leave now."

Sarah slung her purse over her shoulder, and picked up her laptop case.

"I'm sorry, you'll have to leave the laptop," the agent said.

"But...it has my personal information on it, too," Sarah said. "Personal e-mails, financial records—"

"That's fine," the agent said. "We'll return it to you when we've retrieved the information we need."

Sarah's face felt slick with sweat. She walked on wobbly legs to the door of her office.

"Sarah?" one of her team members said. "What are we going to do?"

Sarah shook her head. "It's over," she said, more to herself than to the other lawyer. Isn't that what all this meant? she wondered. Wasn't the entire career she worked so hard to build now suddenly and irrevocably over?

"Good luck," she told the cluster of people watching her. She swallowed and forced herself to look each of them in the eyes. "I really mean that—good luck to all of you."

The interview at the "command post" lasted approximately twenty minutes. The agent in charge asked whether Sarah had worked with a particular collection of lawyers at the firm, and whether she ever worked for a particular list of clients.

The only name she said yes to was the attorney who promoted her: Richard.

"Did you ever work directly with him for any of these clients?"

Sarah shook her head. She knew the client names, but they were too big and important for her to have been trusted with their files yet. Thank God.

The agent let her go, warning her they might need to be in touch again in the future.

Sarah nodded blankly. From what she counted as the agent read off the attorney names, there seemed to be twenty-two members of her firm involved. Almost all of them at the very top of the heap. Thank goodness no one from her own team had made it onto that list.

Sarah left the fourth floor, rode the elevator down to the garage, and then walked away from the life she had meticulously built from her first interview during her second year of law school.

No, she corrected herself as she shuffled toward her car —a car that would be confiscated within a week as the feds seized more of the firm's assets—Sarah had just lost everything she'd worked for since she was a teenager. Since the night she helped her mom clean the insurance agency office, and saw the ad for a secretarial position the owners were planning to place the next morning. Sarah called as soon as they opened the next day and pretended she just happened to be looking for a job. She never told anyone at the agency that her mother was their cleaning woman, or that Sarah had been her helper since she was a little girl.

And now look at her, she thought that day: the little girl in her grown-up suit, turning the ignition on her grown-up car, holding back the flood of tears that she promised herself she could drown in as soon as she made it safely back to the sanctuary of her pretty little grown-up apartment.

Sarah's heart had been broken twice in her life: first by Joe Burke, second by her job.

But maybe this chance she'd been given would help knit together the wounds from both. Get her back on her feet, earning money, building a fresh résumé once again.

And finally helping her erase whatever last vestiges of Joe Burke might still lay hiding in her heart. She'd thought there were none until she saw him that morning. Now she had to admit there were still splinters of him everywhere. She would find each one and pull it out. And in the end, even if it took all five months, she would walk away feeling whole and new again.

Finally free of the first and only man she ever loved.

6

The traffic on the way to the deposition in Pasadena the next morning wasn't too bad, so she couldn't blame her anger on that.

But she could easily blame it on how well-rested Joe looked, how nicely he smiled at his client, that familiar laugh of his she heard just as she opened the door to the hotel conference room.

Joe looked up, met her eye, then went back to talking to the young woman sitting next to him. She must have been in her early twenties, Sarah guessed, and whatever damage had been done to her hair had been long enough ago that it looked thick and lustrous now, covering her shoulders like a brown faux-fur throw, and Sarah had the brief thought that she would happily set it on fire again herself for the way the young woman was staring at Joe.

Hero worship. Sarah had seen it before. Not from anyone she had represented, but usually from women gazing with that same sort of stupid look, a stupid grin to go with it, at some smooth-talking lawyer who said all the right things and seemed to know all the answers.

Sarah wasn't having any of that.

"How's it going today, Number Eight?" she asked Burke.

He took his time shifting his eyes from the young woman to Sarah. "Just fine, Seven." Then he went back to smiling at whatever his client was saying.

Sarah grunted in disgust.

"What's seven and eight?" Paul Chapman wanted to know.

"I.Q." Sarah answered. Then she went back to unpacking her laptop and files.

"You two know each other?" Chapman asked. "Before this?"

"No," they both answered.

Chapman looked from Sarah to Joe. Then he smiled like the last kid to be let in on a joke. "I don't get it."

"I used to play professional ball," Joe said. "Sarah obviously looked me up. Eight—it was my jersey."

"What kind of ball?" Chapman asked.

Joe looked to Sarah for that one.

"Volley," she said without missing a beat. "Shall we get to it, gentleman? And ladies," she added, nodding to the court reporter and Joe's attractive, worshipful client.

"Did you really play volleyball?" the young woman asked. "Me, too!"

"No kidding," Sarah muttered.

She couldn't help seeing the amusement on Joe's face. She planned to wipe that off before the morning was over.

"WHERE WERE YOU BORN, MISS LEE?"

"Objection, relevance," Sarah said.

Chapman turned to her. "Excuse me?"

"Just making my record."

She waited until his next inane question—"What were your parents' occupations?"—and objected again.

"Are you going to do that the whole deposition?" Chapman asked her.

"Yes, I am."

"Off the record," Chapman said to the court reporter, who promptly lifted her hands from the keyboard.

"What are you doing?" he demanded.

"You spent two hours on irrelevant questions yesterday," Sarah answered, "and so I'm making my record. If the time comes when I need to bring this before a judge, I want to make sure I've preserved all my objections."

"You can't keep doing that," Chapman said.

"Of course I can," Sarah answered, motioning for him to continue.

Chapman scowled, then told the court reporter they were back on.

"Where did you go to high school, Miss Lee?"

"Objection."

And so the next few hours unfolded.

After a break, it was Sarah's turn. Rather than ask her few simple questions from the day before, she decided to expand her line of inquiry.

"Miss Lee, hi. I'm Sarah Henley, defending Mason Manufacturing, the subcontractor." She said it all quickly, just to tax the young woman's brain. "You've made a claim for emotional distress—are you aware of that?"

Joe's client looked at him uncertainly.

"I can show you the complaint," Sarah offered, already handing the file across the table.

Joe flipped through the pleading and pointed to where there was a separate claim for emotional distress.

"Yes," Miss Lee said.

"Yes, what?" Sarah asked.

"Yes, I am aware I asked for that," the young woman answered, scowling at Sarah.

Joe leaned over and whispered something to his client.

"The record will reflect that Mr. Burke is whispering to his client," Sarah said.

Joe cast her a look of disapproval, but didn't say anything.

"Now, Miss Lee," Sarah continued, "can you please describe for me all of the elements of your emotional distress claim?"

"All the...elements?" she asked.

"Yes," Sarah said.

Again the young woman looked to Joe. He said, "Off the record." Then, "Sarah, where are you going with this?"

"Investigating the claim," she said.

"Lawyers write the pleadings, their clients don't," he said.

"Are you saying you didn't discuss the lawsuit with your client before filing it on her behalf? Back on," she told the court reporter.

Joe did not look happy, Sarah thought. Good.

"Miss Lee, what kind of emotional distress did you experience as a direct result of the incident you described to Mr. Chapman here?"

"Well...I was..." Again she looked to Joe.

"Were you scared?" he suggested. "Sad? Depressed?"

"Record will reflect plaintiff's counsel is answering for his client," Sarah said.

"I'm not answering for her," Joe said, "I'm clarifying your question."

"The record stands," Sarah said. "Miss Lee, did you seek any psychological counseling as a result of your emotional distress?"

"Psychological?" the young woman said. "You mean like a psychiatrist?"

"Psychiatrist," Sarah recited quickly, "psychologist, psychotherapist, therapist, trained counselor..."

"Oh...no." The young woman turned her eyes to Joe again, obviously hoping for some kind of help.

But he was too busy staring at Sarah.

"So, no medical expenses to support your claim of distress?" she asked.

"No, but I was really scared," the young woman said. "Really, really scared."

Finally Joe turned and gave his client an encouraging smile. "Remember what you told me about being afraid to use even a blow dryer for several months?" he asked.

"Off the record," Sarah said. "Would counsel be more comfortable if he could stick his hand up his client's backside and move her lips for her?"

"Sarah!" Joe growled, pushing his chair away from the

table. "Can I speak to you outside?"

"Certainly," she said.

Sarah casually closed the lid on her laptop, then took her time following Joe out into the hall. She felt the flush of triumph flooding through her veins. She'd gotten to him. And it was only day two.

"What the hell are you doing?" he asked her.

"My job," she answered pleasantly.

"Like hell you are," he said. "You're harassing my client."

"And you're trying to answer every question for her. She's a big girl, Burke. Plaintiffs have to be able to back up their own claims."

"You're over the line, and you know it."

"Take it up with the judge." Sarah started to open the door again, but Joe shoved it closed.

"Is this is how it's going to be?" he asked.

Sarah didn't bother pretending she didn't know what he meant. "Worried, Number Eight?"

"They only let you beat me because the chief judge liked your tits."

Sarah's eyes widened in surprise. "Ha! So there it is! *That's* what you've been telling yourself all these years?"

"I don't think about it, Sarah. Obviously you do. Whenever you're ready to stop pouting and act like a real lawyer again, you come back in there and let's keep working."

He yanked open the door and left her standing alone in the hall.

Fuming.

That hadn't gone the way she'd envisioned it—at *all*. And now he was sitting in there smug and superior, probably holding Miss Lee's hand and comforting her over the terrible treatment she received from that bad lady lawyer.

Disgusting, Sarah thought. And not something she could let continue.

She pulled open the door and calmly returned to her seat. She opened her laptop again, pretended to consult her notes, then asked, "Is there any history of mental infirmity in your family?"

CHAPMAN CAUGHT up to her as she waited at the stoplight outside the hotel. There were several different restaurants in the plaza across the street, and Sarah was starving.

"That was good stuff," Chapman said, chuckling. "Have to say, thought you were being a real obstructionist bitch with all your objections to my stuff, but the way you handled that girl?" He shook his head and chuckled again. "Man."

The fact that the worst lawyer in the room was complimenting her did nothing to make Sarah feel better. She knew she'd gone too far—she knew it the minute she asked her first question.

If only Joe hadn't looked so good that morning in his charcoal gray suit. If only he didn't look so much better than she remembered. If only the young woman hadn't been so *adoring...*

Sarah shook it off. That was just one deposition, and it wouldn't happen again. Didn't have to—she'd made her point. She wasn't there to make friends, least of all with Burke.

"Where you going?" Chapman asked when they reached the other side.

Sarah pointed to the salad place.

Chapman made a face. "See you later then."

Sarah was just sitting down to a massive bowl of greens and tofu when a familiar body entered the restaurant. She almost felt him before she saw him.

She cursed under her breath.

There was no use pretending she hadn't seen him when it was clear he was looking for her.

But he took his time about it, first standing in line, consulting the menu behind the counter, then ordering a southwestern chicken salad.

"Sarah." He didn't even ask, just sat down. He pushed the plastic fork out of its wrapper and took a few bites of his lunch.

Sarah continued chewing her own salad, which was now completely tasteless on her tongue.

"Shall we start again?" he asked.

A wave of cold sluiced over her skin. She narrowed her eyes. "What do you mean?"

"I don't know about you," he said, taking another bite, "but I'm not up for five months of that. I'm too old."

"Yeah, you're ancient," she said. "Buck up, Burke. Take some vitamins."

"*Sarah.*"

The way he said it, she couldn't help looking at him. "What."

He raised his eyebrows in a way that was so familiar to her, she could have predicted the exact lines that formed on his forehead as a result. She knew every inch of that face. She'd held it in her hands, gazed into it, pressed her own soft cheek against it, lusted after it, kissed it, adored it—

"We're already in purgatory," he said. "Let's not make it worse."

"What do you mean?" she asked, wishing she could come up with a snappier line.

"You think I like this?" Joe asked. "You think this gig is a reward of some kind for a job well done?"

Sarah hadn't considered that. She'd been so focused on what the job meant to her, she hadn't wondered how Joe might feel about it. Or why he might be there.

"So what happened?" she asked.

"What, are we going to talk about our hopes and feelings now, Henley?" He threw her own line back at her, but with a shade of humor in his voice, obviously trying to make his point that they should treat each other better.

She softened ever so slightly. "So why are you stuck with this job? Did you make an enemy?"

"A few," Joe said. "I won't bore you with the details." He spread his arms and looked around the tiny restaurant. "And now here we are, both of us hitting the big time."

"Who'd have thought it, Number Eight?" Sarah asked, trying to make up for digging it in earlier.

"Me, sure," he said. "But you, Number Seven? What's the world coming to?"

"That judge was not looking at my chest."

"He definitely was," Joe said, spearing a chunk of chicken and popping it into his mouth. "Couldn't blame him—we all were."

It was actually worse this way, Sarah thought. She gazed across the table to where Joe sat with his afternoon client, a woman in her fifties who seemed just as worshipful as the young woman had been that morning, and all Sarah could think was that she got it—she completely understood.

She'd felt that way herself at one time.

Not at first—at first she thought he was a cocky, over-confident, over-privileged frat boy type who was too good looking for his own good. The fact that he turned out to be a serious student who had never stepped foot into a frat house —let alone participated in any of that kind of drunken, idiotic college boy behavior Sarah resented so much because it meant they could afford to blow off school while she'd worked for years to afford every single credit—meant that Joe had at least a shot at her not hating him. In those days, that was something.

She came to law school with a chip on her shoulder. She

knew that. She had a lot to prove to herself and everyone around her, and she spent night and day proving it.

Which was why she'd joined Moot Court in both her second and third years. It was an extra-credit class for students who wanted to learn appellate lawyer skills and compete in mock appellate arguments around the country.

Some students signed up just for the extra credits, some to pad their résumés, but Sarah was in it for the fight. She wanted to show everyone how fast she was on her feet, how articulate, how unbeatable in an open-court battle.

And it didn't hurt that the major law firms she hoped would notice her had partners who served as Moot Court advisors and who often sat in on their practices to act as judges.

It was how she'd gotten her summer internship in her second year, and how she ended up working for the same firm once she graduated. Because she had a quick, smart mouth, and a quick, smart brain to back it up.

That was where the Number Seven and Number Eight came in: at their final national competition, in the fall of their third year, Sarah and Joe competed on opposite sides of the same case. And while neither of their teams won, Sarah and Joe had been awarded individual honors for their own performances. Sarah won spot number seven, Joe the slot behind her.

She never once rubbed that in when they were still dating. In fact, Joe liked to tease her about it in a way that made her think he was actually proud of her.

But they weren't dating the morning they competed in

that small, chilly town in southern Illinois—not yet, anyway. Their relationship didn't begin for a few more hours.

And it lasted only a month and a half after that.

Too short, Sarah mourned at the time.

But once she understood what kind of man he really was, she realized she had gotten in too deep, too fast, and for far too long. She should have kept things the way they were in the beginning, with just some harmless flirting and a curiosity about what he might really be like if she got to know him.

Well, she got to know him, all right.

Sarah let Chapman drone on in his regular way. She didn't bother objecting as he fleshed out the plaintiff's entire childhood scholastic career from grade school on. She didn't complain when Chapman asked follow-up questions about the woman's waitressing jobs twenty years ago, or about when she and her husband divorced, or about what college her son now attended.

Instead, Sarah wrote sarcastic notes to herself throughout the entire testimony.

That's a great question—I'm stealing that. Oh, did she really work at Target two years ago? That's fascinating, Paul. I wish I were as good a lawyer as you are. I could be a partner and drive a fancy car and fly first class—oh, wait, you were in the back of the bus last night, weren't you? What happened, Paul? Are you in purgatory, too?

Sarah wondered what the story was there—not about Chapman, who cared about him?—but about Joe. If he really was being punished by making him be the road lawyer for this case, what was his standing at his firm? And what had it been before he made whatever enemies he did? What exactly had gone down?

"Sarah?" Joe asked, checking his watch. "Do you have a lot of questions, or should we keep going without a break? I know we all have to drive back to the airport—"

"I'll be fast," Sarah said, holding back the sigh that almost accompanied the statement. It was only day two, and already she was bored out of her mind with the actual work. The idea of making life hard for Burke had added some fun to it at the beginning, but Sarah was already realizing that what he said at lunch was right: five months of this was going to be brutal.

Maybe Burke was right—they were too old. Even though she still had a few more months before she'd turn thirty. This past year of hers could have aged anyone.

It was one of the reasons she insisted on taking such good care of herself. Once she knew how good she could feel with proper food and sleep and exercise, she wanted to stay that way. She'd seen colleagues give in to the pressures of the job and walk around perpetually sleep-deprived, on the brink of some illness, their eyes always red and raw as they tried to pump themselves up with yet another cup of coffee. Or harder stimulants, in some people's cases.

Until a year ago, Sarah had been one of those people constantly fighting off or giving in to a cold. It didn't help her image to always be sniffling into a tissue—she already looked delicate enough. But ever since her trainer Angie had pushed her to make the necessary changes, Sarah started feeling too well to ever give it up.

"Hello, Ms. Jordan," she said, introducing herself to Joe's

client. "Thank you for coming in today. I just have a few questions." She asked her eight best ones, then the deposition was over.

The traffic that time of day from Pasadena back to Los Angeles was going to be horrendous. But her flight—and, she assumed, the others'—was less than three hours away, so she knew she had better get to it.

Her new best friend Paul Chapman took it upon himself to walk with her to the parking garage near the hotel. Sarah remembered where she'd parked, but pretended she didn't.

"You go ahead," she told Chapman. "I'll see you later."

He lumbered off toward an enormous black SUV that looked almost new.

Sarah forced back the bitterness in her mouth.

Then she saw Joe, walking at the opposite side of her row, clicking the remote for his shiny silver Audi and throwing his luggage and briefcase in the back.

He must have slept in his own bed the night before, too, Sarah thought. The driver who met him at the airport had taken him home, then Joe drove to the deposition that morning just like she did.

She wondered where he lived. Someplace expensive, no doubt, from the look of his car. He always had more money than she did. His parents were a lot better off than hers.

Joe looked up just then and saw her watching him. Sarah quickly pretended to search for her keys. Lunch with him had been all right, but she wasn't in the mood for any more interaction. Especially since now she needed him to drive away before he saw the twenty-year-old Saturn she was about to climb into.

She moved against the concrete wall of the garage and waited for him to swing past her. When he did, he gave her a nod of acknowledgment.

It wasn't fair, Sarah thought, none of it was fair.

But she knew she could tell herself that as much as she wanted, and it wouldn't change a thing. Better to swallow whatever last little bit of pride she still had, and be grateful she had a car at all. Be grateful she had work. Be grateful Mickey had recommended her for the job.

Although she couldn't help wondering now if the fact that Burke was on the other side of it might have been the reason why Mickey had suggested her in the first place. Did he think that would make Sarah more effective, more aggressive?

Or was it just one more move in the long-running game the three of them had been playing since that night in Illinois?

8

Mickey Hughes had sought her out.

He made no attempt to hide why.

"I want you on my team. You're beautiful and you smell good, and you know we'll kick their asses. Which one do you want to go to?"

The Moot Court meeting had only just ended, and Sarah was looking over the list of national competitions taking place that fall. There were ones all over the country, each focusing on different areas of the law. The one that caught her eye was a patient confidentiality issue in a health law case. The competition would take place at Southern Illinois University School of Law at the beginning of November.

"That's the one I'm doing," she said, pointing to the description.

Mickey gave it a quick read. "Fine. Great. Whatever. Let's go grab a beer."

Sarah glanced around the room at the other potential

partners she might have asked to work with her. She knew Mickey from their first year Torts class, and had been in Trial Prep with him their second year, so she had seen enough to know he wasn't stupid. Maybe not the best choice out of everyone in the room, but not an awful one, either.

"You sure you're up for it?" Sarah asked him. "I'm not just doing this for the credit—I'm doing it to win."

Mickey flashed her a smile. "Counting on it, Henley. Why do you think I picked you?"

While Mickey bought their beers, Sarah looked over the paperwork she picked up at the meeting. It included a longer description of what the case was about.

She passed it across to Mickey and took a sip of pale ale. "Which side do you want to take?" she asked him. "Petitioner or respondent?"

He didn't bother reading the sheet. "Whatever you say. I'm just your dog, Sarah. Tell me what to do and I'll do it."

"Huh-uh," she said, setting down her glass. "First of all, I hate group work, because someone—me—always ends up doing most of it. Second, you need to decide right now if you're willing to work as hard as I am. Because if you're not, let's just enjoy our beer and part friends. No harm, no foul, we'll just go find other partners."

"Don't be so touchy," he said, smiling. "Of course I'm going to work. I just meant I'm not going to fight you on anything. I know how good you are at this, and I'm not one of those guys who can't take their woman showing them up every now and then."

"*Their woman?*" Sarah repeated, her voice thick with sarcasm.

"Okay, 'moot court partner'—you like that better?" Mickey asked.

Sarah sipped her beer and took a few more moments to consider. Her partner the year before had been an older woman who was an excellent writer, and had done a great job on her portion of the brief, but who began to fall apart the moment they argued their case in front of the judges. Catherine had barely gotten out two sentences of her prepared statement before the judges began firing questions at her, one after another.

That was how Moot Court was supposed to go—it was an imitation of arguing an appellate case in front of a panel of judges primed to interrupt and ask questions, and generally to overwhelm and challenge the lawyers. And for the past two months Sarah and Catherine and everyone else in Moot Court had been rehearsing exactly how to deal with that.

But suddenly Catherine seemed very tired. She rested her arms against the podium and her head started to droop. The next thing Sarah knew, Catherine was swaying to the side, and both Sarah and one of her opponents from the other team leapt up just in time to catch the woman before she fainted. They helped her back to her seat, and Catherine folded her arms on top of the counsel table and laid her head there. Her breathing sounded ragged. Sarah hoped her partner wasn't going to throw up.

"You'll have two minutes, counsel," the chief judge informed her. "If you don't resume by then, you forfeit."

Sarah wasn't sure her partner would recover in time. Her

face—what Sarah could see of it—was still deathly pale, and Sarah could hear a soft moan.

"Catherine?" she whispered. "Are you going to be all right?"

Catherine gave a slight nod.

Sarah glanced at the timer ticking away in front of them. What a disaster. If only the rules allowed her to take over for Catherine, it would have been all right. But as it was, all Sarah could do was rub the woman's back and say soothing things to her, like, "You can do this. It's almost over. You only have to argue a few more minutes."

When the chief judge warned of the last ten seconds, Catherine slowly rose to her feet. Sarah helped steady her back to the podium. Then Catherine made a valiant—and successful—effort to remain on her feet until the allotted time was over. Then she sank back into her chair and laid her head on the table again.

Needless to say, they lost.

But Mickey Hughes didn't seem the fainting type. If anything, he looked like he'd enjoy the spotlight while judges tried to hammer holes in his argument.

"You'll have to make time for this," Sarah warned him. "I don't care what your class load is, I want to meet at least three times a week."

"Sounds good," Mickey said.

"We'll divide up the briefing and decide who researches and writes which part."

"Great," he said.

"And before you start saying yes to everything," Sarah

added, "let me tell you this is strictly professional. This isn't you getting into my pants."

"All right," Mickey said with a grin, "I'll deal with that separately, on my own time."

"I'm serious, Hughes, it ain't happening. I'm here to work."

He gave her a salute and downed the rest of his beer. "Want another?" he asked, getting up. "I have the feeling you're more fun when you're drunk."

Just to prove her point, Sarah pushed away her still mostly-full glass. "Time to go study," she said, also rising to her feet. "See you tomorrow. We'll divide up the work then."

"See you, beautiful," he said.

"That's the last time you say that or we're done right now."

Mickey chuckled. "I meant see you, scrawny, high-strung girl with the big brain."

Sarah smiled at that. "I'm never high-strung," she said. "You'll see. And you'd better be a lot cooler in court than you are trying to pick me up."

"I definitely am," Mickey assured her.

She held out her hand for him to shake. "Guess you'll do for now."

THE NEXT TIME Sarah checked the sign-up sheet, she could see Joe Burke and his partner Ellen Kiptar were the other team working on the same case. They had signed up to represent the respondent—the hospital which had failed to protect sensitive patient information from someone who hacked into the computer database—whereas Sarah and Mickey represented the petitioner, a woman whose medical records had been exposed. The question was whether the patient had a constitutional right to privacy that the hospital violated by being so lax with its computer security. Sarah liked the patient's side of the argument better than the hospital's. She thought she could do a lot with that.

She knew Joe Burke only by name and sight. And all she knew about his partner Ellen was that she was on the Moot Court board and acted as treasurer. Even though they were all third years, UCLA's law school was big enough that students only got to know the people in their smaller classes, and so far Sarah hadn't had any of those with either Joe or Ellen.

Although Sarah did remember one incident involving Joe in her second year, when they were both in the same Federal Tax Law class. He always sat in the back of the large, theater-style classroom, on the opposite side of the room from Sarah. On this particular day he looked like he was sleeping.

Which was exactly why the professor called on him. But instead of proving the professor's suspicions that he was another one of those lazy students caught partying too much instead of studying, Joe completely nailed the question the professor threw at him. Then he kept on going and gave the professor case law that hadn't even been cited in the textbook to back up what he was saying.

Sarah, along with most of her classmates, had a good laugh at the whole exchange. Then Joe Burke went back to slouching into his seat like a slacker, even though his cover had just been blown.

Sarah had also seen him around school with a variety of different female companions. And that right there crossed him off whatever list she might have had. She didn't like players—never had. Like she told Mickey Hughes, she was there at the school to work.

She would make time for a personal life later. Once she had gotten everything she came for.

THE FIRST TIME she watched Joe Burke argue his side of the case during one of the practices, she should have known.

He was that good.

That electrifying, that charismatic, that smart.

Trouble.

"Wonder if any of the other teams have thought of that argument," Sarah murmured to Mickey, who sat beside her in the audience watching.

Even though the two teams were dealing with the same case, they wouldn't argue against each other at the competition. Each of them would be matched with a team from another school.

And Sarah had to admit she was grateful.

Burke was that good.

Maybe even better than she was.

"He's not that great," Mickey muttered back. "We could take him."

"His partner, for sure," Sarah said. Ellen underwhelmed them both.

But Burke...

When the guest judges were finished questioning him, Joe thanked them all and headed back to his table.

But not before looking straight at Sarah. And smiling.

She looked away as if she'd been caught at something. Because she had.

Mickey nudged her with his elbow. "Let's go grab a beer."

Sarah stared at the back of Joe's head a moment longer before answering, "Not tonight."

And maybe that was the start of it, she thought later. The moment when she might have faintly written Joe's name down on her imaginary list.

Like the *Flourish* list: things she might want but didn't necessarily need.

Maybe, Sarah thought as she watched him walk out of the room—saw him once again glance her way and deliberately look her in the eye—a guy like Joe Burke could be interesting to know.

But not now. Maybe later.

After she beat him and everyone else in the competition.

9

The October depositions rolled past, one by one: the northern California ones—San Francisco, Sacramento, Oakland, San Jose—most of them places Sarah had never visited before. Then on to Las Vegas and Reno. Denver and Colorado Springs. Albuquerque, Phoenix, Tucson—the airports and hotels all became a blur, each one interchangeable as she checked into a new one every night, sat in a conference room all the next day, then flew out again to a new city where she would rinse, repeat, ask her same list of questions.

By mid-November, Sarah spent a weekend compiling some of the information she had gathered: a range of dates for when the product had been purchased, a list of stores or Internet sites where the plaintiffs bought the hair iron, and a spreadsheet detailing how long they used it before it set fire to their hair.

Not a pretty picture.

She e-mailed the information to Mickey's boss, Calvin, and asked him to forward it to the client.

And then asked for some information in return.

Sarah noticed a pattern: the only claims were for hair irons bought within a specific time period. It was something any lawyer on the case should have noticed already if they had taken the time to read all the complaints Joe's firm had filed, or if they'd read the interrogatory answers the plaintiffs had sent back.

But Sarah had seen this kind of waste before. It was easier sometimes—and definitely more lucrative, since it meant more billable hours—to have an attorney take a series of depositions in person, rather than ask questions on paper. If Sarah had been hired to work the case from a desk, she might have gathered all this same information more easily and cheaply than having to fly from city to city and stay in hotels and eat bad food on the road.

But she wasn't in charge of any of that. And, she reminded herself, she never would have been able to negotiate the salary she was getting if she just sat at a spare desk in the law firm offices and typed up interrogatories and reviewed documents all day.

So she was on a plane to Salt Lake City the Sunday before Thanksgiving, and would see Boise and Pocatello, Idaho before heading home Wednesday night. Then she would have four long days all to herself, to drive home to see her parents and sleep in her childhood bed.

If she could make it that long.

She had been feeling a little tired. More tired than usual. When she saw Angie on Saturday for their now once-weekly workout sessions, Sarah dragged from one exercise to the next. Finally Angie called a halt to the whole thing and told Sarah to stretch.

"You need a break," Angie said. "Fifteen hours of sleep. A bad-TV marathon. Something."

Sarah had dutifully kept up with her exercise on the road, running on the hotel treadmills every morning, then doing pushups and lunges and squats in the privacy of her own room.

Now she lay sprawled on the padded mat while Angie stretched her aching limbs.

"I think you're right," Sarah told her. "I need to turn off my brain for four days. Just sit in a chair and stare at the wall. Or read all the trashy magazines my mom saves up for me."

"How's Joe been?" Angie asked.

Sarah shrugged. "You know." Then she grimaced as Angie angled her leg into a brutal hip stretch Sarah always both loved and hated.

She had kept saga of Sarah and Joe to herself for a few weeks, but finally she couldn't resist telling Angie about their history. The trainer approved of Sarah's overall plan to make the man suffer.

"Glad you'll get a little break from him next week?" Angie asked as she pushed Sarah's straightened leg practically over her head.

"Yes," Sarah grunted. "Definitely. And that other guy—Chapman. I can't wait to not hear his voice for four long days. What a luxury."

Before leaving the gym, Sarah pulled a stack of bills out

of her wallet.

Angie looked at the amount. "Are you sure? This much?"

"Of course," Sarah said. "Thank you."

She had been paying Angie off a little more every week, not only for the current sessions, but for all the ones Angie gave her for free during Sarah's six months of unemployment.

"I know you'll find something soon," Angie always told her, and then finally one day it was true. Sarah never forgot generosity like that. She planned on giving Angie a big bonus at the end of the year, once she paid down some of her other debts. Angie was just a small business owner like Sarah's parents, and Sarah knew very well the risk Angie had taken in giving her credit for so long with no guarantee of repayment.

If only everyone who dealt with Sarah's parents felt the same way about compensating them for their work, Sarah thought. But she knew that wasn't how the world worked. All she could do was her part.

"What time do you leave tomorrow?" Angie asked her as Sarah pulled a sweatshirt over her sweaty T-shirt.

"Around three," Sarah said. "I want to get settled in Salt Lake and have some dinner so I can go to bed early."

"Get some sleep tonight, too," Angie said. "You've got circles under your eyes."

"Yeah, but you should see the other guys," Sarah joked. It was true, Chapman looked like he had put on weight over the past six or seven weeks, and all of them could probably use more fresh air than they were getting, but Sarah had been disappointed to see how well Burke held up. He still looked fit and rested, even though they had just crammed in five different cities in five days so they could make Thanksgiving week a short one. The guy was indestructible. Still.

Sarah stopped by the grocery store on the way home from her workout to buy herself something healthy. She picked out a few pieces of fresh fruit and a couple of lightly-fried vegetable samosas she found in the prepared foods section. She missed Indian food. Good food of any kind, in fact, and her own cooking even more. She made one more stop, dropping off her dry cleaning and picking up clean suits so she could pack for the next day's trip.

Sarah hadn't bought new clothes in over eight months now. It was a luxury that was no longer on her list. She promised herself a full new outfit when these depositions were all over, but until then she could make do with all the designer suits she purchased back when she was feeling flush. As long as she continued to take good care of them, they should last, no matter how many times she folded them, ironed them with crappy hotel irons, wore them, perspired in them, and subjected them to the cleaners.

As soon as she returned to her apartment, Sarah checked her e-mail, answered one or two, then headed for the shower. Now that she had sweated up her hair at the workout, she was safe giving it the full and laborious treatment: shampooing, conditioning, treating, blowing it out with the dryer, then straightening it with the iron. It was a process that could take as long as an hour and a half sometimes if her hair was being particularly difficult. She hoped today wasn't one of those days. Angie was right: she needed more sleep. Sleep and a long weekend off.

And a break from looking at Joe across a table all day long every day.

"BEAUTIFUL, HUH?" the court reporter, Marcela, said as Sarah gazed at the Wasatch mountains from the window of the hotel conference room. "Have you ever skied here?" she asked.

"No, I don't ski," Sarah said. "Do you?"

"Once," Marcela said. "That was enough. I forgot snow was so cold."

Sarah smiled, just to be friendly, even though she didn't really feel like it. She hadn't slept well. She felt edgy, irritable.

Joe's Salt Lake City client was a woman in her thirties, well-groomed, but with an unfortunately short haircut. It wasn't the woman's choice.

"I used to have hair down to here," she cried, tears slipping down her cheeks. Chapman had finally gotten around to asking a few relevant questions, and was rewarded with copious weeping.

Oh, boy, Sarah thought, this one's going to kill us in front of a jury.

And then the room started to go black.

It started at the edges of Sarah's vision, like black bars, slowly closing in. Then her ears began to buzz. She could feel sweat beading on her face.

Sarah glanced down at her legal pad and tried to concentrate on the few words she had written there, but the letters swam and wriggled out of focus.

When Sarah looked up again, she found Joe staring at her. She scowled, but he wrinkled his forehead and kept looking.

"Off the record," he said. Marcela stopped typing. "Sarah, are you all right?"

"Of course I'm all right." Even though she could feel the sweat covering more of her body.

"Come with me," Joe told her. To the rest of the people in the room he said, "We're taking a break."

When Sarah didn't immediately stand up—and why should she? He wasn't in charge of her—Joe came over and clasped her by the arm. "Come on," he said. "Now."

Sarah slowly rose to her feet. "What are you—" But she couldn't get the rest of the sentence out. Because suddenly the room swayed, and Sarah swayed with it. Joe braced his arm around her waist and escorted her out into the hall.

As soon as the door closed behind them, Joe said, "You're sick."

"No, I'm not."

"Sarah, look at you. You're bleach white. There are black circles under your eyes. You're dripping sweat. Come on, where's your room?"

It was true, she didn't feel well—at all. But he had no right taking charge of her like this. Sarah wrenched herself away. "I'm fine. I just need to rest for a few minutes."

As if accepting that as a signal, her legs began to give way. She leaned back against the nearest wall and started to sink down.

Joe bent over, scooped his arm behind her knees, and lifted her off the floor. Sarah drooped in his arms. Joe wrestled open the door of the conference room and called to Marcela, "Get her things. Come with me."

"What's going on?" Chapman called, but Joe let the door swing shut again.

"What room are you in?" he asked her again.

Sarah shook her head weakly. She wasn't trying to be difficult, she just honestly didn't remember. After staying in so many different hotel rooms over so many weeks, she had no hope of keeping it straight. She started storing each day's key inside the little envelope the clerk at the front desk gave her. That way she could always refer to the room number written on the outside.

Marcela now joined them, holding Sarah's purse and laptop case. Sarah pointed to the purse.

"Key."

Even that much effort felt monumental. Sarah had to rest her head against Joe's chest.

"Sarah?" He sounded so far away. "Sarah." Joe shifted her in his arms so that he held her more securely.

"Got it," Marcela said, showing Joe the key she found in Sarah's purse. "Room four-eighty."

"Would you come with us, please?" he asked Marcela as he started carrying Sarah toward the elevator. "I need you to bring those things to her room. But I'd keep your distance," he added. "We don't know what she has."

"What about you?" Marcela asked him, no doubt noticing that Sarah's sweaty face was just inches from his.

"Indestructible," Joe told her.

Sarah heard it, but felt too weak to respond. It was a line

he had used on her more than a few times. And it still made her mad because it always seemed to be true.

As they rode the elevator, Marcela asked, "What should I tell the others?"

"Tell my client we have to reschedule. And tell Paul to cancel the afternoon. I don't think Sarah's coming back. At least not today."

"Yes, I am," Sarah forced herself to say. "I just need to rest. Don't cancel…"

But she couldn't say anymore.

Her stomach was starting to move.

"Oh, God…" Sarah pressed her sweaty face into Joe's shoulder and held on to one thought only: *Not here, not here, not here…*

Her room was just a few doors down from the elevator.

"Hurry, Burke," Sarah urged.

Her stomach lurched.

"Oh, God…"

As soon as Marcela got the door open, Joe raced with Sarah into the bathroom. Her knees barely hit the floor before her mouth exploded over the toilet.

Everything she had eaten since high school, it seemed, tried to come out of her. One wave after another, gushing, exploding.

In between heaves, Sarah fumbled at the buttons of her jacket. She peeled it off and tossed it to the side where she hoped it would be safe from any splatters. Then she tugged at the bottom of her silk top, desperate to lift it over her head.

"Sarah, what are you doing?"

"Get out!" she yelled, then vomited more. Including all over the shirt.

Now she was crying, in between heaves, as she twisted open the button on her pants. They were wool, lined, one of her nicest pairs. And she still had two more days of depositions when she'd have to wear them.

"What are you doing?" Joe asked again. "Leave those on."

"I can't—" but then another wave hit her, and her gut exploded once more.

Sarah rested for a moment against the toilet seat, and reached up to push down the handle. The bathroom reeked of vomit, and still Joe Burke stood in the doorway.

Sarah resumed trying to take off her pants.

"You'll freeze to death," Joe said. "Stop it."

"Just help me," she said.

Without asking why, he did. He pulled them off in one quick move, leaving Sarah in just her black bra and matching underwear, sitting on the cold tile floor.

"Here." Joe spread out bath towels beside her and helped her shift her knees on top of them. Then he disappeared for a moment, and returned with the thick white hotel robe that had been hanging in the closet.

Joe helped Sarah thread her arms through the sleeves, then he wrapped it around her and tied the belt. Just that little bit of jiggling against her belly had Sarah twisting toward the toilet bowl again and losing so much of her insides, it felt like it included whatever she'd eaten since junior high, and maybe even elementary school.

When the wave passed, Sarah reached up and flushed

again. Then she rolled onto the towels Joe spread out, curled her legs up into her for warmth, and let out a low moan.

She felt Joe lifting her head, then placing a soft pillow beneath it. He laid another towel over her bare legs and feet.

"Go away," Sarah moaned.

"I will," Joe said.

But meanwhile he swabbed her face with a washcloth.

"It's disgusting," she mumbled.

"It is," he agreed.

"It stinks," she said.

"It does."

"Why are you here?" Sarah murmured.

"I wanted to see you in your underwear."

Sarah couldn't help chuckling, just a little. "You're sick." But then she felt the next wave coming.

"Oh, God…"

"I've got you," Joe said as he lifted her toward the bowl.

Sarah vomited until she could have sworn she got all the way down to her mother's milk. When she finally—finally—felt empty, she flushed for the third time, then rolled onto her side again and pulled her knees up to her chest.

"I think I'm done," she managed to say.

She felt Joe lifting her up.

She didn't care that it was him. All she wanted was what he was doing, carrying her to the bed, pulling the sheets back, laying her between them and covering her up. He pulled the covers all the way to her chin.

"I'll be back," he said. "Will you be all right for a few minutes?"

Sarah nodded. She kept her eyes closed. She stayed curled in a ball.

She heard Joe closing the drapes in her room until the light was mercifully blocked out. He didn't turn on any of the lamps, but left the room dark. She heard the door click closed behind him. Then she shivered miserably in her bed.

A COOL HAND on her forehead. She reached up to touch it. It felt dry, a little hairy around the knuckles.

She peeked open one eye. "Still here?"

"Here again," Joe said.

He laid his hand against her neck. "You're burning up. Here. Take these."

He shook two ibuprofen tablets into the palm of his hand and offered them to her along with a glass of water. Sitting up seemed impossible. Sarah didn't move.

"You'll feel better," Joe told her. "Come on, I'll help you."

Her body felt pummeled by a thousand aches. She really was sick, she realized—as if the puking hadn't been enough to convince her.

"What about the depositions?" she asked.

"Cancelled." Joe helped lever her into enough of a sitting position that she could swallow without choking. Then he helped her lie back down again.

"Don't be nice to me, Burke."

"I won't," he said.

"I mean it. You're pissing me off."

"I can see why."

He got up and went into the bathroom, and returned

with a damp washcloth. He wiped away the sweat on her face and the back of her neck.

Sarah felt the sting of tears. And the pang of anger.

"Don't," she said again, this time feeling one of the tears escape.

"It's just today," Joe said. "Then we can go back to being enemies."

"Promise?" she sniffled.

"Promise. Go back to sleep, Sarah. I've got you."

Sarah looked at the clock. 5:02. AM or PM? Which day was it?

Her body ached. Her mouth felt...disgusting. There was no other word for it. Her throat was raw.

She fumbled for the lamp switch beside the bed. The light burned her eyes, so she turned it off again.

She was in her hotel room, she knew that much. Dressed in the courtesy white robe, which smelled like she hadn't treated it very courteously. She cautiously pushed herself out of bed, then unbelted the robe and let it fall to the floor. She would deal with it later, she told herself, once she felt like she might live again.

She padded into the bathroom and reluctantly turned on the light. She looked like hell. No, worse than hell: hell's monster, the one with dark red frizzy hair and a freakishly white face to scare all the sinners. She must have sweated through every hair treatment she gave herself the day before

—or was it the day before that? And Joe had been right about the dark circles under her eyes: Sarah looked like she'd been punched.

She pulled her toothbrush out of its travel case and attacked her sour mouth. She gave it two separate applications, finally tasting more normal after the second. Then she reached into the shower and turned it on as hot as it would go. She might need to stand there for a long time before she started feeling even halfway well again. She had the flu, she didn't doubt. That sick, passed out man on the plane the previous Friday must have given her the bug. Sarah had never been one of those germaphobic people who wore face masks out in public, but she could understand the appeal. She hadn't been sick in nearly a year. This wasn't the time or the place for it.

She unhooked her bra, slipped out of her underwear, and stepped into the shower. The tile was dingy, the bathtub floor chipped in places, but it was glorious, and she never appreciated hot water more. She stood there soaking up the heat, letting it penetrate her skin and bones, letting it wash away the sweat and sickness until she began to feel almost human again.

She thought she heard a sound, but the water muffled it. She opened her eyes and stuck her head out of the stream. There it was again: a soft knocking on the bathroom door.

Sarah jerked the shower curtain aside just in time to see Joe Burke enter with an armful of towels.

"Burke! Get out!"

"Good morning to you, too." He calmly laid the stack of towels on top of the toilet seat.

"Get out!" Sarah said again.

"I've seen you in the shower before."

"Not lately. What are you doing here?"

"I thought you'd want a towel when you got out."

"No, what are you doing *here*—in my hotel room?"

"Don't you remember?" he asked.

For one panicked second, Sarah thought maybe she'd blacked out—maybe they'd...but no. The last real memory she had was of puking her entire life into the bowl of the toilet. Even the most desperate man wouldn't have wanted a woman in that condition.

And she doubted Joe Burke was desperate.

"I slept on the couch," he said.

"What couch?"

"Yours. You walked right past me—didn't you see me?"

"When?" Sarah asked, still clinging to the edge of the shower curtain, wondering how sheer its thin white fabric looked from the other side.

"Right after you took off your robe," Joe said.

Sarah replayed the scene. It couldn't have been more than ten minutes ago. Had he really been right there? And why?

"You slept here?"

"Yep," he said.

"Why?"

"Mission of mercy."

"No one asked you, Burke."

"I know, but it seemed more fun than watching TV."

Sarah closed the shower curtain again and took a moment to collect herself under the hot water. Just that little bit of sniping had left her exhausted. She needed to crawl back into bed.

"I'm getting out now," she said, even though she'd planned on taking a much longer shower. "Do you mind leaving?"

"I do mind," he said, "but I'll do it."

She stuck her face out again. "You really slept here? All night?"

"Uh-huh."

"Why? Was I...that bad?"

"No, you mostly slept," he said. "Except for the times when you talked in your sleep."

"I don't talk in my sleep."

He shrugged. "Must have been my imagination."

She narrowed her eyes at him. "You know I don't talk in my sleep."

"Whatever you say, Red."

"Don't call me that."

Joe sighed. "I can't do anything right today. I bring you towels—"

"You barge in while I'm naked—"

"I clean up your vomit—"

"You didn't," she said, horrified. "Please tell me you didn't."

Joe shrugged. "Feeling better?"

Sarah thought about it for a moment. "Some. Yes, a little."

"You slept like the dead," Joe said. "I was hoping you'd wake up better."

"The dead don't talk in their sleep," Sarah said, hoping he really had been joking.

"I heard my name a few times," Joe said, "but it might have been something else."

"Shut up." She jerked the shower curtain closed again and stood there for five seconds more. Then she finally shut off the water. "I'm getting out," she called, knowing he was still in there.

"Can't wait."

"Burke, this isn't funny now. Thank you for the towels. I mean it—I appreciate that. But now you've had your fun..."

Had he really cleaned up her vomit? Fun. Right.

"Sure you don't need some help in there?" Joe asked.

Sarah's jaw tightened. "Very sure. Get out."

"I had them bring you a new robe, too," he said. "I knew the other one would probably be a toxic waste site."

"Shut up," she said again, feeling like a child for saying it. But he was egging her on like they were twenty years younger. If he was going to act like a fifth-grader, so could she.

"I'm going to order some coffee," Joe said. "Interested?"

Sarah stood behind the shower curtain, shivering. She needed a towel more than she needed to win the point.

She pulled the curtain back enough so that she could reach out toward the toilet seat, but Joe beat her to it. He handed her one of the thick towels, and smiled when she met his eye.

"I like your hair," he said.

Her hand flew to the mass of curls the water had activated. She was on the verge of saying, "Shut up" again, but stopped herself. Instead she closed the shower curtain again and began toweling off.

"I'm sure I've looked wonderful the whole time you've been here," she said. "Barfing over the toilet..."

"Hallucinating in bed..."

"I didn't," she insisted.

"Okay, if you say so."

The truth was, there might have been a dream right before she woke up. And he might have been in it. If she'd said any of that out loud...

"Burke, why are you messing with me? Do you think I'm feeling up to it right now?"

"I don't know, that's what I'm testing," he said. "I'm trying to gauge whether you can fly back home today, or whether you need to stay here."

Sarah paused in her drying. "We have depos in Idaho."

"Not anymore," he said. "Not this week, anyway."

"Why?"

"No one wants what you have," Joe said. "Especially right before Thanksgiving. Paul saw you go down yesterday morning, and he was on a flight home by the afternoon. The court reporter, too. We've all agreed to reschedule."

Sarah stepped out of the shower with the towel wrapped around her torso. She used one of the other towels to hide her spiraling hair. "Rescheduled them when?" she asked, feeling less self-conscious now that they were talking about work again. "We don't have time."

"We'll stop by here again as part of Montana next week," Joe said. "The flight from Missoula to Billings goes through Salt Lake anyway. And we'll squeeze in Idaho after that. Don't worry, Henley, it's all taken care of."

She liked it better when he called her "Henley" than

when he called her "Red." She almost felt like they were back on normal footing now. Except for the fact that he was standing in her bathroom wearing loose cotton pants and a T-shirt, and she wore nothing but two towels.

"Chapman left yesterday?" she said, finally processing that bit of information.

"Yep."

"But you didn't."

"Nope."

She looked at Joe in the small space between them. He gave her an easy look back, not trying to get credit, it seemed, but just stating the facts: he had taken care of her. He had stayed to watch over her. And he was still there.

Sarah shook her head. "This doesn't change anything."

Joe looked her in the eye. "I know." Then he turned to leave, saying, "Coffee, Red?"

Sarah bit back her first response. She forced herself to be pleasant—for her own sake, not his. Yes, what he had done was very kind. Above and beyond, even. But if he expected anything in return—anything more than the most basic, polite gratitude—he was deluded.

"Tea would be better," she said.

He walked over toward the bed and picked up the hotel phone. While he ordered breakfast for them both, Sarah closed the bathroom door and changed into the white robe. Her hair was appalling, but she didn't have the strength to do anything about it. And like Burke said, he'd seen her straight out of the shower—and in it—before.

"I let your office know yesterday," Joe said when she emerged again.

"Know what, exactly?" she asked, her pulse jumping.

"That you were sick and the depositions were off." He cocked an eyebrow at her. "What did you think I meant?"

That we used to be lovers, that you carried me to my room, that you helped me undress, that you held me so I could vomit, that you spent the night with me despite how disgusting that must have been—

"What did they say?" Sarah asked, deflecting his question.

"I spoke to your secretary."

"Not mine," Sarah corrected. "I'm just sharing her—"

"I spoke to someone," Joe continued, "and I told her you'd call her when you were feeling up to it."

"Oh. Okay." Sarah sat on the edge of her bed. Sleep was calling to her, but she needed to deal with business first. "Thanks for letting her know. That was...probably right."

"I try to be right," he said, looking amused at how hard it seemed to be for her to give him any compliment or a thank you.

He pulled on the sneakers lying next to the couch she hadn't even noticed before. All the hotel rooms seemed so alike to her now, all she cared about was whether they had a bed and a bathroom.

"I have to go down to my room for a few minutes," he said. "I'll be back before room service is here. You should get into bed."

Sarah decided he wasn't ordering her around if it was something she wanted to do anyway. She wrapped her robe more tightly around her, then slipped back between the sheets. Joe stepped over to the bed and tugged the blanket and bedspread up closer around her shoulders.

"Burke?"

"Yeah?"

"I think...that was good, what you did for me yesterday." She nodded, convincing herself. "Thank you. I doubt Chapman would have done the same."

"He would if he'd known he could see you in a black bra and panties."

"Shut up," Sarah muttered before diving deeper beneath the blanket.

11

S arah sat up and ate toast and tea in bed while Joe had coffee, eggs, and a bagel at the desk in Sarah's room. At the same time, he worked on his laptop and made a few phone calls.

"I don't know," she heard him say to whomever he was talking to. "At least another day, maybe two."

He listened, then said, "I can't talk about that right now. I'll send you an e-mail."

"What did you tell people?" Sarah asked when he hung up. "About why you're still here?"

"I said I wanted to get in some skiing."

"You don't ski, do you?"

"No." Joe dialed his phone and asked for a lawyer whose name Sarah recognized. She took another sip of tea, then leaned back against her pillow and closed her eyes.

"You're going to have to talk to Luke about that," Joe said

to the person on the phone. "He's taken over all my cases for a while. I'm on the road now."

Sarah opened her increasingly-heavy eyes and peeked over at Burke. He was hunched over the desk now, elbow resting on the surface, his forehead leaning against his hand. "Yeah, well, there's a lot going on," he told the person. "I can't talk about it right now. Call Luke. He'll get you what you need."

He set his phone down and stared glumly at it. When he looked over at Sarah again, she gave him a small smile.

"Purgatory?" she asked.

Joe nodded.

"Feel like sharing?"

"Not really. How was breakfast?"

Sarah laid her hand on her stomach. "It's staying down, so that's good. But I think I need another nap."

"Do you mind if I work in here?"

"No." In fact, Sarah was surprised by how much she wanted that. She liked hearing his voice in the background. She liked feeling him close by.

Which should have been reason enough to tell him to leave. But she wasn't feeling up to that.

Sarah slid back down to horizontal and closed her eyes. But then she turned to her side again and looked over at Joe.

"Are they trying to push you out?" she asked. "At your firm?"

"Yes."

"So why don't you quit? I'm sure someone like you could find a job right away."

As opposed to someone like me, Sarah thought, with the

stain of the FBI raid and all the partner indictments following her everywhere on her résumé.

"I will," he said, "eventually."

"But why would you keep doing this?" Sarah asked him. "I can understand me, but not you—"

Joe's phone rang. He looked at the screen and answered the call. "Joe Burke. Yeah, thanks for getting back to me, Todd. I heard Judge Lewis issued an order, and I wanted to let you know that Luke Tanner is handling that for me now..."

Sarah's eyes drifted closed again while Joe's familiar voice carried on in the background. One of the last things she thought before giving in to the tired was that she missed this—missed him, missed having him around.

It wasn't your choice, she reminded herself. *You could have gone on like that forever.*

He's the one who broke your heart.

But it was getting harder and harder for her to stay angry about it.

Now all she felt was the loss.

When she woke again, Joe was gone. He left the drapes closed and all the lights off, so once again she wasn't sure of the time. The clock said 12:42, and she guessed it must be afternoon, since she couldn't imagine sleeping sixteen hours straight. Still, it was worth checking.

Sarah climbed out of bed, testing her legs. They felt better, less shaky. Her stomach felt better, too, and in fact growled a little with hunger. Sarah pulled back the heavy drapes and let the light shine in. The sky was a brilliant blue, and looked particularly beautiful against the snowy white peaks of the mountains.

This place really was stunning, Sarah thought. She would have loved to stand outside and breathe in some of the fresh air. But the only clothes she had were her suit, which may or may not have survived the vomit, and the workout capris and T-shirt she brought along. She had packed pajamas, too, one of her nice satin sets she bought during the period of *Flourish*, but none of those clothes in combination gave her an outfit she could wear outside. Maybe she could use the hotel robe as a coat.

But Joe had already thought of that.

Resting on the low table in front of the couch was a bag. And inside were a sweatshirt and matching sweatpants, both with "Utah" written across them. He also bought her a pair of fuzzy socks, the kind with little plastic circles dotting the bottom to keep the socks from slipping on the floor.

Sarah sank onto the couch and examined the loot. Why was he being so nice to her?

She had the chance to ask him when he returned within the hour carrying two sacks of food: a burger and fries for him, hot oatmeal and a banana for her. He also handed her a cup of tea.

"Burke, what is this?" she said. "The clothes, the food, the knight in shining armor..."

"Just doing my duty," he said.

"What duty?" she asked, almost afraid of his answer.

"Taking care of opposing counsel. I think it's somewhere in the rules."

"Right," Sarah said, but she didn't press him any further.

She opened the lid on the Starbucks oatmeal and shook out the brown sugar packet on top. She left the nuts and dried fruit alone—she thought they might be too rough on her recovering stomach.

Joe sat on the couch and laid his own feast out on the table. Then he started scrolling through his phone.

"Thanks for the clothes," Sarah said. She had noticed Joe's the minute he walked in. He wore jeans—button-down Levi's—which was unfortunate. Because she always thought he looked particularly great in jeans—the way they hugged his backside just perfectly. For some reason they always made him look especially masculine. Or maybe it was just because he'd been wearing them the night she always thought of as the beginning of everything between them.

Along with his jeans this time he wore a fleece pullover on top, charcoal gray over a white T-shirt. And sturdy sneakers that might have qualified as hiking boots. It was a good look, overall, Sarah thought. It made him look strong and tall and outdoorsy. Like a man who had just come in from chopping wood.

"You really need to start packing for the weather," Joe told her. "It's going to get colder the next few months where we're going, not warmer. You should always have something as backup."

"Thanks for the advice," she answered dryly. But she bit back anything more in favor of eating the soothing food he'd brought her.

"Something else," Joe said, getting up. He went to Sarah's bag resting on the luggage cart. She realized he must have gone through there to know she hadn't packed anything warm. But before she could complain about that, Joe reached into her bag and pulled something out.

"What are you doing with this?"

Sarah's face heated up. And not with fever this time.

"It's none of your business."

"Sarah, are you crazy?"

She stared at the hair iron in Joe's hand. Not only was it an Atheena, it was the exact make and model that had lit all those women's hair on fire.

"I know you're not stupid," Joe said, "so why are you being so stupid?"

"I believe in the product."

"Cut the crap," Joe said. "Have you not been listening to every one of my clients? This thing is dangerous, Sarah. I should have thrown it out when I found it."

"Don't you dare," Sarah said, getting out of bed and grabbing it away from him. "I know what you think, but this is the best product I've ever had. You wouldn't understand—you've never had to deal with hair like mine."

He looked at her frizzy mop. "I like it the way it is—right now. Why do you have to do anything to it?"

"Right," Sarah said, shoving the hair iron back into her bag. "What do you have to do to your hair, Joe? Run a bar of soap over it and you're done? You wouldn't understand."

"You called me Joe."

"It was an accident."

"Sarah, please don't use that thing anymore. You may hate your hair the way it is right now, but it's a hell of a lot better than burning it all off."

"That's not going to happen to me."

"How do you know?" he asked.

"Because I have a theory. And it's none of your business. *Counsel.*"

It was true, she did have a theory, and it wasn't one she was ready to share with him or even her new boss yet. She knew she might be grasping for an answer, simply because she couldn't bear giving up something that really had proven to be a miracle for her hair. But if she was right, it could mean a dramatic shift in the case.

Sarah scooped up the plastic bag that held the sweatshirt and sweatpants. "But thank you," she said. "For these. I can finally get out of my robe."

"What do you wear to bed?" Joe asked.

"Excuse me?"

"I was looking for some warm flannel pajamas or something. You looked like you were freezing last night."

Sarah paused on her way to the bathroom and pulled out the satin pants and camisole she would have worn to bed if she'd been lucid the night before.

"Oh, I thought those were...never mind," Joe said, shoveling in a few more fries. He waved for Sarah to continue on to the bathroom.

"Thought they were what?" she asked.

"You never used to sleep in anything like that."

"I couldn't afford it," she said.

"You didn't sleep in much at all," he said, making sure to look her in the eye.

"Ancient history, Burke." She stepped into the bathroom and shut the door behind her. Then stayed where she was for a moment, leaning against the wood, eyes closed as she tried to block out the image Joe had just planted in her mind.

He didn't sleep in anything, either. And it had been cold then, too.

But neither of them had seemed to mind.

12

It took two flights to get them to Carbondale, Illinois, to the law school where the competition was held. It was the first week in November, and already temperatures were below freezing at night. Sarah had underestimated the weather and brought only a light jacket in addition to the suit she would wear for the actual oral argument.

It was the same suit she'd saved up to buy for the competition the previous year. Even though that particular day had ended so badly with her partner practically having to be carried from the room, Sarah still had faith in the outfit to help her win this time. Besides, she hadn't gotten her wear out of it yet, and for what she spent, she'd better.

She wore jeans, a cotton sweater, and her jacket on the plane, but as soon as she stepped into the Carbondale airport she knew they wouldn't be enough. Even in that closed environment, she was already freezing. She couldn't imagine what it would be like once they were outside.

"Let's get the car," Ellen told them, and marched off toward the rental counter. She had taken it upon herself to make all the travel arrangements for the group, and as treasurer for Moot Court, she was very budget-conscious. She announced that morning when they met at the L.A. airport that the men would be sharing one hotel room, the women another. Sarah had been very sorry to hear it.

As an only child, she wasn't used to having to sleep in a room with anyone else. Even when she went to college, the Cal State San Bernardino campus was close enough that she could still live at home rather than in a dorm. And the place she rented while she was in law school was a tiny guest house in Westwood, too nice for what the owner charged her, but the woman took pity on Sarah the first time they met. Sarah knew some of her classmates had roommates— sometimes multiples—and she couldn't imagine having to deal with all that distraction.

So she wasn't looking forward to having a roommate even for the three nights they would be there. Especially not that night, when she wanted to make sure she was fresh and well-rested for the oral argument the next day.

"Yes, Ellen Kiptar," Ellen told the person behind the counter. "I've reserved a compact."

"A compact?" Mickey said. "Joe and I are both over six foot."

"It's cheaper," Ellen said, waving him away. "And it's just a short drive."

Sarah stood off to the side, trying to warm herself. Her jacket had pockets, but she wished she brought a hat and gloves. None of the others seemed to be as cold as she was.

Joe Burke wore just jeans and his UCLA hoodie, and he looked perfectly comfortable with his hands buried deep in the single pocket.

He must have noticed her look of longing, because the next thing she knew, he was standing in front of her, reaching for her hands. Without a word, he covered them in his own warm ones and brought them back with him into the cocoon of his hoodie pocket.

Sarah looked up and met his gaze. "Thanks."

"Sure thing."

They hadn't spoken very much. Just a few words that morning at LAX, then a few more as they waited in St. Louis to switch planes.

She wasn't sure why they didn't talk, but she also didn't mind. The two of them weren't competing against each other directly—teams from each school would be randomly assigned teams from other schools to go up against in the preliminary rounds—but Burke felt like her competition nonetheless. She had sat through three of his and Ellen's practice arguments, and was impressed with him each time.

He never seemed to feel rushed or nervous. The guest judges could bark questions at him one after another, and he always took the time to offer a patient explanation of why the judge's point was a good one, but didn't change the outcome Joe was arguing for. He always acknowledged any case law that seemed to hurt him, but then explained why it didn't apply to this situation.

Sarah listened to those answers carefully, using them to prepare her own arguments for the other side.

Joe sat in on a few of Mickey's and her rehearsals, too,

Sarah noticed, although he always left before they finished. She assumed he was doing the same thing she was, scouting the arguments for the other side so he could better prepare for the competition.

But now all that preparation was over, and it was time to see how far they could all get. Preliminary rounds would begin the next morning, with the top two teams advancing to the finals on Saturday. There would be an awards banquet Friday night, announcing the finalists, then another banquet Saturday, then everyone would leave Sunday morning to return to their classes the next day.

"Trying to steal my girl?" Mickey asked as he came over to stand too close to where Joe warmed Sarah's hands.

"Not your girl," Sarah reminded him, "and I'm freezing. Thanks, Burke," she said, starting to withdraw her hands. He gave them one more squeeze before he let them go.

"Ready?" Ellen asked, holding up a key.

"You go ahead," Joe said. "I'll see you all tomorrow."

Ellen scoffed. "What do you mean, you'll see us tomorrow?"

"Seven AM breakfast at the school, right?" Joe said. "I'll see you there."

He stepped up to the rental counter while Ellen continued gaping at him. "Joe, what are you doing? Let's go."

He told the man behind the counter his name, then turned back to Ellen and answered her with that same calm voice Sarah had heard him use on judges trying to rattle him. "I'm taking care of this myself. Don't worry, it's my own money. I'll see you all tomorrow. Have a good night." He offered that last sentiment to Sarah alone.

"But...what about the hotel?" Ellen asked. "We'll see you there, right?"

"Nope, taking care of that, too," Joe said. "I stopped sharing rooms when my brother moved out."

Ellen had a few more things to say, but Joe ignored her. Instead he slipped Sarah a relaxed smile before turning around again to deal with the rental agent.

"Come on," Sarah said, tugging Ellen by the arm. "It's too cold to keep standing around. Let's get to the hotel."

As the three of them walked toward the exit that would lead to the garage, Sarah looked back one more time and saw Joe watching her. She gave him a single, approving nod. Then she turned and followed her classmates out the door.

"I HAVE *HAD* it with that guy," Ellen said as soon as she and Sarah were alone in their room. Sarah tried to seem busy unpacking her clothes and hanging them in the closet. "You have no idea how obstinate he is," Ellen said. "I've had to fight him on absolutely everything."

"Like what?" Sarah asked. She couldn't remember any fights she'd had with Mickey.

Ellen counted them off on her fingers. "Who should brief which arguments. Who should lead at the oral argument. Which cases we should include and which we should wait for the judges to bring up." Ellen shook her head. "It's too long to go into. I wish I had your partner."

Funny, Sarah thought, she'd been thinking the same thing about Joe. From what she had seen of him during practice, the two of them would have made a much stronger team than either of them with their existing partners. Not that Mickey or Ellen wouldn't do well, but maybe not as well as Sarah and Joe together.

"You saw how he is," Ellen said. "He never even told me he was going to get his own car. And I went to all that trouble with the hotel rooms."

"But you only told us about that this morning," Sarah pointed out. If she'd thought of it—and had the extra money to spare—she wouldn't have minded booking a room all to herself, too. So far every move of Joe's was one she wished she had made.

"Are you and Mickey dating?" Ellen asked.

"What? No."

"I heard what he said to Joe about stealing his girl."

"We're just teammates," Sarah said. "Mickey likes to joke around."

"Wish we could switch," Ellen said. "I think Mickey's a lot smarter. And he's obviously a lot easier to work with."

"Hm," Sarah answered noncommittally. Ellen could think whatever she wanted.

Sarah escaped into the bathroom to wash her face and brush her teeth. She would save the shower until the morning so she only risked getting her hair wet the one time. She had gotten up early that morning to give it the maximum attention before she had to rush to the airport. Now if it would just behave for the next twenty-four hours, that was one less detail to worry about.

"I hope you brought ear plugs," Ellen called from the other room.

Sarah had a bad feeling. "Why?"

"I don't really sleep," Ellen said. "So you might hear me practicing during the night."

"Great..." Sarah answered herself in the mirror.

She hoped Mickey and Joe were both enjoying having their rooms all to themselves.

At two-thirty in the morning, Sarah had finally had enough.

"Ellen, either go downstairs or shut up."

"I *told* you," Ellen said, as if that made up for all the mumbling and pacing and gesticulating she'd been doing on and off for the past several hours.

Sarah groaned and pressed the pillow over her head once more. She could still hear Ellen whispering, "Yes, your honor, but as you know, the constitutional right to privacy must be always balance the needs of the individual against the interests of the state—"

"Ellen!"

"I'm sorry, I'll try to be quieter."

But Sarah could still hear her for the next hour or two until one or both of them finally passed out.

"Shit," Mickey said when he saw her.

"Don't say *anything*." Sarah was still trying to contain her rage. She knew her pale face looked blotchy. She knew the pillow she pressed to her head all night had left her uncontrollable hair even unrulier than usual. And she knew her eyes looked as red and raw as they felt. "That woman is the devil."

Joe Burke walked up to Mickey and Sarah in time to hear her assessment.

"Took me longer to figure that out," he said. "By then it was too late to find a new partner."

"At least you didn't have to sleep in the same room with her," Sarah said.

"A gentleman can always say no," Joe said.

"Are you kidding me?" Sarah said with a harsh laugh. "Are you saying she actually tried?"

"You know how it is," Joe said, looking from Sarah to Mickey.

"No," she answered emphatically, "I don't."

Mickey wrapped an arm around Sarah's shoulders and gave them a squeeze. "Too bad, Burke. You should be more careful who you link up with."

It wasn't hard to catch the territorialism behind Mickey's gesture. Sarah wasn't in the mood. Her nerves felt so close to the surface she was having a hard time being pleasant to anyone. She stepped out of Mickey's embrace.

"Have they announced the assignments?" Joe asked her.

"Not yet," she said.

"I'm getting coffee," he offered. "Want some?"

"Yeah, that'd be great. Thanks."

"Black for me," Mickey said.

Joe gave no sign that he heard him.

While Joe drifted toward the breakfast buffet table, Sarah continued to fume. "You'd better pray we don't go on until this afternoon," she told Mickey. "Then at least I can go back and get some sleep."

"You can stay in my room, if you want," he said.

"Very funny," she said.

"I'm not being funny, Sarah."

"What did I say?" she reminded him. "This is not an opportunity to get into my pants."

She didn't realize she said it so loudly until she saw a few heads turn in her direction.

One of them was Joe's. He caught her eye and gave her an amused smile.

Sarah turned her back to him and lowered her voice. "I'm *this* close to losing it, Mickey, so don't push me today. And I'd better see you doing your rosary or whatever that is for an afternoon slot."

But when the schedule for the preliminary rounds was finally announced, Sarah groaned and dropped her forehead against Mickey's chest. "Ten-thirty? Why?"

Mickey wrapped both arms around her and pulled her in close. Sarah lifted her head up again and gave it a hard shake.

"Okay, we can do this," she said, extricating herself from Mickey's arms. "I just need about fifty more cups of coffee."

She went in search of Ellen to get a ride back to the hotel. Both of them still needed to change and get ready.

Ellen was busy arguing with Joe. "I *told* you you should have stayed with us!"

"What's the problem?" Sarah asked.

"Our argument's not until eleven," Ellen said. "We'd still have time for one more practice, but Mr. Defiant here is at some hotel way on the other side of town, and won't be able to get back until right before we go on."

Joe looked at Sarah and shrugged.

But there was something about the look he gave her that she didn't quite understand.

"Ellen, we need to get ready," Sarah said. "Let's go."

"In a minute," Ellen said. "I want to go look at the list first."

"We already know who we're all paired with—" Sarah started to say.

"I can take you," Joe interrupted.

"No," Ellen told him. "You'll be too late. Just go back and change and meet me here as soon as you can."

Joe ignored her and kept his eyes on Sarah. "Ready to go now?"

"Yes."

The idea of getting away from Ellen even for the space of a short car ride to the hotel sounded too good to pass up. Even being free of Mickey for a little while would be good for Sarah's nerves. She needed quiet and solitude, without people picking at her and talking to her. Burke didn't seem to need to fill the air with noise. And he wasn't constantly touching her the way Mickey was lately.

"I'll meet you back at the hotel," she told Mickey. "The three of us can ride back together."

"Okay, but I'll need at least an hour to do my hair and makeup," Ellen warned her. "So try to be out of the bath-room before I get back."

Try not to strangle you with my bare hands, Sarah thought, but she was too tired to bother answering.

"Ready?" Joe asked her.

Sarah led the way from the room.

Once they were in the car, she leaned her head back against the seat and closed her eyes. "I hope this isn't too out of your way."

"It's not," he said. "My hotel's right next to yours."

Sarah looked over at him. "But I thought you were way across town?"

Joe gave her a look back.

"Oh," she said, smiling for the first time that day. "You just don't want to have to practice again."

"Would you?"

"God, no," Sarah said.

They rode in silence for a few minutes before Joe said, "I tried to get you, you know."

"What do you mean?"

"As a partner. I was going to ask you at our first Moot Court meeting, but Hughes beat me to it."

"Really?" A warmth flushed over Sarah's face. But her nerves were still too raw to enjoy the sensation. She felt ready to jump out of her skin.

"So I did the next best thing and signed up for the same competition."

"Joe, are you serious?"

"Hundred percent."

"That's...nice. But why?"

"You're great at this," Joe said. "I like watching what you do. I think we would have made an unbeatable team."

"I like watching you, too," Sarah admitted. She leaned back against the headrest again and closed her eyes. "Oh, well." She tried to make it sound light, but the regret actually felt heavy.

"But we're here now," Joe said. "So let's make the best of it."

"How?" Sarah asked, yawning.

"For one thing, you can come take a nap in my room."

SHE PROTESTED, but only a little. Joe waited in the car while Sarah returned to her room and quickly gathered up her suit and all her toiletries. Then he drove them the extra five minutes to the hotel where he was staying.

"This isn't some trick, is it, Joe?" she asked as he let her into his room. "Because if it is..."

He flipped on the light. "We have a little less than two hours before I should take you back. How long will you need to get ready?"

"Um...maybe a half hour, forty-five minutes."

He set the alarm on his watch. "Go lie down. I'll wake you up when it's time."

She hesitated for a moment, then had to ask him again. "This isn't some trick, is it?"

"Why would I trick you?"

"I don't know, let me oversleep and miss the argument so your team can win?"

"You may find this hard to believe," he said, "but I'm not like you and Ellen. I don't need to win everything."

"Neither do I," Sarah protested. "Just...most things. I've worked really hard for this."

"And I promise I'll get you there on time," Joe said. "But

every minute you're still arguing with me, you could be sleeping. So get into bed while I take a shower."

Exhaustion pulled at her like a weight around her bones. She hung her suit in Joe's closet, then kicked off her sneakers and lay down on his bed.

"Under the covers," he said. "Go on, it's warmer."

She felt odd about it, but went ahead and crawled in, still dressed in her jeans and sweater. Joe turned off the light.

"Why are you doing this?" Sarah asked into the dark.

"Because I like you, Red. And I want you to do well, despite my psychotic partner." Then Joe closed the bathroom door and turned on the shower.

SARAH HAD HAD power naps before: those twenty-minute wonders that could take the edge off exhaustion and let her study long hours into the night.

But a full hour of complete, restful sleep in Joe's bed felt so healing, by the time he woke her up she almost felt whole.

"You should probably call Mickey," Joe said when she opened her eyes.

"Why?"

"I'm going to take you straight to the school, not back to your hotel. You can tell him you'll meet him."

Sarah rubbed her eyes and reached for her phone. She dialed Mickey.

"Where are you?" he asked.

"With...Joe. I took a nap."

There was silence on the other end.

"Mickey?"

"Yeah. Whatever. See you there." Then he hung up.

"He thinks we had sex," Sarah told Joe. She surprised herself by saying that out loud.

But Joe took it in stride. "He's married, you know."

"*What?*" Sarah stared back at him . "No, you're joking."

"Married, with a kid on the way. You should ask him."

Sarah's mouth still hung open. "Unbelievable." Then she laughed.

"You don't care?"

"Not in the least—except he's a douchebag for always hitting on me."

"It wasn't going to work one of these days?" Joe asked.

"Hardly."

"How come?"

Sarah pulled back the covers and swung her legs over the side of the bed. "I'm here to work, Burke. Thanks for letting me sleep. Now I need to get ready for battle."

13

When Sarah emerged from Joe's bathroom with her hair done, makeup on, and wearing the most expensive outfit she'd ever owned—a navy blue pencil skirt and snug-fitting jacket, with a crisp white cotton blouse underneath—Joe took a step back and made a fist at his heart.

"Shut up," she said, but the gesture pleased her.

"Red, you're a total knockout."

"Stop calling me that."

"Okay, Henley," Joe said, "but you're not actually going out like that, are you? Give the rest of us a chance."

She smoothed her skirt over her thighs. "You think I look okay?"

Joe looked her up and down once more, and let his eyes linger at her chest.

"Nice fit," he said.

She crossed her arms.

"Don't ever be embarrassed of having a great body, Henley," Joe said. "You're doing a public service walking around like that."

"Can we go?" she asked dryly.

He stepped closer and pressed a kiss to her cheek.

"Great. Am I going to have a problem with you, too?" she asked. She tried to sound irritated, knowing the flush on her skin might give her away.

"Can't help it," Joe said. "You're that beautiful."

Sarah glanced at her watch, just to have something to do. He wasn't making her nervous, exactly, just...distracted.

Joe lifted his own suit jacket from where it hung over a chair, and met her at the door. He opened it for her, then followed her out into the hall.

"You're gonna kill," he told her. "And not just because all the male judges will be salivating. I've listened to your argument, Sarah, and it's great."

The compliment pleased her even more than any of the ones about her looks. "Yours, too, Joe. You're one of the best I've seen."

"In a lot of respects," he said, and when she raised an eyebrow at him, showing him how unimpressed she was by what was obviously a line, he added, "But we can talk about that after one of us wins."

Mickey was obviously not happy.

Joe wished Sarah and Mickey good luck, then left to find Ellen.

"What are you doing with him?" Mickey muttered, pulling Sarah off to the side.

"Sleeping," she said. "Literally sleeping. You should be happy I did, too—I feel fine again, thanks for asking."

Mickey swung his arms back and forth in front of his chest and hopped in place a few times like he was about to go in there for a weight lifting competition instead of an oral argument.

"Are you ready for this?" Sarah asked, giving his arm a squeeze.

Mickey nodded and blew out a breath. "Sure. Ready. Absolutely."

Their opponents, two men from Georgia State University, stood several feet away, talking in low voices. Every now and then they looked up at Sarah and Mickey, then went back to muttering between them.

Finally the door to the classroom opened, and the two teams ahead of them emerged. One of the women looked like she had been caught in a rainstorm, her hair was so matted to her head with perspiration. Sarah could see dark patches under the woman's arms where she'd sweated through her suit. One of the men on the other team didn't look much better. It made Sarah wonder how she and Catherine must have looked to people last year when the two of them came stumbling out, Sarah supporting Catherine around the waist in case she collapsed again.

Mickey stared after the people who had just left. He had a pale look to his face.

"You'll be fine," Sarah told him. "You're ready, Mickey. Come on. Let's go do this."

For all his self-confidence over the past two months—not just self-confidence, Sarah thought, but cockiness—the guy looked like he was starting to lose it. His eyes seemed jittery. And she could see beads of sweat above his lip.

"Mickey." Sarah took him by both arms and tried to steady him with her gaze. "I'm going first, right? So you can watch me."

She stopped talking while the team from Georgia State passed by and headed into the room.

"Then we'll go have a beer afterward and it'll all be fine," she said. "Just do it exactly the way we've practiced, all right?"

Mickey nodded. More sweat had pooled above his lip. He wiped it away with his sleeve.

Sarah wondered how Joe would have been in these few minutes before the argument. Somehow she doubted she'd have to give him a pep talk right now.

"We have to go," Sarah said. "Come on." She pulled Mickey into the room.

"How was yours? I thought we did really well," Ellen said, not waiting for an answer. She and Joe found Sarah and Mickey still talking outside in the cold, Mickey pacing back and forth to work off all his excess stress.

Mickey kept taking his jacket off, then putting it back on every time the wind got to be too much. He had sweated through his jacket just like that woman, Sarah noticed, although Mickey's stains reached halfway to his waist. At times during the argument, his sweat was so epic, it actually ran down the sides of his face like blood pouring from a head wound.

"Either of you have a cigarette?" Mickey asked Joe and Ellen.

"You smoke?" Sarah asked.

"Used to," Mickey said. "Going to again."

"How'd you do?" Sarah asked Joe quietly.

He shrugged. "Not bad. You?"

Sarah nodded. They both seemed to understand they wouldn't be able to talk about it honestly until they were free of their partners.

"So," Joe said, "how about lunch?"

"And a beer?" Mickey said to Sarah.

"Right. I promised."

"Good news," Ellen said in a cheerful, almost giddy voice. Sarah wondered if it was because she did well during the argument, or because she was just so relieved it was over. "Since breakfast was free," Ellen told them, "we still have all that money, plus the rest of our meal allowance for today. So we can eat anywhere we want."

"How much?" Joe asked.

"We can even have a few beers," Ellen said, not looking at Joe.

"How much is the allowance, Ellen?" he repeated.

It was the first any of them had heard of any allowance.

"A hundred a day," Ellen said. "It's what the Moot Court board voted all the teams would get this year."

"A hundred per team?" Joe asked.

"Per...person," Ellen said, clearly uncomfortable being pressed.

"And where is all this money?" Joe asked.

"I have it," Ellen said, sounding less cheerful by the moment.

Joe held out his hand. "I'll take mine now. Sarah, you want yours?"

She had watched the whole exchange without realizing it might mean anything to her. "Oh. Sure. That would be good."

Ellen made a face as she pulled open her purse. She obviously didn't like giving up control. She took her time removing the envelope and counting out four fifties.

"But you're coming to lunch with us, right?" she asked.

"Sure, we'll come for a beer," Joe said. "What do you say, Sarah?"

Sarah noticed the "we." Somehow in the last few minutes she'd gone from being Mickey's companion to being Joe's. She wasn't sure when the shift had happened, but she knew it had.

And she didn't mind.

"A beer sounds good," Sarah said. "Come on, Mickey. We'll even find you some cigarettes if you need them."

Then it seemed natural to follow Joe to his car, rather than to go with Ellen and Mickey.

"How about that steak place near the hotel?" Ellen called after them.

"Sure," Sarah said. She and Joe continued walking.

"Mind if we make a stop first?" Joe asked her.

"No." She didn't mind anything at the moment. It felt good to be back around someone who wasn't freaking out, wasn't rehashing everything that he'd said in front of the judges, practically begging Sarah to tell him again how great he had done and that no, he didn't screw up.

"How'd it really go?" Joe asked her.

"So-so. Yours?"

"It had its moments."

Sarah looked at him and smiled. "Were you any good, Burke?"

He shrugged. "Good enough. You, Red?"

"I think so."

He reached down for her cold hand and pulled her in closer. "Wish I could have seen you."

Joe parked in front of the Walmart.

"Okay..." Sarah said.

"This will only take a minute," Joe told her. He waited until she came around her side of the car, then slipped his hand in hers again.

"You think this is okay?" she asked him, holding up their joined fingers.

"I think so," he confirmed, "don't you?"

She shrugged, trying to appear indifferent. But the truth was, her heart was pounding. And she wasn't sure what to do about it. She also wasn't sure what had happened in the last ten or fifteen minutes to take them from where they'd been with each other that morning, to where they were right now.

Once they were inside, Joe tugged her toward the left, into the clothing section. He wandered a few aisles before finding what he wanted.

"Take your pick," he said, "although I think this one looks nice."

He let go of her hand and reached for a soft pink fleece hat hanging from the display rack. He pulled it gently over her head.

"Maybe you don't like pink," he said.

Sarah looked in the nearby mirror. "Pink is fine, but it's kind of cliché for redheads."

"Try blue," Joe said, handing her a replacement.

He kept his arm around her waist as they both looked at the hat in the mirror. Sarah found it hard to concentrate.

"Blue's fine," she managed to say.

"Here, try these on." He handed her the matching one-size-fits-all gloves. "Get the whole set for five-ninety-nine."

The gloves looked more like a child's size than an adult's, but as Sarah pushed her fingers into them, they expanded to fit perfectly. She wriggled her fingers to model them.

Joe stood in front of her and gently tugged on the hat, pulling it lower around her ears. And with him that close, that kind, after a whole string of kindnesses all morning long, Sarah couldn't resist twisting her gloved fingers in the lapel of his suit jacket and pulling his mouth down to hers.

Their hunger for each other shocked her. As if they'd both stood coiled, ready, waiting for the other to make a move. Joe captured her by the hips and pulled her hard against him as Sarah locked her hands behind his neck. He was at least half a foot taller, but in her heels she narrowed the distance. He spread his hands along the sides of her ribcage, practically lifting her body into his. She pressed against the length of him, feeling the unmistakable hardness that pressed back, and she kissed him, devoured him, made out with him there in the Walmart accessories aisle, both of them in their suits, Sarah in her powder blue hat and gloves, Joe with his hands buried now in the ends of her hair, tugging her head back while he took her mouth, neither of them caring who in that town might see them or what they might think.

Finally they came up for air. The two of them stood staring at each other, panting. "We were supposed to meet those guys," Sarah said, surprised she could even think anymore.

"We will," Joe answered. "In a minute."

But instead of taking her mouth with his again, he reached down and clasped her hand. "Come with me."

Sarah tried not to panic when she saw where they were going.

"A little fast, wouldn't you say, Burke?" she joked, trying to sound unconcerned.

"I told you, a gentleman can always say no," Joe answered, pulling down a package of condoms. "But if you ask me, Sarah, I'm not going to say no."

Was he really going to leave it up to her? she wondered. Although considering what she'd just started, he probably didn't have too many doubts.

"Joe, I'm not sure..."

He squeezed her hand as they walked toward the check-out. "I just don't want to have to come back here in a hurry."

He studied her face as he paid for their items. At the last minute, Sarah realized he'd just pulled out one of the fifties Ellen had given him. "No, here," Sarah said, reaching for one of her own. "I'll buy my own hat and gloves." Then she blushed, thinking how obvious she had just made it that the condoms were on him.

"Next time," Joe said, gently pushing away her money. "You can buy my lunch." He finished paying and they left.

On the way back to the car, Joe said, "I'll never try to rush you, Sarah. I've already waited all this time."

"All what time?" she asked, thinking it had only been a few hours since that morning.

Joe smiled. "A long time." He leaned down and kissed her again, and as Sarah deepened it, Joe braced the two of them against the side of the rental car. Someone driving by honked. Joe raised a hand and waved, and kept right on kissing her.

MICKEY AND ELLEN were already two beers down apiece and nearly finished with their meals by the time Sarah and Joe arrived.

"We ordered a pitcher," Ellen said, "but obviously we weren't going to keep waiting. Where have you two been?"

"Can't you guess?" Mickey said. He took a long drag on his cigarette.

Sarah held up her hands. "Gloves." She patted the hat on her head. "I was tired of being so cold."

"Oh, you don't seem so cold right now," Mickey said. "What do you think, Burke?"

"I think I'm going to get us some food. Sarah? What would you like?"

While Joe hunted down the waitress to order them both a few burgers, Sarah excused herself to go to the restroom.

Once she was safely inside, she let her face finally unleash the huge smile she had been holding back—even in front of Joe. What she felt was too adolescent to let him see. She duplicated the move she saw Mickey make that morning, hopping in place a few times. Then she gazed at her face in the mirror. Her makeup was smeared and her lips looked puffy. Her eyes were bright and alive. Such a different face than the one that had greeted her first thing in the morning, blotchy and ragged with sleeplessness.

But was she really going to sleep with him?

Sarah wasn't a virgin, but she might as well have been for all the experience she had. One awkward night when she was in high school, then two more very uninspiring encounters with different guys when she was in college. Either they didn't know what they were doing or she didn't, and she was willing to believe it was both.

But she guessed from the string of girls she'd seen Joe with since she started paying attention to him that he had at least some clue how to do things better. And their long makeout session in Walmart had certainly backed that up. Even just kissing him, clothes on, was already more arousing than anything anyone had ever done to her before. If that was what they could accomplish in public, she could only imagine what they would be like in private.

Actually, Sarah thought, she couldn't imagine it. But she didn't want to. She'd rather be surprised by what Joe would show her if she really gave herself to him.

By the time she returned to the table, a plate of food awaited her.

"I'm not that hungry," she whispered to Joe. Then she reached underneath the table and gave his hand a squeeze.

Joe signaled to the server and asked her to box up the food.

Mickey gulped back his beer and poured himself another.

"So...you two?" he said, taking another drag on his cigarette.

Sarah didn't answer.

"We'll see you tonight at the banquet," Joe told Ellen and Mickey. He threw down what was left of his fifty after buying a hat and gloves and condoms.

Ellen scowled and shook her head. "Typical."

"Typical what?" Sarah couldn't resist asking.

"Horny students after Moot Court. Happens every year."

"I'm surprised you don't get more people signing up, then," Joe said. "You ought to mention that at orientation."

14

They drove back to Sarah's hotel to retrieve the rest of her luggage. She wouldn't be staying in a room with Ellen again, no matter what. Even if she and Joe ended up sharing his bed platonically.

Although at the moment that seemed very unlikely.

Joe came with her up to her room, and as soon as they were behind the closed door, the two of them rushed at each other, mouths and hands exploring, jackets falling, pants unzipped, skirt hiked up, underwear yanked away.

"Oh, my God," Sarah laughed on a rush of breath. Then she helped him unbutton her blouse because he was taking too long.

"Are you sure about this?" Joe asked. "Because if you're not, you'd better back away right now."

But instead Sarah pushed her pelvis into his and wrapped a leg around his hip.

"Wait a minute, wait a minute—" Joe's hand shook as he tried to rip open the package.

Sarah felt remarkably calm. She laughed again as she popped the condom free and helped smooth it over Joe's erection.

Then he was inside her, and Sarah felt a sensation she'd never felt in her life, at least not when a man was touching her: purity. Mixed with elation. She kissed him hard while the two of them rode each other, her back against the wall, Joe supporting both of her legs now so she was free to thrust against him as he thrust into her.

"Would you please stop laughing," Joe said at one point, burying his head against her shoulder.

"I can't help it." Her smile was too big, and there was no other way to release what she was feeling than to mix laughter in with her moans.

But she was wrong about that: there was another way. She just hadn't known it before.

As the orgasm ripped through her, Sarah gasped and pulsed against Joe. Then, as surprising as the laughter, came a wash of tears streaming down her face, wetting her mouth as she kissed Joe with even more hunger than before.

"Sarah," he said, his body tightening, his mouth pinning hers as he erupted right after. Then he held her where she was, the two of them still connected, until finally he gently lowered her to the floor.

Sarah looked up into Joe's face. He swiped his thumb below one of her eyes.

"Oh, my God," she said, chuckling soft and low, as amazed as she'd ever been in her life.

She looked down at her clothes, the wrinkled skirt, the beige cotton bra. He hadn't even taken it off—there wasn't time.

Joe stood looking equally disheveled, dress shirt hanging over his thighs, his pants and underwear pooled at his feet.

"Let me take care of this," he said, stepping out of his pants and moving into the bathroom to flush the condom. Then he was back, hands smoothing over Sarah's shoulders, mouth kissing hers.

"Now this doesn't seem right," Joe said, finally taking the time to release the clasp on her bra. He cupped both breasts in his hands, then leaned forward to run his tongue over each one in turn.

Sarah pulled at his hair. "No, you can't," she said, trying to catch her breath. "Let's wait. Let's go to your hotel."

"There's a bed right here," Joe said.

"But I don't want to have to get up again—not until tonight." Ellen would be coming back at some point, she knew, and Sarah had no desire to put on a show—or to have to stop.

Joe eased back into his underwear, kissed a breast, pulled up his pants, licked the other breast, tucked in his shirt, dipped his finger in Sarah's slickness.

"Ugh, come on," she said, backing away. "What time is it?"

He checked his watch. "A little after three."

"We have to be there at six," Sarah reminded him. "Come on—we can be in your bed in fifteen minutes."

"Too long," he murmured, pulling her to him again.

Sarah agreed, but one of them had to keep their heads. She pulled her blouse closed again and buttoned it, but threw her bra and the wad of underwear into her bag. There was no point in making it harder to get undressed as soon as she could. She added the few other items of clothing from her side of the room, made sure she got everything out of the bathroom, then zipped the bag closed and handed it to Joe.

He watched her the whole time, eyes dark with lust.

"Can you drive like that?" she asked.

"Like what?"

She pointed to his obvious erection.

"I should have asked you to bring everything over with you this morning," he said. "We'd already be in my room."

"Why didn't you?"

"You think I knew?" Joe asked.

"Didn't you?" Everything seemed so perfectly timed, so perfectly planned, from holding her hands inside his hoodie the night before, to offering her a bed to sleep in that morning, to pulling a hat onto her head so that his mouth was so close to hers she had no choice but to kiss it.

"Sarah, I haven't known for months," he said. "Believe me, this is a fantasy come true."

Sarah stared at him, amazed.

"Come on," she said, grabbing him roughly by the arm. "We're wasting time."

And she was done with that, Sarah thought. From now on she wanted every minute with him they could spare.

It took a little effort to make her suit presentable again for the judges. They would be mingling with all the students that night at a cocktail party before the actual awards banquet. Sarah wondered how on earth she was going to keep a straight face.

She had never thought of herself as a sexual creature, but it was obvious to her now that all she needed was for someone to show her the way. And Joe Burke was the perfect candidate for the job. The way he peeled away her clothes slowly the next time, tasting as he went, making her gasp more than laugh, making her moan in agony, punch his arms with irritation when he wouldn't give her what she wanted, but just kept drawing it out, making her suffer and wait, building her higher and higher until she finally exploded with the kind of complete, pure pleasure she'd read about in books but never, ever understood.

The two of them lay sprawled naked and wet across his sheets. Joe grunted as he sat up to pull the covers up over them. "Can't have you cold," he told Sarah, kissing her softly on the lips.

Sarah squinted toward the bedside clock. "I should shower."

"Mm, sounds good."

"Alone," she said, thinking of the shower cap she was going to have to pull over her hair. She always looked horrible in that thing—did anyone look good?—but she didn't have time to blow dry her hair and straighten it before the dinner. At most she'd have time to quickly wash, reapply her makeup, then erase all the evidence of sex from her one nice outfit.

She walked naked to the bathroom, very aware that Joe was watching her. "I like your tits," he said.

"Thank you."

"I like your ass."

"Thank you."

"I like every inch of your skin."

"You're not making this easy," Sarah said, poking her head out of the bathroom again.

"I'm not trying to. I want you to come back here."

"Later," Sarah said. "Don't you want to know if either of us are going to the finals tomorrow?"

"No."

"What if it's me?" Sarah asked, leaning naked against the bathroom door frame.

"I'll come watch you."

"What if it's you?" she asked.

"I'll be too busy in bed with you."

Sarah laughed. "I'm sure Ellen would love that."

"We didn't win, Sarah. She was horrible."

Sarah grew serious. "Was she really?"

"With a capital H for help me."

"That's too bad," Sarah said. "I'm sorry."

"Who cares?"

"You really don't?" she wanted to know.

"Sarah, I've already gotten everything out of this trip that I could possibly dream of."

Sarah didn't try to hide her smile.

"But not you, right?" Joe asked.

"What do you mean?"

"You'd like to win."

"Well, sure," she said.

"That's what I like about you, Red."

She waited, hoping he'd fill in the rest of the sentence himself. When he didn't, she asked him shyly, "What do you like?"

He reached for her.

"Huh-uh. Tell me from here."

"No deal," Joe said. He continued to hold out his hand, waiting for her.

Why should she resist? Sarah asked herself. Why should she ever resist anything Joe wanted to give her?

He gathered her in his arms and pulled her tight against his chest. "I like that you're smart and you're never embarrassed about that. But at the same time, you're not like other people at our school, constantly going around telling everyone how great you are. You let us all figure that out for ourselves. And I did figure it out—first year."

"First year?" Sarah said. "But I didn't notice you until second."

Joe pretended to stab himself in the heart.

Sarah laughed. "It's just...I wasn't looking. At anyone. But then that day in Federal Tax Law..."

Now it was Joe's turn to laugh. "So that impressed you?"

"Do you know what I'm talking about?" Sarah asked.

"Of course I do. Didn't you see me look at you? I was showing off for the redhead across the room."

"No, you weren't. You didn't even know me," Sarah said. But inside she really hoped it was true.

Although a part of that smart brain he claimed to admire also reminded her that she had seen him with plenty of other women since that day, so if he was pining for her, he found a way to deal with it.

But why should she think about that, she asked herself, when she was naked in his arms and he was already tasting her again, flicking his tongue over her body in that way that had already driven her mad?

She dove away from him in one quick move and rushed into the bathroom. Then she locked the door behind her, tucked her hair into the hotel shower cap, and washed away the evidence of their afternoon.

Wishing they didn't have to go anywhere, and could just stay in his bed until their flight home on Sunday.

15

Was it Sarah's imagination, or did Ellen look a little disheveled herself?

Sarah glanced from Ellen to Mickey, then dismissed the idea.

No way he'd do anything with her. No matter how drunk he might have gotten.

And from what she could see right now, that was plenty drunk.

"Mickey, maybe you should just have water for a while." The two of them stood off to the side of the room, both dressed in their suits again, or maybe still, in Mickey's case, and all around them were the various superior court, appellate, and supreme court judges who had listened to the preliminary round of arguments all day long.

Sarah saw one of hers and Mickey's judges over by the bar. He was a short, balding man with thick-rimmed glasses and an easy smile. Sarah never minded his questions, because he nodded as she spun out her answers, encouraging her, it seemed, rather than staring at her stony-faced the way the other two judges did.

"So I heard a rumor," Sarah said to Mickey.

"Yeah, what?"

"That you're married and your wife is pregnant."

He looked at her, eyes not nearly as focused as they'd been earlier in the day. "Yeah, I guess that's right."

"You guess that's right?" Sarah said, laughing. "How far along is she?"

"Seven months."

"Congratulations."

"Cut the crap," Mickey said. "Did you sleep with him?"

Sarah took a sip of her drink. And decided not to lie. "Yes."

"Why?"

That question was harder to answer. And she wasn't sure it was any of Mickey's business.

"Did you sleep with Ellen?" she asked.

"No."

"Are you sure?"

"Positive," Mickey said.

"Did she try?" Sarah asked, looking over to where Ellen stood gesticulating and monologuing to one of the judges, obviously hoping to impress him.

"You heard what she said," Mickey answered. "All those horny students. Happens every year."

"But not you," Sarah said.

He swallowed what was left of his drink. "Maybe with you, Sarah, but not with anybody else."

"Somehow I doubt that's true."

Mickey shrugged. "I'm a good Catholic boy. Do I wish I was single? You bet. People should be more like animals. Come together to mate, then leave and go out on their own until next year."

"How long have you been married?"

"Summer between college and law school. So I'm a third-year there, too."

Mickey swirled the ice cubes in his cup, then tipped it back again to suck up the last drops.

"We should probably mingle," Sarah said. "Go talk to our judges or something."

"Why? You know I crashed and burned today."

"No, you didn't," Sarah said. "You were a little nervous at first—"

"A little nervous?" Mickey chuckled in a way that sounded both sarcastic and miserable. "I had no business signing up for this, Sarah—you know that. You probably saw it at our very first practice. You could have told me, you know. Saved us both a lot of embarrassment."

"You're blowing this way out of proportion," Sarah said. "Let's wait and hear the scores, all right? I guarantee you didn't do that badly."

"I'm going to get another drink," Mickey said. "Want anything?"

"No. Thanks." She looked across the room. Joe and Ellen stood talking to another one of the judges.

No, Ellen stood talking, Sarah corrected herself. Because Joe wasn't even paying attention. He waited until Sarah locked eyes with him, then subtly raised his glass.

Sarah smiled and turned away. She couldn't spend the whole night with her heart racing over every little look or gesture or touch the two of them might find secret ways to exchange. They agreed to stick with their partners for the evening, and go through the banquet the way they would have if they never met.

It was a stupid agreement, Sarah thought, glancing back at Joe and finding him once again watching her with the same hungry expression she'd seen on his face all afternoon long.

Sarah checked her watch. Then she held up two fingers, meaning they only had to stay two more hours.

Joe pointed to the exit.

Sarah shook her head.

He pointed again, and she laughed. And then went in search of Mickey before the poor guy drank so much he passed out before the ceremony.

Although in Sarah's heart she knew he was right: they really didn't need to hear the announcement to know their team wasn't advancing. Oral argument would never be Mickey Hughes's strength. And even though Sarah thought her own performance had gone well, her scores would be averaged with Mickey's to determine the team's ranking, so that was the end of that.

Although she had to agree with Joe: winning the competition wasn't nearly the best thing that could have come out of it. She'd already gotten more out of that trip that she ever could have dreamed of.

. . .

"Congratulations, Number Seven," Joe told her as soon as they were alone again in his car.

"Nice job, Eight."

The two of them grinned at each other. Even though neither of their teams advanced, the judges gave out individual scores, too, and both Sarah and Joe made it into the top ten.

"That's not bad, huh?" Sarah asked.

"A lot better than I expected," Joe said.

"What should we do to celebrate?"

"I think you know my answer to that."

Just hearing the way he said it made Sarah's insides flare with heat. She wondered whether the seats of the rental car folded down.

"Tomorrow's Saturday," Sarah said.

"Uh-huh." Joe had her hand in his, and was swirling his thumb against her palm. She found it very difficult to think.

"Final arguments in the morning, then the luncheon, then another dinner tomorrow night."

Joe didn't say anything, just began stroking higher up her arm.

Sarah gasped on a laugh as he scooped his hand inside her jacket and began stroking the breast he found there.

"Joe?" she managed to get out.

"Hm?"

"Let's skip all of that. Stay inside."

"Sounds good." He pressed his mouth to hers and unbuttoned the top of her blouse. Then he slipped his hand inside the fabric until he found bare skin.

Sarah moaned.

Joe pulled his hand free and started the car.

Sarah leaned her head back, too aroused to keep her eyes open. She wanted the ride to be over, wanted not to have to walk across the hotel parking lot, in through the lobby, take the elevator upstairs. She wanted to be instantly transported now, straight into his bed, straight into his arms and not leave there for hours and hours.

"Sarah?" Joe said after a while.

"Hm?"

"Congratulations. You really deserved that."

She looked over at him and laid her hand on his arm. He rested one of his hands on top.

"You did, too, Joe," she said. "I'm really happy for both of us."

It was one of the nicest nights they had together, in a whole series of amazing nights. Nights followed by days in which Sarah fell harder and harder for him by the minute. And she thought he fell for her, too. Didn't he tell her so?

But it was all over seven weeks later. And Sarah still didn't understand why.

16

Sarah woke on the Wednesday morning before Thanksgiving feeling better than she had in days. Her body didn't ache the way it had, and she felt well-rested instead of lethargic from all her hours in bed.

She went into the bathroom and splashed cold water on her face and brushed her teeth. The dark circles under her eyes were gone. She still looked paler than normal, but she hoped a little food and tea would help.

While she waited for room service, she booted up her laptop. She hadn't checked e-mail since Monday morning. There were the usual garbage messages she deleted without reading, but a few of them grabbed her attention.

The secretary she shared with three other lawyers in the firm had e-mailed her several sets of scanned documents, all with the subject line "Mason Manufacturing." Sarah opened one of them and found purchase orders and other internal documents and memoranda. She would have plenty to read over the Thanksgiving weekend.

As soon as she signed for her breakfast, she took a cup of hot tea and a piece of dry toast with her into the bathroom. She needed a shower badly. Her hair looked like someone's beginning attempts at dreadlocks, and her skin felt coated with a layer of dried sweat from the fever she knew had finally gone away. She ducked out of the Utah sweatshirt Joe bought her and pulled off the matching sweatpants. They had been perfect sleepwear the night before, but now she wanted the feeling of clean clothes against a clean body.

A fresh hotel robe hung from the back of the bathroom door. She didn't remember putting it there, and wondered if Joe had, since housekeeping hadn't been in there for days. Joe kept the Do Not Disturb sign on Sarah's door, and she agreed with that, since she didn't want to pass along the flu to some poor worker like her mother, who would then have to spend her holiday flat out in bed instead of relaxing with her family.

Sarah thought again of Joe saying he had cleaned up after her. It had to be true. She knew the Monday morning explosions left splatters everywhere. Now there was no evidence of it. Why would a man—any man—do that? And how was she supposed to feel about Burke going so above and beyond the call of duty? Especially since it wasn't his duty to take care of her at all.

Sarah took another bite of toast and drank half a cup of tea. She wanted to take it slowly, to give her stomach time to settle with each new addition. But so far, everything felt fine.

She stood under the hot water for a long time. Shaved her legs and armpits, both of which had grown stubbly in the last few days. She washed her hair with the special shampoo she brought from home, rubbed conditioner into the ends, let the rough curls slip through her fingers as she separated them and sorted them out. She felt well enough that she thought she could bear standing at the sink for half an hour or so while she blow-dried her hair straight. She wouldn't bother with the hair iron—that sounded like far too much effort at the moment—but at least she could do the minimum to bring her mop back under control.

She came back out of the bathroom wearing the hotel robe and toweling off her hair. She found Burke sitting on the couch working on his laptop.

Sarah glanced over at her own laptop, still open on the bed. She casually walked toward it.

"I like how you just come and go as you please," she said.

"You haven't seemed to mind it."

"I assume that's my room key you're using?"

"Didn't think you'd need it. But I can see you're feeling better."

"I am," she answered as she closed the lid on her laptop.

When she turned around, Joe was looking at her.

There was no mistaking the anger in his eyes.

"You don't really think I'd do that, do you?" he asked her.

Sarah thought of the documents she'd been reading and left open on her screen when she went to take a shower. But the idea that Joe would sneak a look while he heard the water running didn't actually ring true. He had plenty of opportunities over the past few days to go through all of

Sarah's files if he wanted, and to read anything on her laptop since she hadn't bothered to password-protect it, but Sarah couldn't believe he would do that. Joe Burke might be a lot of things, but unethical wasn't one of them.

"No," Sarah admitted, feeling slightly ashamed of herself, "I don't."

Joe held her gaze for a moment more, then nodded and went back to work. But Sarah could still feel the tension in the air.

"I am feeling better," she said, hoping to shift things back to normal. "I looked up the schedules, and there's a nonstop tomorrow morning at eight o'clock. I think I'll book it."

"Good," Joe said. "I will, too."

"You don't...have to stay today if you don't want to," Sarah said. "I'm sure you have plans tomorrow for Thanksgiving."

"I doubt I'll be able to get a flight out at this point," Joe said. "It'll be easier to go in the morning. Fewer people traveling."

"Right," Sarah said. "I'm sure you're right."

"I try to be right," Joe said almost automatically.

Sarah knew she should say more: thank him for everything he'd done. But she couldn't seem to form the words. They felt like too much of a concession. Too weak. Too...honest.

She listened while Joe made arrangements with his office to change his return ticket. Sarah called her own office and did the same. Her hair had dried into a thousand mini spirals by the time she realized it, and she wondered how she lost track. She usually obsessed over every little thing her unruly hair was doing, especially if there were anyone else in the vicinity to see it, but for some reason she forgot to be self-conscious about it around Joe.

Of course, it could be because what he said before was true: he had already seen her. In and out of a shower, in and out of clothes, hair perfect, hair wild, Sarah laughing, Sarah in ecstasy, Sarah crying. What did she possibly have to hide from him anymore? At least where it concerned her appearance.

As soon as he hung up the phone, Joe leaned back against the couch and linked his hands behind his head. "Feel like getting some fresh air today, Red? You look like you might be up for it. Get out of this hotel room, go for a drive."

"Yeah, actually, that sounds nice," she said, already loving the idea of it. She had work to do, but that could wait. Her parents wouldn't mind if she spent some of the time she was with them that weekend poring over documents. She knew they liked to see her doing her law work, the same way they liked watching her study over the holidays while she was in law school. They took great pride in Sarah's accomplishments. She liked knowing that.

On the other hand, it was why she found it so impossible to call them right away after the events of April 6. She waited days to build up the courage to tell them. By then they already knew, of course—it had been all over the news both locally and nationally—and they left phone messages checking to see if she was all right. All she could do when she called them back was stutter a few words before she spent the rest of the phone call sobbing.

"It's cold out," Joe said. "You'll want to layer as much as you have."

Sarah pulled from her luggage the workout capris and T-shirt.

"That's a start," Joe said. Then he dialed his phone to make another business call.

When it became obvious he intended to wait there while she changed, Sarah dug into her luggage for a fresh pair of underwear and her workout bra. The black lace one still bore traces of her illness, and she intended to give it a thorough scrubbing once she got home. She took the workout clothes and the Utah sweats with her back into the bathroom and shut the door.

Once she was dressed, she evaluated her hair again in the mirror. She could take the time to wet it down and then straighten it, but decided she'd rather get outside sooner and feel the wind on her face instead of the breeze from the blow dryer.

She did, however, take the time to add a light layer of makeup, just mascara, a little blush, and some lip gloss, so she wouldn't look so sickly even to herself. And in a way she intended it as a gift to Joe, who was probably tired of seeing her look so pale and clammy over the past few days.

Joe wrapped up the call when he saw she was ready, then closed his laptop and left it on the table.

"Where are we going?" Sarah asked him.

"Up the mountain," Joe said. "I just need to make one quick stop along the way."

. . .

As soon as Sarah saw which parking lot they were pulling into, her throat went dry.

"Burke…"

"You're never dressed for the weather," he said. "Come on. This will only take a minute."

He led the way into Walmart while Sarah hung back. Then she realized she was being stupid. She could walk into a Walmart with Joe. She wasn't a child.

He didn't wait for her, but headed off toward a familiar section of the store. When Sarah arrived, he already had a set in his hands. "Blue still good?"

She nodded, not trusting her voice. Joe handed her the hat and gloves, then started walking again.

If he heads for the condoms…

But of course he didn't, Sarah realized a moment later as Joe angled toward the shoe section. He scanned the shelves until he found what he was looking for.

"They don't have to last forever," he said. "Just today."

Sounded like his philosophy in a nutshell, she thought.

Sarah reached for a pair of light hiking boots in her size. She kicked off one of her sneakers and tried it on. Then she put it back in the box.

"Ready?" Joe asked.

Sarah nodded.

She knew she should say something about all of this, but her tongue felt glued to the roof of her mouth. If they had no history together, all of this would seem perfectly normal —nice, even. Opposing counsel taking his sick but recovering colleague to a discount store where she could buy a few items to make her more comfortable. Perfectly cordial.

They walked together to the checkout lanes, Joe leading the way. He waited beside her while the cashier scanned her items.

And finally daring to look Joe in the eye, Sarah could see the mischief there. The clear understanding of what he was doing. The invitation for her to call him on it, to say something real for a change instead of always weighing her words.

"Burke."

"Yes?"

But at the last second she decided not to give him the satisfaction. Instead she stared at him blandly as he looked back at her with an innocent smile.

"Bastard," Sarah couldn't help mumbling.

Joe rested his hand against the small of her back as he leaned over to whisper, "I just wanted you to remember it wasn't all bad."

Of *course* it wasn't bad, Sarah wanted to tell him. That was exactly the problem: it was *great*. Just that brief touch to her back was enough to remind every cell in her body how much she wanted him before, and how easy it would be to want him again.

Sarah paid for the merchandise, then the two of them left together, side by side. Not holding hands, like the first time, not desperate to fall back into each other's arms, no making out against the side of the rental car this time, no one honking in approval.

A part of her wanted to call off the outing. Have him take her back to the hotel where she could spend the day reading through documents and pretending the last ten minutes hadn't happened.

He had to know it would affect her. He could have taken her anywhere: Target, a sporting goods store, probably even convenience stores there carried winter wear. He had to know her eyes would have widened at the Walmart sign, her heart would have sped up, her heart would have hurt.

Was he trying to hurt her? It was hard to believe after all the care he'd taken of her the past few days, but why else would he would want her to relive a moment like that with him when he knew everything else that flowed from it?

If their relationship had ended differently, if they'd parted friends, then maybe Sarah could have joined him in a happy little walk down lovers' lane, pointing out the landmarks: *"Yes, this is where I first couldn't get enough of you. Over here is where we lost our minds over each other. Oh, look, there's where you first told me that you loved me."* But it was like returning to the scene of the crime with an arsonist: *"Remember that beautiful house you used to live in? How did you feel when I burned it all to ashes?"*

Sarah stared out the window as Joe drove them up the mountain. Watched the pine trees going from unspotted green to laden with heaps of white. The higher they climbed, the more snow on the ground and the windier the road.

Sarah noticed that Joe was taking it slowly. A few cars passed them, but he kept a steady pace. She wondered if that was for her sake, to spare her stomach from any more trauma. If so, then he was one of the most considerate men she'd ever met, and his compassion should never fail to impress her. Or maybe he was one of the cruelest men she knew, and she didn't understand any of his motives at all. Her assessment of that could change every minute.

"Warm enough?" Joe asked. He tilted the vent so it blew on her more directly. Sarah clasped her gloved fingers together, feeling the soft fleece against her skin. Yes, she was warm. Yes, it was nice of him to make sure she had the proper clothes—the hat and gloves, the boots, the sweatpants and sweatshirt he bought for her earlier. Nice, nice, nice.

Except nice guys didn't tell their girlfriends how much they loved them, how crazy about them they were—didn't ask their girlfriends to *marry* them, for God's sake—then go away for the winter break and return completely changed. Never answer a phone call, avoid any attempts to speak in person, and finally, because Sarah obviously hadn't gotten the message, grabbing the ass of that very willing second-year he pulled into a dark corner of the library with him, and pressing her against the wall and grinding up against her while he explored her mouth and her breasts, knowing Sarah stood only ten feet away because she finally tracked him down.

And it wasn't just that one. In the five months they had left of school, Sarah saw him with two, three, four different girls. Maybe there were even more—those were just the ones he made a point of kissing in front of her, until Sarah did everything in her power to stay as far out of his range as she could so she never had to witness any of it again.

And meanwhile her heart became molten metal, pooling at the bottom of her lungs, then freezing again, then breaking into shards at the slightest reminder of anything he'd said, any way he touched her, anything she had ever felt for him. Her last semester of law school passed like a fog, blotting out everything but what she had to do this minute, this class, then go home and not think about him, go to sleep and not remember him, go to school the next morning and never, ever look his way.

At graduation she braced to hear his name, then purposely stared at her program while he took the long walk to receive his diploma. When it was her turn, she kept her eyes locked on the dean, afraid that if she glanced even a fraction of an inch to the side, she might see Joe there in his cap and gown and realize this was it, she never had to see him again anywhere. California was a huge state. The chances of ever running into him again were small. She would be safe, if she could just make it through that one last day.

But her eyes were too used to finding him. So even though Sarah had done everything she could to spare herself, still her gaze shifted just enough to see him off in the distance after the ceremony, standing with his father and brother, all three of them hugging, his father crying.

Tears burned Sarah's own eyes as she turned back to her parents and let them tell her again how proud they were of her.

"Come on," she said, taking her mother by the arm and leading them both away. "Let's go eat Mom's pie."

When what she really wanted to do was get drunk.

17

J oe pulled in to the Snowbird ski area and found a parking spot at the end of a long row. The ski area had already opened the week before, and Sarah could see figures up on the mountain zigzagging their way down.

She traded her sneakers for the boots, then stepped out of the car onto the cold ground. The air felt so dry it was almost powdery. It seeped between the threads of her clothes like fine dust, making her wish she wore at least one more, thicker layer.

"Here," Joe said, reading her mind and taking off his coat.

"No, you should wear that."

"Sarah, you don't have to fight me on everything, you know." He helped her into the roomy coat, which really did feel wonderful, she had to admit. It reached down to middle of her thighs, blocking out the wind. She rolled the sleeves up, then put her gloves back on.

"Hot chocolate?" Joe asked.

"Sounds good." Now that they were somewhere else, somewhere unusual and new, Sarah found she could speak again. Any minute she would feel like herself again, and regain her footing with Joe. But right now she still felt like she was catching up.

They trudged up to the base area where there were rental shops and restaurants. Joe pointed to one with outside seating. "Will you be warm enough?" he asked.

"We'll see," Sarah answered. Joe left her at one of the picnic tables while he went inside to buy their drinks.

He returned with a cup of hot cocoa topped with an enormous mound of whipped cream.

"Oh," Sarah said. "I don't really do that anymore."

With anyone else, she might have worried about hurting his feelings, but Sarah needed this, she realized. Needed to feel on top of her game again.

She carried her cup to the nearest trash can and scraped off the whipped cream. Then she sat back down across from Burke and sipped the nearly boiling drink.

He took a swallow of his and studied her. "I already guessed vegetarian," he said. "From the tofu in your salad. But vegan?"

"Yep." Usually Sarah let people think she was a vegetarian because vegan sounded so extreme. But she didn't care what Joe thought about it.

"Can I ask why?" he said.

"I wanted to make some changes last year."

Joe nodded. And cast a look from her face down to her body. "I noticed."

"Noticed what?" she said.

"When you were in your underwear. Puking. You looked good."

Sarah couldn't help but laugh. "I don't usually get that compliment."

"I'm surprised," he said. "Because you deserve it."

Sarah allowed herself a moment of staring into his eyes across the table. Then something in her couldn't stand the charade anymore. Didn't want to let another minute go by without saying something true for once.

"Burke, what is all this?" she asked quietly.

To his credit, he didn't ask, "All what?" He didn't try to stall or make Sarah uncomfortable by pretending he needed her to restate the question.

"My apology," he said.

The answer sucked the wind from her lungs. Her lips parted and she forced herself to draw in a few small breaths. She was sure her eyes must have looked shocked and wary and afraid, because Burke reached across the table to cover her hand in his as if she needed the comfort.

She pulled both of her hands into her lap.

"What if I don't want it?" she managed to choke out.

He never took his eyes off hers. "Then that's your choice. I'm just doing what I think I should."

Sarah bolted up from the table and took off across the snow. Her boots squeaked as they pressed footprints into the white. She'd been stupid to let him bring her up there, she realized. So far away from where she could simply take her key away from him and lock him out and not have to speak to him again. Not personally, anyway. They could meet across a deposition table any day, and she would learn how to stop letting it affect her.

The air was cold, and it was thin. They were thousands of feet higher than where they had been in the city, and Sarah began to feel the effects. She had barely eaten that morning, and even less the days before. And she was having a hard time breathing, both because of the altitude and because of Joe.

There was a mound of snow above her, close to one of the buildings. If she could make it that far she could rest. But her legs felt heavy, like she was trying to walk through pudding, and she felt a familiar blackness at the edges of her vision.

Not again.

She turned around to find Joe trailing her. He wasn't so far away. He stood there looking like a lumberjack, not a lawyer, in his jeans and boots and sweater, slight stubble on his face, so handsome and masculine and concerned.

Sarah shook her head at him, even smiled weakly, acknowledging what she knew was about to happen.

Then her legs folded beneath her and she melted onto the snow.

SHE AWOKE feeling sweaty and feverish and foolish.

A woman bent over her, shining a small penlight into her eyes.

"Did she hit her head?"

"No," Joe said, "I don't think so."

"Did she lose consciousness?"

"Yes," he answered, "briefly."

"It may just be dehydration," the woman told him. "You said she's been sick? Vomiting? She's probably lost a lot of fluids in the last few days, and then coming up here…"

Joe rubbed his hand down his face. "God, Sarah, I'm so sorry."

She shook her head. She was such an idiot for storming off like that. She should have known her body wasn't up for it. She hadn't worked out in days, and she let her nutrition completely fall apart. She had been learning her physical limits all year long—and learning to push them—but this? This was just stupidity.

Sarah started to sit up and felt the room sway a bit. Joe steadied her, one hand on her back, another holding her arm.

"She should be fine," the woman said. Sarah couldn't tell if she was a nurse or a doctor. The woman wore heavy canvas pants, a long-sleeved T-shirt, and a down vest. It was obviously a proper uniform for medical personnel up on the mountain, since Sarah looked around the clinic and saw several others dressed that way, but it didn't give a patient much information.

"Can I take her home?" Joe asked.

"Let her have a few sips of water while she's here and I'll be back in a few minutes. But if she seems fine, then yes, you can take her."

Joe reached for Sarah's hand, and she let him. And as easy as it would have been for her to let him take the blame and feel guilty about what had happened, Sarah knew she couldn't do that.

"I'm not a delicate flower," she told him as soon as they were alone. "I'm actually very strong. You're just catching me on a very bad week."

"Sarah, I never should have…"

But he let the rest of the sentence trail off, and Sarah understood why: never should have told her the truth? Never should have tried to apologize? Neither of those was right.

"You just took me by surprise," Sarah said. "Classic mistake. I asked a witness a question without knowing the answer first."

Joe clutched her hand harder, then leaned forward and gently pressed a kiss to her lips.

Too soft, Sarah thought somewhere in her animal brain, too soft when there was obviously a deeper kiss hidden behind it, and all she had to do was reach for him, pull him toward her by the back of the neck, angle her head, open her lips, feel his tongue and his teeth, block out reality for just a moment and take comfort in a feeling that she missed and remembered too well.

But he was careful, too careful, and that was right. *I try to be right.*

The kiss lasted only a moment, but its effects lingered on. Sarah's stomach felt queasy. She had to close her eyes and bend her head forward while she pressed her finger against a spot between her brows. It helped her sometimes to get rid of headaches. Right now the only thing it accomplished was sparing her from having to look at Joe.

He handed her a bottle of water. Sarah took a few sips. She looked around the clinic at the people who obviously needed to be there—people in leg splints and arm splints, presumably doped up since they were sleeping instead of screaming.

"Let's go," she told Joe. She waved to the doctor or the nurse, whichever it was, across the room. "I'm fine," she said. "We're going home." Then she let Joe put his arm around her as they walked toward the door.

The cold air hit her again, drying the sweat from her face. It felt good, bracing, alive.

"I know you won't believe this," she said, "but I'm still glad we came up here. This is better than being in my room all day. I felt like an invalid."

Considering that she was slowly shuffling away from the medical clinic, she knew that probably didn't make much sense.

Joe hadn't said anything for a while. Sarah glanced to the side to gauge his condition.

"Burke. Stop. Look at me."

She knew she was too cold to stand there for long, but what she needed to say couldn't wait until they finally reached the car. He might have broken her heart once, but she wasn't looking for revenge. At least not so much anymore. Regret? Yes. She'd love for him to feel regret, and lots of it, if she could help it. But she wanted him to suffer for legitimate reasons, not this one.

"You've been a saint this whole week," she told him. "Nobody in my life except my parents would ever do what you've done for me. Thank you. I'll never be able to thank you enough. But it's for this, all right? This is separate. No matter what you did in the past, this was something good."

"Sarah," Joe growled. His eyes flashed with intensity. He grabbed her by both shoulders, and she could feel the tension in his hands radiating through her body and practically lifting her from the ground.

Then Joe seemed to stop himself from whatever he was going to say or do, and instead looked up at the sky and shook his head. He let go of her arms. Then he turned to the side again and curved his arm around her waist and steadied her toward the car.

What just happened? Sarah wondered. She could still feel the energy pulsing through his arm and his hand, electric against her back and her hip.

She moved closer to him, maybe only an inch or two, until her leg bumped against his as they walked. It was better for her balance, she told herself. This way he could hold her more closely and brace her.

When they reached the car, he opened her door and held her hand while she got inside. Then he knelt down and unlaced her boots. He removed one and closed his fingers over her toes, warming them in his hand.

"Joe, I told you, I'm fine—"

"Would you stop arguing with me for once, Henley, and just take it?" he snapped.

Sarah jerked back in surprise, but then let him do what he wanted. Which was to remove her other boot and warm the toes of that foot, too.

"Burke," Sarah said on a laugh when he came around the

car and got in on his side. "You have a really unusual way of getting people to let you help them."

But Joe wasn't smiling. "I'm not your enemy, Sarah. And I can take some of this, but not all of it. You need to decide how you want things to be. Until then I think we should keep our distance."

18

The drive down the mountain from Snowbird seemed to take three times as long as the drive up, even with gravity in their favor. Sarah stared out the window the whole way. She curled and extended her toes under the warmth of the floor vent, replaying how nice it felt to have Joe's big, warm hands rubbing them.

Replaying the sensation of his lips on hers.

Then blinking hard to clear the image from her mind, even though it didn't work.

When they returned to the hotel, Joe asked her if she needed anything, and when she said no, told her good night. Even though there was still plenty of daylight left outside.

He was gone before she remembered he had her key. She stopped by the front desk and showed her I.D. to get another one.

Maybe she didn't forget he had it, she admitted to herself

as she rode the elevator. Maybe she hoped he would still use it.

When she opened the door to her room, she saw that he had: his laptop was gone. Her key lay in its place on the table.

Sarah sank onto the couch.

"You need to decide how you want things to be."

Making it her problem, not his.

Or, if she wanted to feel generous about it—which she didn't—giving her all of the power.

He kissed her.

In the midst of everything else, he might have thought she forgot it, or didn't notice. It had been very quick, after all. But even if Sarah had been as anesthetized as some of those other patients, she felt certain she would have noticed Burke's mouth on hers for the first time in six years.

And the way he looked at her when he gripped her arms in the parking lot.

And the shock she felt when he explained that everything he'd been doing all week, taking care of her, was his version of an apology.

"What if I don't want it?"

"Then that's your choice. I'm just doing what I think I should."

Damn it, Burke, Sarah thought. Don't act like you're the innocent victim here. Like I'm the one being cruel and unreasonable. I was there for you, I would have been there for you, I never would have left your side.

She had played back that image often, seeing him and his brother and father off in the distance at graduation, huddled together all alone. She could have been part of that group, her arms around Joe or holding tightly to his hand, comforting him on what she knew had to be a very hard day. But he didn't want that, obviously. Although she noticed none of his other girlfriends had been around to fill that void, either.

So what was there to decide now? she wondered. Whether to be polite to him during the next three months of depositions? It wasn't as if there were anything else on the table. They weren't lovers anymore, they weren't even friends. Even her relationship with Mickey Hughes had survived the peculiarities of law school, enough so that they got together for lunch once or twice a year, and Mickey had found her this current job.

Was that what Joe wanted, a few lunches every year? A "Hey, how you doing, how are things, what are you working on these days?" kind of friendship where neither of them ever said what was really on their minds, because then they'd be right back where they were now in this kind of stalemate of anger and guilt and yes, a little too much left-over lust for Sarah's comfort, if she had to be entirely honest with herself?

She stretched out on the couch and lay with an arm draped over her eyes. Mickey hadn't done her any favor, she realized. Yes, she appreciated the money and getting back to work again, but this had turned out to be a much more hazardous assignment than she knew when she took it. Look at her now, she thought, laid up in a hotel room, wearing hotel gift shop sweats, rehashing a day when she and Joe had kept their hands and mouths to themselves in a

Walmart, and ended up sharing a chaste kiss in a mountain medical clinic.

The only thing she needed to decide right now was whether to watch a movie on cable while she ate her dinner from room service, or just eat in silence while she watched a mental repeat of the day. Because either could be equally dramatic.

THE SALT LAKE CITY airport was busier than she expected for Thanksgiving morning—she assumed most people traveled the day before—but she passed through the security line fairly quickly and headed for her gate.

There was no sign of Joe. She hadn't seen him since he left her in the hotel parking lot the afternoon before. She wondered if he would even be on her flight after all.

But then she saw him in the distance, looking less like a hardy lumberjack now and more like a person who had slept as badly as she had. His face was unshaven, which was a good look as far as she was concerned, but he also seemed haggard, worn out. And unhappy.

He saw her, too, gave her a quick nod, then found a seat somewhere else.

So he really was going to stick to that "we should keep our distance" thing, she thought.

"I can take some of this, but not all of it." She'd thought about that statement a lot.

Take what, exactly? she wondered. The sniping and the fighting, or the rare moments here and there when they were actually friendly to each other—maybe too friendly—

forcing her and maybe him, too, to remember why they'd been attracted to each other in the first place?

"I just wanted you to remember it wasn't all bad." Damn it, Burke, she thought, looking at him now across the gate area, why did you have to stir it all up again? She'd been maintaining—they both had. Why did they suddenly have to drop all the pretense of being Henley and Burke and go back to being Sarah and Joe again?

The gate agent called for boarding, and Sarah waited for Joe to go first. If he wanted his distance, she could give it to him. Fine. Gladly. Take it.

She sat crowded into her window seat by a mother and child, the child way too bouncy and excited about seeing Grandma. Normally Sarah didn't mind having a few Cheerios spilled on her lap or a sticky hand messing with the armrest between them, but what she really wanted right now was the peace and quiet of a row all to herself, or of the Joe from the previous day—the one who brought her hot chocolate and carried her to the clinic and warmed her toes in his hand—that one, sitting beside her now, offering up a broad shoulder for her to lean against as they both flew home together.

Stop it, Sarah scolded herself. Joe was right. All of this sentimental crap was bad news.

"Seeing family?" the woman with the child asked.

"Yes," Sarah said, feeling no need to tell the woman she was actually heading home from work.

The woman rolled her eyes. "Us, too. I hate the holidays. Nobody ever comes to us, we always have to go to them."

Sarah nodded sympathetically.

Nobody ever comes to us, we always have to go to them.

You need to decide how you want things to be.

She wanted things to be easy—that's what she wanted. But it didn't seem possible anymore.

THIS IS STUPID, Sarah thought, watching Joe walk ahead of her through LAX. She wasn't going to pretend she didn't know him.

She lengthened her stride until she caught up.

"So...have a nice Thanksgiving," she said.

"Yeah, you, too," he said.

"Are you going to your dad's today?" she asked.

Joe nodded. "Your folks?"

"Yeah."

They walked in silence for a few moments more, then Sarah finally took the hint.

"Okay, see you on Monday. Montana, right?"

"Montana," he agreed.

Thank you, was on her lips. *Thank you for taking care of me. Thank you for everything you did for me this week.*

But he'd already moved on.

19

Dinner at her parents' house wasn't until late afternoon, so Sarah used the time in her apartment to catch up on her life. Unpack, do a load of laundry, hand wash a few items, spot clean her suit since it would be a week or so before she could drop it at the cleaners.

She fixed herself a green smoothie with half a bag of prewashed spinach and enough berries, bananas, and orange juice to disguise the taste. She appreciated the effects of all the added greens in her diet, she just didn't always like the flavor.

She answered a few e-mails, then repacked her bag. This time she filled it with jeans, T-shirts, and the kinds of slouchy, stretchy, comfortable clothes she knew she could overeat and relax in.

At the last minute she pulled her Utah sweatpants and sweatshirt out of the dryer and added them to the bag.

Fontana, California was only a few hours away from Los

Angeles and Culver City, traveling inland away from the sea. Sarah listened to music the whole way, not bothering to keep up on the traffic reports. She missed a lot of things about the Mercedes her old firm leased for her, but on long drives like this, what she missed most was the sound system. It was easier to sing along and feel like she was in tune if she couldn't hear herself too well over the music.

But she still sang every tune. Anything to keep from thinking about Joe.

She wondered what Thanksgiving would be like for his family. Just Joe and his brother and his dad. Did any of them cook? Did they go out somewhere? Was it a sad event, spent reminiscing about Joe's mother, or did they do the man thing and sit around watching football all night and talking to the TV instead of each other?

She turned the radio up louder. *Stop thinking.*

Finally she began passing the landmarks of her childhood: the high school, the library, the grocery store. When she turned off onto her old street, she slowed the car. The houses looked the same, just maybe a little more tired. Still bikes left out front, cars with flat tires left at the curb, a few kids skateboarding on the asphalt.

Sarah pulled into her old driveway and parked next to a car she'd never seen. It was obviously her dad's current project. She wondered if all mechanics brought their work home, or if some of them had seen enough of engines and transmissions by the end of the day that they preferred to find some other hobby.

Her mother must have heard the car, Sarah realized, because she came out of the house right away, still wearing her apron, the smells of the kitchen clinging to her hair and her clothes so that Sarah got a her first whiff of Thanksgiving just by hugging her mother close.

"Let me look at you, sweetheart." Her mother drew back and studied Sarah's face. She tucked a misbehaving lock of hair back behind Sarah's ear, then hugged her again. "It's so good to see you. We miss you."

"Hi, Dad." Sarah's father was a few steps behind. She moved into his embrace, enjoying the sensation of one of his bone-cracking hugs. Even when she was a little girl, he never treated her like she was delicate.

"Come on," her mother said. "You hungry?"

"Of course," Sarah answered.

She followed her parents back into the warm kitchen, where Sarah found the oven and all four stove burners fully employed. Potatoes boiled, gravy bubbled, turkey roasted, rolls baked.

"Mom, it smells wonderful. Can I help?"

"No, you sit down," her mother said. "You had a long drive. Dinner'll be ready shortly."

Sarah took her customary seat at the table, across from her father. Her mother always sat between them. It all felt so normal, so regular, so exactly the same as ever, Sarah found it hard to believe how much had happened since the last time she had been home for Thanksgiving, right after her promotion. She'd been bursting with the news then, anxious to share it with the two people she knew would be as thrilled about it as she was. Becoming a partner in one of Los Angeles's most prestigious law firms just days before her twenty-ninth birthday. What a thing to celebrate.

So much could happen in the space of a year, Sarah thought. Or a week.

Or one day on a mountain with Joe Burke.

"Where'd you just come from?" Sarah's father asked.

"Salt Lake City."

"Never been," he said.

"It's pretty," Sarah told him. "You two might like it. Cold, though."

She knew that would be enough to keep her father away from there forever. The man could never abide the cold.

While Sarah's mother busied herself at the stove, Sarah couldn't help noticing how worn out she seemed. Both her parents always looked tired to her these days. She wondered if they had always looked that way, and she just never saw it when she lived at home. But now that months went by between her visits, she could see how they aged. It was one of the reasons she was so happy when they finally started accepting money from her. She had visions of helping them both retire within another few years. It was just one more dream she lost on April 6.

"How's the car running?" her father asked.

"Really well. No problems. That was a good find, Dad. Thanks."

"I'll tune it up for you again over Christmas," he said. "Don't take it to any of those L.A. shops. They'll ruin that car if they touch it."

"I won't let anyone else near it," Sarah promised.

Her father nodded and went back to reading the paper.

"So, how's it going with Joe?" Sarah's mother asked.

Sarah knew that question would come. Ever since she

told her parents who her opponent was, Sarah's mother acted particularly protective.

"It's fine," Sarah said. "It's not a big deal. We're all so exhausted all the time from the travel, no one even bothers talking to each other very much."

She knew she should feel bad about lying that way, but it was better than the alternative. If her mother had any hint of what happened with Joe the day before, she would have lectured Sarah for hours about how untrustworthy he was, how maybe he was trying to take advantage of their relationship so he could win his case, how Sarah was too good for him back then and far too good for him now, and of course he realized that, but too bad, he'd had his chance and thrown it away, he never should have treated her like that...

Only some of which Sarah agreed with.

"I don't know how you're doing it," her mother said, taking the potatoes off the stove and draining them over a colander. "If your father ever left me, I'd never forgive him. You remember that, Gene."

"I'll remember," he said, winking at Sarah.

"I don't know how I'd ever be able to sit in a room with him even once," Sarah's mother said, "let alone over and over, week after week. I'd be so angry I couldn't stand it."

"Oh, come on," Sarah's father said. "Work's work. You can't always choose who's on the job with you."

"That's right," Sarah said, grateful that her father was always so practical. "I'm just glad to make money again. I should be out of debt by the middle of next month. Then I'm going to start sending you some again. *Yes*, I am, Dad," she said before he could argue. "When's the last day off you had? Either of you?"

"We're both taking the whole weekend off," Sarah's mother said.

"Good. That's progress," Sarah answered.

"What do you think will happen when your five months are up?" Sarah's father asked.

"I'm hoping they'll offer me a permanent job there. If not, at least I have something new on my résumé. I'll be fine. Things are already so much better."

Sarah got up from the table before her mother could steer the conversation in the wrong direction again. "Want me to mash those?"

"Sure, honey. Butter and milk in the fridge."

Sarah and her mother had reached a compromise about her food: Sarah wouldn't eat any meat—not the Thanksgiving turkey or the Christmas ham or any of the other standard meals her mother made for every holiday, including the meatloaf Sarah used to love to have any time she came home—but Sarah also wouldn't be such a stickler about butter and cream and other dairy products her mother insisted made every dish of hers as rich and delicious as it was. So she accepted the milk in her mashed potatoes. And the butter dripping on the rolls. And every other off-limits item her mother depended on in her cooking.

Sarah could have another green smoothie when she got home. Until then, she was in her mother's work-worn hands.

"Bet that Joe Burke wishes he could see you right now," Sarah's mother said. "Look how beautiful you are. He probably hates having to take a few days off. I'll bet he wishes all the time the two of you were still together."

"He doesn't," Sarah said, wanting to shut down the topic once and for all. "We're opponents, Mom, that's all. It's business. Lawyers have to deal with this all the time. Sometimes you get along with the attorney on the other side, sometimes you don't. But everyone's just working their cases and trying to win. I'm sure Joe and I will never even run into each other after this is all over. It'll be like it never happened."

Sarah's mother humpfed, but then went back to tending her turkey. She could speculate all she wanted about what was going on in Joe Burke's mind at that very moment, as long as they didn't have to talk about it anymore.

Sarah mashed the potatoes, wishing she weren't wondering the same thing.

20

"There she is!" Paul Chapman bellowed when Sarah walked into the room. "Heard you lost your cookies. Hope it wasn't something I said."

Sarah gave him an unfriendly smile and greeted Marcela instead.

"Thanks for your help last week," Sarah told her.

"No problem," Marcela said. "You looked awful."

"All better now, though," Sarah said cheerfully. "Burke." She nodded to her opponent.

"Sarah."

Joe's client sat at attention, hands clasped tightly in front of her, face tense with anxiety. Joe whispered to the woman, and she nodded stiffly. Sarah felt badly for her. She knew how stressful legal proceedings could be for people outside the profession. Many times she imagined her own parents having to sit through a deposition or a trial and having to face someone like Sarah whose sole goal was to pick their testimony apart and make sure they lost.

But no matter how much sympathy she had for the woman across from her—particularly since Sarah could still see the damage the hair iron had done to the woman's head —she knew it was Joe's job, not hers, to make his client feel better.

"Everybody ready?" Chapman asked. Marcela began typing as Chapman introduced himself for the record.

Then the new workweek began. "Ms. Hopkins, where were you born?"

Sarah had packed better for Montana. She checked the weather in Missoula ahead of time, saw that it would be cold and rainy, and packed tights to wear under all her suits, a full-length raincoat that would cover her past her knees, and the hat and gloves she'd picked up at the Walmart in Salt Lake City. She was done seeming frail and incompetent, too stupid to anticipate the conditions and know how to keep herself insulated and dry.

She also packed a set of resistance bands she borrowed from Angie so she could do some strength-training in her room in addition to running on hotel treadmills every morning. She needed to reclaim her healthy body. Needed to regain her balance.

With Joe as much as anything else.

It was the last week in November already, which meant she had survived eight full weeks of their grueling pace on the road. Montana and back to Utah and on to Idaho this week, Oregon next, then Washington and Minnesota before they all took a holiday break. A week and a half off, then back to work in January.

Looking at the schedule, Sarah couldn't imagine how Mickey's boss thought she'd be done by the end of February. Sarah always knew she wouldn't be traveling to every single state—that would have taken months and months more, and the class certification hearing was already set for March—but still, now that she was on the hunt, she wished she could gather as much information as possible.

Maybe another temporary attorney in her position wouldn't have bothered working the case so hard, but Sarah couldn't help it. She needed to go for the A. It had nothing to do with beating Burke any more, and everything to do with her own pride and satisfaction.

Sarah asked her questions, and they let Ms. Hopkins go. Chapman had been speedier this time, and it was only eleven o'clock when they took their break.

"Wow, at this rate," Sarah said, "we could actually fit in three depositions every day." She said it sarcastically, but she was really feeling out the room.

When neither Chapman nor Burke took the bait, Sarah said, "I'm serious. Let's think about adding more depos. I'd like to make it to the east coast by mid-January."

"Why?" Joe asked.

Sarah turned to face him. He looked tired. He'd looked tired all morning.

"I'd like to do more discovery before the hearing," she said. "If the three of us can agree to that now, then great. If not, I'll file a motion with the judge. But either way, I want to talk to more of your clients, Burke. I'm sure you're not trying to hide anything."

There it is, she thought. He didn't look so tired now. He looked angry.

"On the record," he said to Marcela. The court reporter had to quickly set down her muffin and coffee, and prepare to type again. "Counsel for the plaintiff stipulates to expanding discovery to include additional depositions of parties. Names of deponents, locations, dates, and times to be determined upon consultation with opposing attorneys."

He glanced at Marcela. "Off the record." Then he leveled his gaze at Sarah. "Satisfied?"

"What do you say, Paul?" she asked, turning away from Joe's eyes. "Now that you're warmed up, ready for a marathon?"

Chapman bit down on a danish. "Don't know why you have to make it so hard, Sarah."

"I don't know," she answered, "maybe because they're paying me?"

She'd already drawn up a preliminary schedule while Chapman droned on that morning. She showed the other two lawyers how they could fit in at least five more states, all in the Midwest and on the east coast, between then and the end of February.

Chapman glanced at the court reporter to make sure they were still off the record.

"You know it's going to settle," he said out of the side of his mouth as if letting them in on a secret. "Don't know why you're going to all this trouble."

Burke smiled, but Sarah knew that look: Joe's *You're a*

complete idiot look. "Of course we'll entertain any offers your client wants to make, Paul," he said. "And since I expect the judge to certify this as a class action, you should probably make me an offer soon, before that happens. But until then, if we're in it, we're in it. I don't object to Sarah talking to every single one of my clients if she wants to."

Sarah noticed he didn't look at her. He wasn't doing this for her benefit, she supposed, he was just reacting to the procedural aspects of the case, the same way he would if there had been any other attorney on the other side.

Chapman sighed. "All right, if you two are such gluttons. But I may start sending an associate to some of these. I still have work to do back at the office, you know. I don't even get my weekends anymore."

"You poor man," Sarah couldn't resist saying. "Whereas I go straight from the airport to a spa every Friday night."

"See?" Chapman said to Joe, pointing at Sarah.

"I have the pink toenails to prove it," Sarah added. She and her mother had enjoyed a ladies' pampering night over Thanksgiving, and it was the first time in months any nail of Sarah's had seen any color. Now that she thought about it, the idea of going from LAX to a spa sounded so heavenly—and out of reach—she wished she'd never brought it up.

"I'm going to lunch," Joe said. "We're back at one o'clock."

The man stayed true to his word, Sarah thought. He barely looked at her if there weren't some reason associated with the case, and he'd certainly been keeping his distance all day long. On the way back from lunch she saw him waiting to cross the street, and she knew he saw her, too. But he didn't wait for her, didn't try to initiate any kind of conversation, just pulled his suit coat tighter against the wind and strode back toward the hotel.

Sarah didn't know what she expected. No, that wasn't true, she told herself. What she expected was some kind of recognition that she was wearing *their* hat, *their* gloves, maybe pull some kind of comment out of him, even if it was sarcastic. Anything to acknowledge that yes, they had their moments the week before, and no, neither of them had forgotten.

But midway through Chapman's ridiculous questioning of Burke's next client, Sarah snapped out of it and realized what she was doing.

I'm chasing him again. I'm following him to the library, begging him to talk to me, and there he is with that girl, and he's about to grab her ass—

"Your witness," Chapman said abruptly.

"What?"

He checked his watch. "She's your witness. I need to go make a phone call."

Sarah checked her watch, too. It was only a little after two.

Chapman must have realized what he said, because he looked guiltily toward Marcela and said, "Not that last part—take that off. I meant off the record."

Marcela looked to both Sarah and Joe. Sarah waved it off. "No objection. I don't care."

Joe nodded without looking up. "Fine."

Chapman raced out of the room like he suddenly remembered he had a flight to catch.

"I just have a few questions," Sarah told Joe's client. She was surprised Chapman would let the deposition go on in his absence, but that wasn't her problem. She introduced herself, asked her questions, and they were done twenty minutes later.

Joe escorted his client out of the room, leaving just Marcela and Sarah.

"That sounded so good!" Marcela said.

"What?"

"A spa." She looked toward the door to make sure neither of the men were coming back in, and whispered conspiratorially, "I'll bet we can find one."

"Here?" Sarah asked.

Marcela sat down and started thumbing a search into her phone. "Four of them," she announced. "You have a car, don't you?"

A smile spread over Sarah's face. "Do you want to?"

"I will if you will," the court reporter answered.

Sarah took a deep breath. *Flourish.* She had been so careful with money, even once she started receiving a regular paycheck again, but maybe it was all right to loosen her hold on it every now and then. Maybe she was allowed a few luxuries, especially if a surprise opportunity presented itself.

"Okay," she said. "Let's call and see if we can get in." Then she added, "But you can't tell the boys. Ever. I'm supposed to be as manly as they are."

Marcela grinned. "Our secret."

"YOU AND JOE know each other, don't you?" Marcela asked on the way to the massage studio. "From before, I mean."

"Why do you say that?" Sarah asked, stalling. She didn't really know Marcela, other than their polite interactions surrounding the depositions the past several weeks. Marcela had been the court reporter at more than half of them so far, and Sarah supposed she felt comfortable enough now to ask such a personal question.

But it wasn't something Sarah felt comfortable answering.

"I could tell," Marcela said. "By the way he picked you up and carried you when you were sick. And the way you put your arms around him and put your head on his chest. It looked like you'd done that before."

Leave it to a woman to notice details like that, Sarah thought. She doubted Chapman would have picked up on it.

"We used to date," Sarah confirmed. "A long time ago. But please don't tell anyone—especially Paul."

"What we say in this car stays in this car," Marcela said. "Off the record. But it's not illegal, is it? I mean, you can be an attorney against someone you went out with, right?"

"No, there's nothing wrong with it, technically," Sarah said. "There's an ethical rule about disclosing to your client the fact that you might be married to someone on the other side, or related to them in some other way." She remembered there being something about that on the California bar exam. "But I don't think there's any rule about telling people you dated someone once."

"Then what's the problem with it getting out?" Marcela asked. "I won't tell anyone," she hurried to add, "but I'm just curious."

"I always think it's best to keep our private lives out of cases," Sarah said. "We're all just here to do our jobs. Sometimes if people know too much about you...it complicates things."

Knowing Joe was certainly complicating things for her.

"I heard he stayed," Marcela said. "He didn't go back until Thanksgiving."

"Where did you hear that?"

"From one of the girls at his office."

"See?" Sarah said. "That's what I'm talking about. I don't want people knowing things about me."

"I'm sorry," Marcela said.

"No, it's not you," Sarah said with a sigh. She realized she'd sounded harsher than she meant to. She also knew she was particularly sensitive to the topic of gossip, having lived through a scandal earlier that year. She knew people had all sorts of opinions about her, including whether she had been more involved with the senior partners' crimes than anyone let on. Maybe she was paranoid, Sarah thought, but maybe she had a good reason.

She parked the car and turned to Marcela. "There's nothing between me and Joe now. We're just friends—actually, not even that. We knew each other, then we grew up. The end."

Marcela shook her head. "Didn't look like 'the end' to me. You should have seen the way he looked at you. That's how I knew."

Sarah reached out and clasped Marcela's wrist. "This has to stay between us. Please. It was a bad moment—I was sick. But it isn't how things really are. So please just forget you ever saw it, whatever it was."

Marcela smiled indulgently. "I won't ever tell anyone, but just between you and me? I wish a man would look at me that way."

21

By the time Sarah returned to the hotel, her muscles felt like mush. She forgot how exquisitely painful and wonderful it was to have someone dig their fingers into her sore back and shoulders. And the Missoula massage therapist had fingers like thick wooden dowels, which made her work on the bottoms of Sarah's feet particularly cruel and wonderful.

She lay on the bed in her hotel room for a while, still basking in the aftereffects of the massage, and enjoying the fact that for once she didn't need to rush. Her next flight wasn't until the morning. Unlike the previous weeks of depositions, these next ones were in cities too small to have more than a few flights a day. So they would all stay put wherever they happened to be every night, then catch the first flight out every morning.

Sarah had to marvel again at the insane schedule Paul

Chapman devised. If it were up to her, they would have taken depositions all over the country, drawing from a larger sample, instead of deposing only a few people at a time in these towns all across the west.

But then, she didn't agree with so much of how Paul Chapman ran his case, so that was nothing new.

And besides, she reminded herself, the only reason she had this job in the first place was *because* the schedule was so crazy. Mickey's boss didn't want to waste one of his own in-house lawyers on traveling hither and yon five days a week. So in a way, Sarah had Paul Chapman to thank for her nicely increasing bank account.

That made it a little easier to stand the man. Just a little.

But it wasn't Chapman she was thinking about at the moment, and it certainly hadn't been his hands she imagined working out the knots in her tense shoulders, kneading the muscles up and down her legs—

"Just between you and me? I wish a man would look at me that way."

"Stop it," Sarah said out loud. She never should have let the conversation with Marcela get that far. And she definitely didn't need her own thoughts to spin out the irrational fantasy further.

What she needed to do was work. Hard. Now.

She took a moment to order a baked potato and a bowl of vegetable soup from room service, then she booted up her laptop. The purchase orders and other internal documents she started reviewing the week before were beginning to form a picture.

Every time she found some new piece of the puzzle, no matter how small, she felt a thrill, a buzzing all along her skin. Her eyes softened, and a smile tugged at her lips. It felt a little like lust, she had to admit, which maybe no one but another lawyer would understand. But she couldn't deny the thrumming sensation in her nerves whenever she uncovered something she knew no one else had found—that no one was even looking for yet—and here it was, in her hands, ready to take advantage of whenever the time was right.

She was sure Joe didn't know about it—why would he? And Chapman? The man was completely clueless.

But beyond the shear pleasure of discovery, Sarah felt something else: hope. Because if she was right—if she could prove this—then she felt certain she could save her career. What had begun as a temporary job—a job in purgatory, as Joe saw it—could turn into Sarah's ticket back.

Sarah spent the next hour drafting a lengthy e-mail to one of the other attorneys in Mickey's office who was also working on the case. She provided him with a list of the kinds of information she needed. She would have preferred preparing the interrogatories and requests for documents herself, but she knew it wasn't practical during a week with so much travel. She only hoped that Mickey's colleague could follow her detailed instructions, and get her the final, damaging proof she needed.

Then everything would change.

CHAPMAN WAS in an unusually jolly mood. Sarah and Joe exchanged bewildered glances every now and then as the man chuckled and joked and teased his way through the morning deposition. At one point it seemed as if he were actually trying to flirt with Joe's client, which was made all the worse by the look of horror on her face.

"What was that?" Sarah muttered to Joe when they finally took a break. They weren't finished with the deposition yet —Chapman still had more questions, and then it was Sarah's turn—but their flight from Missoula back to Salt Lake City had gotten them there mid-morning, and now it was already time for lunch.

Joe's client stood beside him, so the most he could give Sarah was a quick, wry smile. But that was enough. It was the first time he had shown her any kind of friendliness at all since their drive back from the ski area the last time they visited that city.

Sarah felt strange being back at the same hotel. She was given a different room than the one where she had been cooped up for so long, but everything else about it felt like déjà vu.

There were a few restaurants nearby, and Sarah found one that served a gourmet sandwich of roasted vegetables and pesto. Now that she had the clothes for it, she decided to sit outside. The day was cold, but sunny. She zipped up her raincoat to keep out the wind, then pulled on her blue fleece hat. She ate by herself, gazing up at the mountains.

What was she doing with her life?

This wasn't where she expected to be a year ago.

She tried not to think too much about what the day meant, but that was difficult.

Today was her birthday. She had just turned thirty. Nothing was the way she planned.

THE WEEPER WAS BACK.

Sarah had forgotten her impression of Joe's client the last time she saw her: that the woman would be great in front of a jury.

Once again, as she had that morning before Sarah had to flee the room, the plaintiff cried as she recounted how long and lux and beautiful her hair once was, and how devastated she was to see nearly half of it go up in flames.

Sarah cringed at the woman's detailed description. The product really was dangerous. Now that she had a theory about exactly what happened between her own client and Chapman's client, the primary manufacturer, she felt even more sympathy for the woman than before.

But when it was Sarah's turn to ask questions, the woman turned on her.

"How would you know what it's like?" she snapped. "Pretty little thing like you? I'll bet you just love running your fingers through that thick red hair of yours. How do you think you'd look with half of it burned off? Think you'd be so pretty then? Men would still look at you, but only because you're a freak—"

"Ms. Tiburon," Sarah said calmly, "please answer the question. What other hair products and equipment were you using during this same period of time? That would include blow dryers, curling irons, gels, pomades..."

"Everything," the woman answered. "I've tried every-thing, I use everything, I'm not going to list them out. Do I have to list them out?" she asked Joe.

"To the best of your ability," he said.

The woman sighed dramatically. And Sarah started thinking she wouldn't look so good in front of a jury after all. Ordinary citizens appreciated real emotions, but not melodrama. Maybe if Joe worked with his client, the woman could learn to keep her performance in line. But Sarah could already see that the more she pushed this plaintiff, the uglier the woman's temper became.

By the time Sarah got through her questions, she felt tired and worn out. Some depositions were easier than others, but this one went into the pain-in-the-ass category.

As she gathered up her notes and packed away her laptop, Sarah couldn't help lingering in the room. Wondering if she'd see some sign of recognition from Joe that he remembered what day it was.

Why would he? Sarah scolded herself. *It was one day six years ago—you really think he'd remember? And so what if he does?* she had to add. *Would that make up for anything?*

No, she thought, but it might at least make her feel good to know that someone besides her parents remembered. So far, their phone call that morning while she waited in the Missoula airport had been the brightest part of her day.

"Good night, everybody," Sarah said, looking at Marcela and no one else. She heard a few mutters in response, then left to return to her room.

It was a little before five o'clock. She could work out,

order room service, and review more documents for a few hours. The flight to Billings, Montana the next morning was scheduled to leave around seven-thirty, so she wanted to get to bed early.

But somehow the idea of doing any more work that night, especially after the hostile encounter she had just had, left her feeling completely uninspired. It was her birthday—couldn't she think of better ways to spend it?

When she packed this time, she included a travel-sized bottle of expensive bubble bath from home, on the off chance she might be in a hotel that week that had a decent-looking tub. The one in her current hotel wasn't particularly nice, but maybe it would do. Stick a shower cap over her hair, roll up a towel for her neck, and soak in the scent of vanilla and lavender while she thought about her life.

She had just sunk into the bubbles when she heard the phone in her room ring. Anyone she wanted to talk to would have called her cell, she reasoned, and so she made no effort to drag herself out of the water to answer. She did, however, get up to turn off the light in the bathroom. She wished she'd thought to bring a candle. But lying in hot, delicious-scented water in the dark was as close to luxury as she was going to get.

WHEN THE BATH was finally too cold to be comfortable anymore, Sarah climbed out, turned on the light, and toweled herself off. She wrapped herself in the familiar white robe that hotel had to offer, then headed for the phone to order room service.

The message light was blinking. Sarah pressed the button and listened.

"Hi. I thought I'd have dinner downstairs tonight," said Joe's voice. "If you're interested, I'll be there around six-thirty."

Sarah glanced at the bedside clock. She had about fifteen minutes to get ready, if she wanted to.

If.

She rested the phone back in its cradle, then sat on top of her bedspread. There was nothing wrong with staying in, and potentially many things wrong with going out.

But she couldn't help her curiosity. And, she admitted, couldn't ignore the heavy layer of loneliness that settled in on her while she bathed in the dark. Maybe it was all right to have dinner with him, just this once. How could it be any more awkward than her fainting up at the ski area and him having to carry her to a clinic? Or, for that matter, what could be worse than him cleaning up after her when she'd been sick all over the bathroom?

The more she thought about it, maybe this was exactly what she needed to balance things out again. Buy him dinner, be pleasant, leave feeling like she was as much of an adult as her thirty years said she should be.

And you're lonely, a voice inside dared to remind her.

But that wasn't a good enough reason. She had been lonely for a long time, and hadn't felt the need to do anything stupid yet. She would allow herself to go if she could maintain a certain distance—just like Joe said they should.

Sarah went to her luggage to find something to wear. And knew she brought the perfect thing.

"It isn't real silk," her mother told her as Sarah opened her birthday gifts over Thanksgiving. "I think it's rayon or polyester."

"It's beautiful, Mom—really beautiful. Thank you so much." Sarah held the royal blue kimono top in front of her for her mother's inspection. The pajama top crossed over the chest in the center and tied at the side. It came with a matching pair of pajama pants.

"That almost looks good enough to wear out," her mother had said.

Yes, Sarah thought now, it did.

Especially when she paired it with her black pumps, earrings, and a thin gold necklace. She smiled at her reflection, thinking how fun it was to have this as her own private secret. As soon as dinner was over, she could simply return to her room, brush her teeth, and climb into bed. It was almost as easy as wearing sweats.

The dining room downstairs looked like every other restaurant she had been to in any of the chain hotels. This one had a bar, and unfortunately, Paul Chapman was sitting at it that moment.

Sarah hid at the side of the hostess's station until someone came to seat her.

"Away from the bar," Sarah requested. "Far away." Then she followed the hostess, watching Chapman the whole time as he guzzled his drink, shoveled nuts into his maw, and stared at the TV above the bar. If she could just get past him, she could relax again.

But she sat in her booth for only a few minutes before she realized she wouldn't be relaxing at all. Because suddenly Joe stood beside her, two glasses of red wine in hand.

Sarah looked up, saw what he was wearing, and immediately said, "*No.*"

"What do you mean, no?" Joe asked.

He stood beside the booth dressed in button-down Levi's and a faded UCLA hoodie. It had to be the same one from six years ago, Sarah thought, since it was tighter across the chest and shoulders now, and the cuffs looked tattered. Which meant that there was the pocket where he first warmed her hands. There was where he first touched any part of her.

She tried to cover her reaction with sarcasm. "Come on, Burke, you're not that sentimental."

"You don't know that," he said, handing her one of the glasses of wine and sliding across from her into the horse-shoe-shaped booth. He lifted his own glass in a toast. "Happy Birthday, Sarah."

She studied his face, searching for some hint of how he expected her to answer. He had to know that showing up there like that—wearing what he was wearing—would catch her off guard. And then remembering her birthday—what did he think she was going to say?

But before she could come up with the right line, whatever it was, Burke leaned forward and said in a low voice, "Come on, Red. Take the night off. It's your birthday—you're entitled."

"Fraternizing with the enemy, huh?" Chapman's booming voice interrupted as he shambled toward their table. "Or is it cavorting?"

Keeping his gaze on Sarah, Joe slowly leaned back. "Both. Want to join us?"

Sarah widened her eyes at him, but Joe ignored her.

"Sure," Chapman said. He made a move for Sarah's side of the booth, but Joe stopped him.

"No, why don't you sit over here, Paul."

Joe made room for Chapman by scooting closer to Sarah's side. She pressed her foot down hard against the top of Joe's. He pretended not to feel it.

But he reached beneath the table for her hand, and gave it one quick squeeze before letting go.

"I'm celebrating," Chapman announced.

"Why's that?" Joe asked.

"You two are going to have to start getting along without me. I made a deal yesterday. Thanks to Sarah here, I'm going home."

Sarah didn't feel like asking any follow up questions, mainly because she knew she didn't need to. Paul Chapman was one of those people who viewed any conversation as an opportunity to monologue.

"I told them, 'If you expect me to start spending even

more time out of the office and traveling to even more cities just because that psychopath Sarah Henley'—no offense," he added, which Sarah thought was uncharacteristically sensitive of him, "—'thinks she's going to show everybody up and act like some hot shot just so she can bill every last dime out of this case before it settles...'" He paused to take a sip of his drink. "'...then you're either going to have to pay me a bigger bonus this year or let me farm it out to one of the associates. Because I am *done* here. *Finito*,'" he said, in what Sarah thought might be an attempt at Italian.

Joe's hand was on hers again under the table. He gave it another quick squeeze, perhaps signaling something, Sarah thought, but instead of letting go this time, he held on.

"So they're sending out one of the underlings, starting next week," Chapman continued. "Good luck with that. Those new kids don't know what the hell they're doing."

The server showed up then, and took their orders. Joe still held Sarah's hand.

"That's all you're eating?" Chapman said after Sarah asked for several sides of vegetables. "No wonder you're skin and bones."

While Chapman instructed the server in the proper preparation of his meat, Joe pretended to study his menu so he could whisper to Sarah behind it. "I like the way you look. Always have. But especially now."

"What happened to keeping your distance?" Sarah whispered back.

"I decided to take tonight off, too."

Sarah allowed herself to hold his hand a moment longer,

then drew it away. Joe let her go. But he widened his legs just enough to make contact with hers. And she let him.

This wasn't the dinner she had dreamed of for her 30th birthday. Exhibit A: Paul Chapman, back to droning endlessly about himself. Exhibit B: Joe Burke, sitting close enough to her now she could feel the heat radiating off his body and that familiar pull of gravity that made her want to slide over one more inch, two, until she could drape her leg over his, let him run his hand up her thigh, up to where there was already evidence that she wasn't as immune to him as she pretended, and her body had its own ideas about what kind of special birthday treat it might like—

Sarah deliberately moved away from Joe again. He might be taking the night off, but she couldn't. Couldn't afford to. Not now, not ever.

Not without losing too much in the bargain.

SARAH YAWNED. She made a point of never drinking on these trips because she knew she'd feel too fuzzy-headed in the morning. But she didn't mind feeling that way now, thanks to the wine, especially since it helped turn Chapman's monologue into white noise in the background while she concentrated on what was happening underneath the table.

She wasn't sure which of them moved first—it could have been either—but it wasn't long before they sat leg to leg again, Joe's hand resting comfortably on top of her thigh.

"Right," he'd say to Chapman, or "Yep," while at the same time letting his hand roam upward on Sarah's slick pajama pants, the heat inside her building with each centimeter he climbed higher, until finally she had to capture his fingers and push them back to safe territory. They sat there that way for a while, fingers intertwined while they ate and drank with their outside hands—Sarah trying to maneuver her fork left-handed, which was a challenge—and then Joe's hand began drifting upward again and Sarah had to guard the gates.

It was a tease and a seduction and a game they both knew, but Sarah had little desire to stop it. Maybe it was the wine, maybe it was the birthday, or maybe it was just the fact that she had let him get this far, and she didn't care anymore where it went. Not tonight. Just this once.

He stroked his thumb across the top of her hand now, the movement slow and rhythmic, and Sarah had to clamp her lips together to keep the moan from escaping. His touch felt as arousing as if he turned to her in the booth, spread her kimono top open, and took her breasts with his hands and his mouth.

Joe must have noticed her yawn. She had tried to be as obvious about it as possible.

"Listen, Paul," he said, "I'm going to have to call it a night. I don't have your kind of stamina."

Chapman obviously liked that. He chest almost visibly puffed out.

"How about you, Sarah—had enough?" Joe asked.

"Plenty," she said.

Joe signaled for the check. As soon as it arrived, Sarah reached for it.

"Not on your life," Joe said, snatching it up. He released Sarah's hand so he could pull his wallet out of his jeans.

Chapman sat there, making no such move.

But Joe wasn't shy. "Come on, Paul, let's have your credit card." He held out his hand and waited.

Chapman dug out his wallet and took his time pulling out the card. He looked over at Sarah. "What about you, Henley? Or are you pulling the female thing?"

"She's pulling the female thing," Joe confirmed. "Dinner's on you and me tonight."

"Unbelievable," Chapman muttered.

Joe ignored him and handed the bill and both credit cards to the server.

"So, you're one of those?" Chapman asked Sarah. His words had grown more slurred throughout dinner, and his eyes seemed to lose their focus.

"One of what?" Sarah asked coldly.

"A 'feminist,'" he said, putting finger quotes around it, "when it suits you, and a 'female' when it comes to paying for anything?"

"That's right, Paul," she said. "You have me all figured out." She started to exit the booth.

"Is that why you went to law school?" Chapman asked.

Sarah paused for the inevitable follow-up insult.

"To get yourself a husband?" he continued. "Only it didn't work out, huh? Too much of a ball-buster."

"Yep, that's right, Paul," she said. "Balls spontaneously exploding everywhere I go. You got it."

Sarah turned to Joe. "Thanks for dinner. It was...unusual."

"I'll walk you out," he said.

"Aren't you afraid for your balls?" she asked for Chapman's benefit.

"I'm a risk-taker," Joe answered.

He signed the receipt, then escorted her out of the restaurant.

"What an asshole," Sarah muttered.

"He never disappoints," Joe agreed.

"Why did you invite him?" She'd been dying to ask him that for the last hour they had been trapped.

"To shut him up," Joe said. "A guy like that would love to tell anyone who'd listen that he saw us having dinner together. I thought I'd spare us the gossip."

Sarah couldn't deny the logic. Even though having dinner with that cretin any night, let alone on her birthday, was the last thing she wanted to do.

They walked as far as the lobby, then the two of them paused. They stood close to each other, but not nearly as close as they'd been in the booth. The elevators were behind them, and it would have been easy for Sarah simply to say goodnight and return to her room.

But instead she looked up at Joe. And waited. She wanted to know exactly what he would say next, and exactly what she would say in response. How this game would play out.

"Feel like taking a drive?" he asked.

"Where to?"

"Not far," he said.

Sarah nodded, as if considering. But there was nothing left to decide. She already crossed that boundary, she realized, by even coming downstairs to dinner. Everything after that felt inevitable.

Still, she kept her eyes locked on his for a moment more, and let the negotiation continue in silence.

The lobby door opened, and a gust of winter wind swept in. Sarah clutched her arms around her chest.

"Here. You're not dressed for it," Joe said, removing his hoodie and handing it to her.

She tugged it over her head. And breathed in. It smelled of laundry soap and Joe—unmistakably Joe. His familiar, masculine scent. Just one more reminder of all of the pleasure she once took in his body. And could take again.

She pulled the hoodie all the way down until the hem of it hung to her thighs.

"Ready?" Joe asked.

Sarah nodded.

The two of them walked together to his car, two colleagues out on a short errand, if Chapman happened to notice, two attorneys giving no indication they knew each other beyond a professional acquaintance. There was no touching, no stolen glance, nothing except a smooth entry into the car, the ignition turning right away, Joe pulling out of the parking lot without a moment's hesitation.

He was right, it wasn't far. Maybe five minutes away.

"You always have to stay somewhere else, don't you?" Sarah asked. But she was quickly reaching the point where she didn't want to talk at all.

They walked into the second lobby together, still not touching or looking at each other, and headed for the elevator. Sarah waited for the doors to close them in before turning to Joe.

"You know it's just for tonight."

"I know," he said.

"It doesn't change anything."

"All right."

Then she told her mind to take the rest of the night off while she let her body take it from there.

23

They were barely inside the room before they went at each other as if no time had passed or too much had. Sarah grabbed him and pulled him to her with nearly as much force as he reached for her. Their mouths crushed together while Joe slipped his hands underneath the hoodie. Sarah lifted her arms so he could tug it over her head. Then she undid the tie on her kimono top and let it fall to the floor.

Joe stared at her naked breasts, his breath ragged. Then he yanked down the pajama pants and found nothing between him and her flesh.

"My God, Sarah, you've been like this all night? Why did you let me sit there so long?" He covered her mouth with his as he cupped a breast in one hand and her ass with another. He pulled her hips into his. Sarah could feel the hardness struggling to escape his jeans.

"Why did you wear a belt?" she gasped, fumbling to undo it.

He took over, and then popped the top button of his jeans for her. Sarah pulled the rest of the buttons free, then reached inside and released his erection. Joe kicked off his shoes and Sarah pushed his jeans and underwear roughly down his legs. It was all taking too much time, and she still had his shirt to get rid of.

She slid her hands under his T-shirt and then spread her fingers across his warm chest, exploring the width and the strength. He was so different from how she remembered, so much firmer and more muscular. She pushed his shirt up to his shoulders so she could feel the unfamiliar muscles there, too. Then she pulled the shirt free, and leaned forward to flick her tongue against his nipple. She took him in her hand at the same time, gripping and stroking him, and Joe groaned as she controlled him from both above and below.

"Sarah..."

He slid his fingers into her wetness and pulled her mouth back up to his. Sarah locked her arms around his neck and pressed as much of herself as she could against him, chest to chest, groin to groin. Joe briefly abandoned her mouth to nip and suck at one of her breasts, but then they devoured each other again as he backed her toward the wall.

He paused for a moment to grab his jeans from the floor and dig into one of the pockets.

"That sure, huh?" Sarah managed to say as Joe found the condom.

"Never sure." Then he was back in position, kissing her,

lifting her from the ground so they could take each other the way they had that very first time.

"No," Sarah said. "Wait." Even though she wanted it that way, too, hard and fast and now. Her heart pounded so hard she had to hold her hand there to steady it. "We're only doing this once, so you'd better make it last."

Joe immediately obliged by carrying her to the bed. He ripped the covers back and lowered her to the sheet.

He met her gaze with a dark and knowing look, then levered her thighs apart and took her with his mouth.

Sarah cried out, arching her back, nearly pushing him away, ready to stop him at any moment because it was too good, too long overdue, and she might not live through it.

Damn right you'll let him do this, her body responded, shoving those insane thoughts right out of her mind. *You shut up and let him go.*

So she shut up and let him go.

All through dinner she imagined what it might be like to be with him again, but her fantasies hadn't done him justice. Here he was, flesh and blood, the best lover she had ever had, and he'd lost *none* of that, only improved on it.

She thought she understood her body, what it liked, what it needed, how long it took to climb up the crest and then take the plunge over. But between his tongue and a hand expertly deployed, Sarah could feel the pressure of a wave building far too soon, ready to take her whenever she let it.

"Joe—"

"I know," he answered, "do it."

And with that she let go, his name on her lips as she let the wave overtake her.

He stayed with her the whole time, still pressing, still tasting, charging every nerve in her body with such wattage and heat she wondered how it could still be safe to touch her.

Then he was above her, with a look of such exquisite need on his face, she didn't wait to hear the words.

"Sarah, I have to—" But she was already pulling him to her, because she needed it, too. He paused only long enough for the condom, then he was on top of her, sliding into her, as Sarah lifted her hips to meet him.

She had waited too long, she knew now. Waited and tortured them both. When really this was for her, had been for her all along, and giving Joe pleasure was no sacrifice when she could have all of this for herself.

They moved together, lovers who had memorized each other's desires once before and had forgotten absolutely nothing. Sarah arched as she came again and Joe drove himself to release. The two of them trembled with the force of it, Sarah's arms still shaking as they held on to each other and waited for their eruptions to subside.

Then Joe rolled to the side and pulled Sarah close against him. She draped her body over his and rested her head against his chest, feeling the strong pulse of his heart against her cheek. She reached up her hand, and he threaded his fingers through hers. Then she lifted her face and pulled him toward her so he could kiss her again.

"*Damn*, Burke," she whispered. Then she collapsed back onto his chest.

He stroked a hand gently down her back.

"Sarah..." But then he must have forgotten what he was

going to say. He covered them both in the blankets, then wrapped her in his arms.

SARAH DOZED for almost an hour before her leg twitched and woke her up. She and Joe had changed positions during that time, and she now lay on her back with her thigh open, resting on top of Joe's. He slept on his back, too, snoring softly, with his hand curled possessively around her thigh, gripping it even in his sleep.

If she was awake, he should be, too.

She drummed her fingers against his arm.

"Subtle," Joe murmured.

"It's still my birthday," she pointed out.

Joe groaned and rolled onto his side. He looked into Sarah's eyes. "You're so beautiful. I never get tired of looking at you." He ran a hand over her shoulder, then down her arm. "You're so different now."

Sarah leaned back and let him explore. She had never been shy about her body around Joe. He claimed it so completely their first day together, she didn't see the sense in trying to hide it.

He cupped her breasts in his hands, kneading them softly, looking at them under the glow of the bedside lamp. He kissed the peak of each breast in turn. "I like how rosy your nipples are. Your lips turn the same color if we've been kissing for a long time—did you know that?"

"No." But she liked that he noticed. He never mentioned that before.

He smoothed his hands down the sides of her waist.

Then he poked the tight muscles of her abdomen. "I like that."

"My trainer said I used to be 'skinny fat' when I first came in," Sarah said. "Thin, but no muscle tone."

"I liked it then," Joe said, kissing along the sides of her belly, "and I like it now." He kissed the pale skin just below her belly button, then turned his head and rested his cheek there. Sarah laid her hand gently on top of his head. She stroked his short hair, then spread her palm softly against his cheek. Joe wrapped his arms around her waist and the two of them lay like that for a while.

It felt completely natural, Sarah thought, to be with him like this: tender, loving, no different from how the two of them had been toward each other all those nights and days of their seven weeks together. She felt no need to be cagey or smart-mouthed or self-protective in any way.

Because once she made the decision in the lobby of her hotel to give herself this one night, she let go of any of the barriers that held her back. She could erect them again in the morning, but for now, for these next few hours, she just wanted to feel him, to let herself be free with him, to give herself this gift and not hold anything back—not from herself, and not from Joe.

She caressed the sensitive area behind his ear, knowing what he would do. He raised his head from her belly and climbed back up to where their mouths could meet once again. She wrapped her arms around his neck, pressing her breasts against his chest, and angled her hips so that she stroked him without taking him in.

Joe moaned. And grabbed her cheeks to control the

motion. Sarah felt a familiar laugh bubbling in her throat. The two of them had become expert at the tease, both trying to hold off longer than the other, to make the other one beg, to be the one who gave in when the other couldn't bear waiting another second more.

Abruptly Joe pulled away and strode toward the bathroom. He returned with a handful of condoms.

"Joe…" Sarah said with a laugh.

"I wanted to be ready," he said. "In case you ever said yes."

"How long have you been waiting?" she asked.

"Six years."

Her expression darkened. And one of the barriers instantly went back up. "I'm serious, Joe. You need to be careful here."

"All right, then," he said, "two months. Does that make you feel better?"

Sarah nodded. And tried to shake off that flash of momentary anger.

"Do you have any good ideas?" Joe asked.

"About?"

"What comes next."

"Lots of them," Sarah said. And if Joe meant something else, she didn't want to know it as she reached for him again to take what she had been missing for far too long.

24

"Sarah."

"Mmm."

"We have to get up."

She snuggled deeper into the cradle of his arms as he spooned her from behind.

"Sarah." He kissed her shoulder. "We really have to get up."

She heard the alarm, too, and knew he was right. They had to be at the airport by six-thirty, and she still needed time to return to her hotel, shower and change, pack, and turn in the rental car.

But it seemed impossible in that moment to leave the comfort of his body.

Joe kissed her one more time, then let her go and climbed out of bed. She watched while he crossed the room to the coffee maker and began brewing a cup.

She studied his naked form from behind. "I like the way

you look now. I like touching all those muscles. I like the way you feel against me."

"Sarah, if you say anything more, I'm never going to be able to leave this hotel room."

He turned just enough for her to see his growing erection. She smiled and rolled onto her back to gaze at the ceiling.

"Here," he said a moment later, handing her the first cup of coffee. He stared at her the way she had been staring at him, taking in all the contours of her body, the slopes and angles, the various changes since they'd last been together.

Sarah liked the attention. It had been a long time since she let someone look at her. She liked the visible effect it was having on Burke.

But he was right, they had to get to work.

"I don't do coffee anymore," she said, "but if you have tea, I'll take it."

Although considering how little sleep she'd gotten, a cup of strong black coffee sounded like a much wiser choice.

She forced herself from the bed and retrieved her pajamas from the area just inside Joe's door. "Can I borrow this?" she asked, holding up his hoodie. "Just for the ride back."

Joe's eyes raked her naked body again. He groaned and disappeared into the bathroom.

Sarah took that as a yes.

She dressed, then brought a cup of tea with her back to Joe's bed to wait. She propped a pillow behind her and pulled the covers up over her legs and spent the next several minutes replaying scenes from the night before. He was a better lover now, in so many ways. More patient, more inventive, more...skilled.

She forced herself not to think of how many women he had been with since her who would have given him that practice. She already knew she couldn't trust him. She would never make that mistake again.

But it didn't mean she had to deny herself the pleasure of a purely physical relationship with him. It was no different from eating right and working out: her body wanted certain things now, and it was up to her to provide them.

And to be smart about it this time.

Joe emerged from the bathroom and picked up his own clothes from the heap by the door. He was dressed within a minute, then asked, "Ready?"

"What do you think?" Sarah asked, hugging her knees to her chest and looking him straight in the eye. "Was this the only time?"

"I sure as hell hope not, but we'll see. Come on, Red, I have to take you back."

SHE HAD NOW BEEN in the Salt Lake City airport far more times than she ever dreamed she would. And she would be back there the next day and the one after that, since it was the hub for all their Montana and Idaho flights. She thought about driving between some of her destinations, but even with all the hassle of trying to bounce from one regional airport to another, it was still faster than traveling by car. And at least she could work in the airport and on the planes, so she accepted the itinerary as planned.

"How are you holding up, Henley?" Joe asked as he appeared at her side rolling his carry-on down the concourse. He seemed absorbed by what he was reading on his phone, and Sarah doubted that anyone watching them would guess they were speaking to each other.

"Exhausted," she said. "I need more than two hours of sleep."

"We should try to get to bed earlier tonight," he said, still not looking at her. Sarah's body flushed in response. She could feel the moisture building from just that one simple statement. The idea of being back in bed with Joe as soon as possible made her want to turn around and return to his hotel, and skip the flight altogether.

"I'll think about it," Sarah said, hoping to sound less affected by him than she was.

They walked in silence until Sarah could see their gate just up ahead. Then Joe asked, "What's your phone number?"

Sarah hesitated, but then gave him the numbers to input into his phone. She could see Marcela to their right, curled up on one of the chairs, snoozing against her wadded up coat.

"See you later," Joe said. Then he lengthened his stride and let her walk the rest of the way alone.

Sarah spied someone drinking from Starbucks cup, and it was one too many temptations for her to try to resist that morning. She reversed course to where she knew she passed one of the kiosks, and stood in line already savoring how that first sip would taste. Angie had been right advising her to overhaul her diet last year—Sarah felt so much better just a week into the experiment—but these were extraordinary times, she told herself, and she was only human.

She returned to the gate area, cup in hand, and stole another look at Joe. He sat looking so serious and adult in his gray suit, dress shirt, and tie. She watched him as he typed into his laptop, his brow furrowed in concentration. Then, whether he sensed her there or just happened to look up at that moment, the two of them locked eyes ever so briefly before Sarah continued on and sat in a different section.

She hated those moments in movies when the characters exchanged secret glances that anyone in the vicinity with half a brain would have noticed. It made her look around for Paul Chapman, wondering what he would make of that one weak moment.

She found him splayed out on a chair, legs wide, head thrown back as he snored. She glanced at Marcela again, too, knowing the court reporter would be more attuned to seeing something pass between Sarah and Joe.

But Marcela still slept, and so Sarah felt safe looking at him again, just for a minute. She took a sip of dark coffee and secretly studied his handsome face.

God, she wanted him. Wanted to hold that face in her hands and kiss that mouth, wanted to feel his hands on her, his skin against hers, the weight of his body, the pleasure of him inside her. Her nerves still buzzed from everything he had already done to her and from the promise there might be more. Was it so wrong to want this time together, here in the purgatory of their lives?

But it wasn't just their history together that warned her of all the risks involved. This wasn't just about her and Joe.

There were still a few minutes before the gate agent would begin calling rows. Sarah fed a search into her phone.

California rules of ethics, conflict of interest.

It took her a moment of scrolling through the list to find the rule she was looking for.

Rule 3-320 Relationship With Other Party's Lawyer

A member of the Bar shall not represent a client in a matter in which another party's lawyer is a spouse, parent, child, or sibling of the member, lives with the member, is a client of the member, or has an intimate personal relationship with the member, unless the member informs the client in writing of the relationship.

There was no denying, Sarah thought, that she now had an intimate personal relationship with the member. In her sleep-deprived state, she almost snickered at the reference to "member." But she knew this wasn't funny. She had crossed a line the night before—they both had. And it wasn't in Sarah's nature to violate the rules.

It was why she hated any suggestion that she had been involved in any way with the illegal activities of her old firm. Sarah's reputation was squeaky clean before, and she intended for it to be again, once the taint of April 6 finally washed away.

A text popped onto her screen.

I missed you.

Sarah closed her eyes. Joe had no intention of making this easy for her. She should have known that from the moment he pulled up in front of Walmart the week before. Should have known it for certain from the mischievous, wicked look he gave her in the checkout line. Or from the soft kiss he planted on her lips while she recovered in the mountain clinic. Or from the way he took care of her when no one else would.

He had been working on her for longer than just last night, Sarah knew, longer than just their time at dinner as he stroked her thigh beneath the table.

He wanted this as much as she did.

Which didn't make it any less complicated, or any less unethical.

Sarah shut off her phone without texting him back.

25

At the deposition in Billings, Montana that afternoon, Chapman rattled off his questions so quickly, Marcela looked like she was having a hard time keeping up.

"Where were you born—what is your work history—where did you go to school—did you graduate—who are your parents ...?"

At one point Joe finally had to say, "Off the record. Paul, you have to give her time to answer."

"I thought we all wanted to speed it up," he answered. "Isn't that what you said, Sarah?"

"Asking only relevant questions would be a big help," she said, "yes."

"You do your job," Chapman said, "I'll do mine. Back on," he told Marcela, then continued reciting questions from his notes.

Sarah resisted exchanging any kind of look with Burke, even if this one was justified by their work. Instead she resorted to writing the word *ASS* on her legal pad and then decorating the letters with dramatic shading and smoke rising out of the A and long tails growing from the Ss. She looped the tails into swirls and circles that then became sinister-looking eyeballs and grinning demons. Yes, she was really going to miss Chapman when he went.

"Hi, Ms. Harowitz," she said when it was her turn. She read somewhere that people in the service industry were familiar with the "post-asshole" customer experience. If someone has witnessed a store clerk or a barista being abused by the customer ahead, by the time the next person steps up, he or she bends over backward to be nice. *"Sure! No problem. Whatever you can do."*

Sarah felt a little of that impulse now. Joe's client had been very tolerant of what was truly a bad example of lawyering.

"Thank you for coming in today," Sarah said. "I know you had to take time off of work, and we all really appreciate it."

Chapman grunted.

"We won't keep you much longer," Sarah said. "I'm interested in just a few things. You said you received the hair iron for Christmas. How soon after that did you use it?"

"The next day, I think," Joe's client said. She still seemed tense from Chapman's questioning, but Sarah hoped to see her relax soon. Being courteous and professional with a witness often seemed to have that effect. Sarah wondered if Chapman had ever tried it.

"How often do you have to straighten your hair?" She

asked. "I do mine about every three days—more often if I've just worked out or I've gotten it wet."

"Oh, *this* is relevant," Chapman sneered. "Thanks for showing me how it's done."

Sarah ignored him. "So how often would you say you straighten yours?"

Now that it was simply a conversation—and about a topic both women had in common—Joe's client opened up. Sarah wasn't pretending: she genuinely wanted to know what steps Ms. Harowitz went through to wash, condition, dry, then iron her hair. It was just woman-to-woman for a while, both of them comparing stories about how difficult their hair had been all their lives, and what they'd gone through to try to tame it.

Chapman made no effort to hide his annoyance. He leaned back in his chair, arms crossed, and kept shaking his head and smirking at Burke, as if the two of them agreed Sarah was wasting their time. Finally Chapman asked, "Are you two girls going over makeup tips next? Because Joe and I might as well grab a beer."

He was too stupid to listen, Sarah thought. All the better for her and her case.

"You said the product caught on fire February thirteenth, right?" she asked.

Joe's client nodded. "I wanted to do an extra good job on my hair that night. You know, for Valentine's the next day."

Sarah winced. "I'm so sorry."

The woman seemed to appreciate a genuine human reaction, as opposed to Chapman's robotic, "And then what happened...and then what happened..."

Sarah consulted her notes. "So, assuming you first used the product on December twenty-sixth, and used it approximately every two days after that, it sounds like you used it about twenty-five times, total. Does that sound right?"

Ms. Harowitz shrugged and looked apologetic. "I never really counted it."

Sarah accidentally glanced at Joe just then and saw him looking back at her with a curious expression. She had never gone this in-depth before, putting a specific number out there, on the record. So far she'd just been keeping that information in her notes.

"Thank you, Ms. Harowitz. That's all I have. We appreciate your time and patience today."

SHE HAD ALREADY SWEATED through two miles on the hotel treadmill that evening when her music cut out to alert her to a text:

The name of a different hotel. And a room number.

Sarah deleted it and kept on running.

This was the problem with reality, she thought. Once it started creeping back in, it tended to crowd out the fantasies altogether. And reality had been intruding on her thoughts more and more as the day progressed.

...an intimate personal relationship with the member...

What she and Joe had done was unethical. There was no other way to look at it. No exceptions, no gray area, none. No, "Oh, but we had a little wine," or "It was my birthday," or "I'm sorry, I was lonely, and opposing counsel was right there—have you seen him? That man is *hot*." There wasn't even an exception for taking up with former lovers rather than starting something new with someone else.

And that was just the legal side of it. What about the personal? Joe Burke was no friend of hers. Yes, he was outstanding in bed. Congratulations, here's your medal. But it didn't change the fact that he'd once stuck a blade in her heart and left it there. The scar tissue may have grown around it, but Sarah had felt the knife every time she even considered getting in too deep with another man. And now if that man was Joe Burke again, run far and run fast.

Sarah increased the speed on the treadmill. It was a start.

They would be back on an easier schedule the following week—easier for Sarah, anyway. There were more flights between places like Portland and Seattle, which meant they could fly every night after the depositions, instead of early in the mornings.

Which meant Sarah would never have a night free.

She picked up the pace and ran flat out for a mile. The sweat poured off her as her heart and lungs pumped. She would feel better in no time, she thought—exercise was always a great release.

Kind of like sex with Joe, her lascivious mind answered.

STOP. It was just one night of weakness, she reminded herself. She could live with that. She had made mistakes before—plenty of them, including falling for Burke in the first place. The key was not to wallow in them, but instead keep moving forward. Move forward and be careful never to repeat that same mistake.

The first step was forgetting the hotel and room number her brain had automatically memorized. The second was forgetting how absolutely perfect it felt to be in Joe's arms again. To pick up where they had left off, as if they'd never been apart.

It was going to be a long night.

THE BILLINGS AIRPORT restaurant didn't open until five AM. Sarah was still a few minutes early. She waited outside the door, hoping they had oatmeal.

The terminal was small enough that she knew there would be no hiding from each other. Marcela had already passed her with a yawn and the greeting, "Just one more morning like this, then we can sleep all weekend." Chapman shuffled by without bothering to say anything. And then she saw Joe.

Damn it, why did he have to look like that? Sarah thought. Although Joe in a suit was nothing compared to him in jeans.

Sarah still had his hoodie. She'd forgotten about it until she unpacked her workout clothes the day before. Now it still sat in her bag, waiting for a convenient and covert time to give it back. She couldn't exactly pull it out of her luggage and hand it to him now. If either Marcela or Chapman noticed, they might wonder.

The restaurant door opened behind her and Sarah quickly ducked inside.

But it was too much to think she would escape him.

"Morning," Joe said, coming in behind her.

"Good morning," she answered without turning her head. She concentrated on the menu, then ordered tea, a banana, and a bagel.

"Sleep all right?" Joe asked her. "I'll take a coffee to go," he told the server.

"Fine," Sarah said. "You?"

"No, I wouldn't say that."

She listened for some tone in his voice, some hint of pouting or anger, but it didn't appear to be there. He was as casual as if they were discussing the weather.

"Maybe tonight," Joe said, and then left it at that. He paid for his coffee and told her he'd see her later.

While meanwhile Sarah's heart beat at a staccato.

She sat at one of the tables and concentrated hard on spreading jam over her bagel. The bread was stale, but she ate it anyway. She needed something to do with her hands and her mouth.

Maybe tonight.

Her body buzzed at the mere suggestion.

See, this was the problem, she thought. You can't have just one. So, tonight in some hotel room in Boise, Idaho. Tomorrow, somewhere else. Was this really what her life was reduced to? Sneaking around with Joe in whatever town they happened to be in, both of them filling up their idle hours with as much sex as they could fit in before they had to fall asleep and go back to work the next morning?

As opposed to what? Sarah asked herself. As opposed to returning to her hotel room alone every night, eating bad food from room service, reading through documents until she passed out and woke up to the alarm and rushed off to some airport to do it all over again?

Chapman had the right idea, getting someone else to do

the dirty work. Sarah would have much preferred being one of the attorneys back in the office, sending out discovery requests without ever having to catch a flight and face another long, tiring day of depositions and being in the same room with Joe for six or seven hours, then having to walk away from him again. And again.

A text popped up on her screen.

Feel like takeout tonight?

Why did he have to make it sound so easy?

Sarah turned off her phone.

But then a minute later, turned it back on again.

And sat staring at the text for a long time before turning the phone off for good.

26

———

It was Thursday, she had to remind herself. The days strung together now like reruns of the day before. Every plane ride felt the same. All the hotel conference rooms looked alike. All the food tasted equally bad. *Feel like takeout tonight?* Of course. And a whole lot more than that.

Chapman continued with his new style of questioning, firing them off so rapidly Joe's client barely had a chance to answer. Clearly Chapman was already done with the job. He had been a bad lawyer at the beginning of their travels together, but at least Sarah could tell he thought he was good. Now, he clearly didn't care.

"Objection," Joe said again. He'd already objected several times that afternoon, always with the same complaint. "Please repeat the question slowly and allow my client sufficient time to answer."

Chapman scowled and did as he was asked, but in an exaggerated way, enunciating every word and speaking extra loudly as if Joe's client, an elegant woman in her 70s, were both mentally deficient and hard of hearing.

The woman was neither, Sarah noticed, and so far had been extremely tolerant of Chapman's boorish behavior.

"My husband and I moved to Boise after our son graduated from high school," the woman said in answer to Chapman's question, and Sarah wanted to throw something at his fat head when she saw him roll his eyes and pretend to be bored by what he was hearing.

Then don't ask! Sarah wanted to scream at him. *Stick to the facts of this case!*

But Chapman was like so many other lawyers she'd come up against: convinced of his brilliance, in love with the sound of his own voice, and immune to anyone's helpful suggestion that he pull his head out of his rear end and actually learn to do the job well.

"Objection," Joe said again after another pair of rapid questions. "Let the record reflect counsel is not allowing my client sufficient time to answer."

"Fine!" Chapman said, leaning back. "Take all day." He twirled his hand at the woman. "Please, speak."

Joe's client looked at him coldly, but then answered him in her unfailingly dignified manner.

Sarah hid a yawn behind her hand and tried to tune out Chapman's voice for a few minutes while she studied Joe's client instead.

Sarah wondered if she would still be going to so much effort with her hair when she was seventy-three, like Mrs. Barrett.

Didn't there finally come a point when people said forget

it, take me or leave me, my hair is a kinky frightful mess and that's just the way it is? When they gave up on makeup, too, and accepted the fact that their eyelashes were too pale, their nose too wide, their lips too thin, their cheeks not nearly defined enough?

Although looking at Mrs. Barrett, who had obviously taken great care with her appearance that morning, wearing not only makeup, but also simple, elegant jewelry and a colorful scarf to go with her sweater and long skirt, Sarah saw the appeal of not giving up too soon. Mrs. Barrett probably enjoyed her own reflection in the mirror. And her husband probably enjoyed her, too.

Sarah found her thoughts straying more and more to the personal lives of the people in that room. Chapman didn't wear a wedding ring, which was no great surprise, since Sarah couldn't imagine who would have him, but did he ever date? Was there anyone who could put up with him for even a single hour?

And she assumed Marcela was single, based on her comment about wishing someone would look at her the way Joe looked at Sarah—

"Objection," Joe snapped. "Paul, if you keep this up, I'm suspending the rest of the deposition. Your firm is the one that scheduled all of these in the first place. If you didn't want to hear from my clients in person, you should have handled it with interrogatories."

"Wish I had," Chapman answered. "Not my problem anymore. Mrs. Barrett, please take as much time as you need to answer the question," he said, sickly sweet now. "We have nothing better to do all day long than to listen to you reminisce about your years in the Navy."

"Off the record," Sarah said. "Paul, if you don't want to know someone's work history, don't ask. If you don't want to know about her schooling, don't ask. But don't be rude to a woman who has taken time out of her life to be here and sit through a deposition all afternoon just because your client's product blew up and set her hair on fire." She could feel her face getting hot, and knew she needed to maintain control, but she was sick of this man and his obnoxious behavior.

"Because of your faulty part," Chapman returned.

"All subject to litigation," Sarah said. "But if you don't stop abusing these plaintiffs—"

"Then what?" Chapman said. "You going to file a bar complaint against me, Henley? Try to get me sanctioned? You think anyone's going to listen to you, with your history? Word is you got off lucky. You should have been indicted with the rest of them."

Sarah felt her blood pressure spike. Her eyes flashed toward the court reporter to confirm that none of this was being taken down.

"That's enough," Joe said calmly. "We're taking a break. And you're done with my client now, Chapman. If you have any more questions, submit them in writing. Ms. Henley, I assume you have a few questions?"

"I do." Sarah continued to stare furiously at Chapman. He smirked back at her.

"We'll be back in a few minutes," Joe said, then he escorted Mrs. Barrett from the room.

Sarah forced herself to control her temper. She had been in this position many times before, under personal attack for one reason or another, and she knew without a doubt that the best and only response was to win her case and grind the other attorney into the ground. To win so soundly and unequivocally, her opponent would know he made a mistake underestimating her, and especially made a mistake trying to bully her.

But it was so tempting to grind him into the ground right now, face first, preferably against asphalt and broken glass—

Sarah took a very slow and deliberate breath. And let a cold kind of calm overtake her. She felt the muscles in her shoulders and face relax. A few more breaths and her hands finally unclenched and opened again.

By the time Joe and his client returned to the room, Sarah had composed herself, and could stare at Chapman blandly now, no longer visibly fuming at his gloating, despicable face.

"Hello, Mrs. Barrett," she said, offering the woman a genuine smile. "My name is Sarah Henley. Thank you so much for your time today. We really appreciate it."

And as Chapman once again scoffed at Sarah's polite and unnecessary introduction, Sarah thought, *That's all right. You enjoy yourself today.*

Because the time is coming when I'm going to bury you.

Sarah rolled her bag toward her new room. She still felt the stench of Chapman on her, the slime leaking out of his pores, the grin on his face as he so clearly relished trying to humiliate her in front of Joe and everyone else.

But she'd already begun her revenge. The questions she asked Mrs. Barrett continued to lay the foundation for the defense Sarah was mounting. And if Chapman was too stupid or arrogant to see that, then all the better for her.

She unlocked her door, still feeling agitated and angry. No matter how calmly she had been able to conduct the rest of the deposition, the fact was she still wanted to rip that man's face off. She'd already endured two months of his insufferable, overconfident behavior. She was happier than even Chapman could be that they wouldn't have to sit next to each other in a tight, closed room anymore.

And she couldn't believe she had had to waste even a minute of her thirtieth birthday listening to that fat, drunken blowhard drone on about himself, bragging about how clever he was. She should have grabbed Joe by the hand and pulled him out of the restaurant right away, and gotten straight to the best part of the night.

Sarah stood just inside her room, tapping her finger against the handle of her luggage. What she needed was a hard workout. Something to burn off all that anger and irritation. She should change into her exercise clothes right away, and go sweat in the hotel gym.

She tapped her handle a few more times, then made a decision. She pulled out her phone.

And texted: *Now. Where?*

The answer came back in less than a minute, naming the hotel and room number.

As you are, Sarah texted back, hoping Joe would understand what she meant.

When she arrived and found him standing in the doorway still fully dressed in his suit, Sarah smiled.

A wicked smile, just like the one he'd given her.

The door closed hard behind her and Sarah grabbed his tie to drag his mouth down to hers. She kissed him deeply, angrily, twisting his shirt inside her fists and not minding if she wrenched some hair and skin in the process. Then she released him and shifted her hands down to his belt.

"You going to need all these clothes, Burke?"

"I doubt it." He undid the button on her jacket and yanked it from her shoulders. Then he pulled her shirt over her head and helped himself to the breasts rising out of her bra.

"I like the black," he said appreciatively, running a finger over the lace before reaching behind her and undoing the clasp. He needed both hands to work the zipper on her pants, but as soon those fell Joe could bring his attention back to her breasts while Sarah finished stripping them both of everything below the waist.

"You'd better go get one," she said, "because it's happening right now."

Joe chuckled softly, then unzipped the luggage he hadn't had a chance to unpack.

"Burke, I mean it—"

It was on in a flash, and then Sarah pushed him to the ground, straddled him, and swiftly took him inside. She gave herself three or four hard, vicious thrusts before she had to pause and tell him, "Stop laughing."

"Can't help it," Joe said. "You don't know how much I love you like this."

"Say that again and I'm leaving," Sarah said, but they both knew she wasn't going anywhere. Instead she closed her eyes and flattened her palms on his chest and rode him the way she'd been thinking about all day. If he was going to play with her, then fine, she would play with him back.

She leaned forward, teeth teasing his earlobe, the whisper hot against his ear. "I could stop now, you know. Get up and walk away."

Just like you did, you prick.

Joe's eyes were dark and hungry with desire. She liked that. She wanted that.

He grabbed her hips and anchored her down harder, then flipped and rolled her onto her back. He pinned her body with his as he slowed the rhythm, angled more, made her take her time and let the sensation build. When finally her back arched and her lips parted and she bucked her hips up into his, he gave her what she wanted and drover harder, steadier, until Sarah pulled him down to her mouth and clenched him in her legs and the two of them exploded together. Then he kept on thrusting, even after he could have stopped, and forced even more pleasure from her.

"Stop, you have to stop," she gasped, her body trembling with the force of it all.

He lowered his mouth to her breasts and continued to give her more.

"Joe, no you can't—" But then she was coming again, completely against her intentions, and he helped her ride it as long as she could before finally letting her go.

It was a long time before her breathing calmed and she could peel open her eyelids to look at him.

"You can't keep doing that."

"Why not?" he asked.

"You know why." Although at that moment, Sarah was having a hard time explaining why to herself.

Because it's too good, was the truth, but that didn't seem like a very persuasive argument.

Joe traced the outline of her breasts with his fingers, then leaned forward and warmed the tips of each with his mouth. Then he scooped her up from where they had been lying on the floor, and carried her to the bed. He pulled back the covers and pretended he was going to softly lay her down, but at the last minute jolted her upward again and then dropped her onto the mattress.

Sarah cracked half a smile. "Does that make you feel like a man?"

"Sure does."

He braced both arms on either side of her and pushed her back with the force of his kiss. She wrapped her legs around him and trapped him against her to remind him who, exactly, was in charge. They wrestled and rolled and teased for several long, energetic minutes before Sarah finally pushed him away so she could breathe.

They each lay flat on their backs, still linked by intertwined hands.

"I was promised takeout," Sarah said.

"You'll get it."

"I want pizza."

"You'll get it."

"All veggies, no cheese."

"What other way is there?"

Sarah smiled to herself and let her fingers play against his palm. Then she rolled toward him and draped her body half on his. She looked into his face and kissed him. Then she rolled away again.

"Burke?"

"Hm?" He rolled toward her this time, pulled her closer to him, and lightly stroked his hand across her belly, just the way she liked it.

"We shouldn't do this anymore," she said.

"I disagree."

His hand strayed upward toward one of her breasts, and he seemed content to play there for a while.

"What if anyone finds out?" Sarah asked.

"They won't."

"They might, and then what?"

Burke propped himself up on an elbow and looked into her eyes. "Then we'll deal with it."

"You really don't care that this is completely wrong."

"I don't think it is wrong."

"Burke, read rule three-three-twenty."

"I already have."

"And?"

"We'll deal with it," he repeated. "But I'm not giving this up, Sarah. Not if you and I both want it. That's how it is."

She shook her head in disbelief.

"You'd risk your career for sex?"

"No."

He got up and went to the pile of discarded clothes. He

found his cell phone in the pocket of his suit jacket and brought it back to the bed.

He scrolled through it for several minutes before finding the closest pizza place that delivered. Then he handed the phone to Sarah to complete the call. She ordered only the toppings she wanted, without consulting Joe: sauce, no cheese, artichokes, red onions, garlic, tomatoes, and mushrooms. Joe kept busy the entire time continuing to stroke her body.

"If you're going to touch me like that," she said once she disconnected, "you'd better be prepared to back it up."

"In a while," he said.

"No, now. You have thirty minutes before pizza is here. See what you can get done before then."

27

Sarah ate pizza wearing only Joe's dress shirt, loose and unbuttoned. She didn't mind the splash of sauce she left on the pocket, any more than she minded that the shirt didn't smell clean, but smelled of Joe's perspiration from the day.

She liked the scent of him.

He reached out and pulled one of her feet onto his lap. "When you said that in the deposition the other day about painting your toenails pink..." He got a lustful, faraway look in his eye that made Sarah laugh.

"You like that, huh?" She wriggled her toes until he closed his warm hand around them. With his free hand he reached for another slice of pizza.

"Could you get used to this?" Sarah asked.

"I already am."

"No, the pizza," she said, resisting the urge to answer *Me, too.* "I mean without pepperoni or sausage. Would you ever order it that way?"

"No, too healthy. But I know better than to cross you today, Henley. Why do you think I hustled my client out of there before you unleashed Armageddon on Chapman?"

"Armageddon's too easy," she said. "He's just going to have to wait for it. He'll forget about me, then one day it will become absolutely clear to him that he messed with the wrong person."

"Does that go for me, too?" Joe asked, looking her in the eye.

Sarah shifted her gaze away and shrugged.

"I didn't forget," Joe said.

"We're not talking about this."

Sarah pretended to be very interested in the pizza. She lifted out another slice, even though she was already full.

Joe stroked a hand along her calf, then ended again at her toes. Sarah let his hand rest there. She liked the strange comfort of it. She had always liked all the various ways he came up with for touching her.

"Just out of curiosity," she said, unable to stop herself from taking the conversation one step further, even though she knew she was treading into dangerous territory, "do you have a strategy here, Joe?"

"Somewhat."

Land mines all around, she thought, but she took another step.

"What's it involve?" she asked.

"Being nice to you."

Sarah swallowed her surprise, then tried to cover it with another bite of pizza.

"Good luck," she said, hoping to sound unaffected and tough.

"Thanks. Turns out it's quite a project."

She narrowed her eyes at him. Joe smiled.

"Good thing I enjoy my work," he added, pushing the pizza aside and tasting her instead.

THIS TIME when the alarm rang, Sarah settled back into the cradle of Joe's arms and gave herself a few minutes more. She didn't have to run out of there so early the way she had the other morning, because this time she brought her luggage with her and left it in the car until she was sure she was staying.

By midnight, when she was too tired to do anything but hand Joe her keys and ask him to please go get her bag, she knew she was staying.

Now she rolled over to face him and found his lips immediately on hers.

"Where are we going today?" he murmured.

"Pocatello."

"Why's that again?"

"To give us something to do," Sarah explained. "Otherwise we'd just stay in bed all day."

Joe hugged her to him. Her nipples were still sensitive from all the attention he'd given them the night before, and they seemed to like the combination of his warm skin and the soft dark hair on his chest. She draped her thigh over his and they stayed there kissing for far longer than they should have, considering they had another crack-of-dawn flight.

While Joe made coffee for himself and tea for her, Sarah closed herself in his bathroom for a quick shower. At the last second she locked the door before slipping the hotel shower cap over her hair. He had seen her in many conditions, but wearing a shower cap still wasn't one of them. She wanted to keep her streak alive.

"Why do you get to stay in such nicer hotels?" she asked when she came out again, wearing a softer, thicker robe than the kind she was used to, and rubbing a thick lotion on her hands instead of the watery concoction she found every night in her hotel rooms.

"The firm gets a discount at certain chains," Joe said.

For a second Sarah thought she saw some sort of look flash across his face, but then decided it must have been her imagination. Joe handed her the cup of tea and took his turn in the shower.

Sarah stood in the steamy bathroom at the same time, applying her makeup and brushing her hair into a more orderly shape. She liked this, too, she thought, the way she was enjoying far too many things about being with Joe again. She could get used to having him around, to sharing a bathroom and a bedroom with him, to going about the routines of her day with Joe's schedule intersecting hers, Joe's voice in the background, Joe's arms around her when she fell asleep at night and still around her in the morning.

Not to mention everything he'd done to her last night, multiplied by seven for a good week. She could get used to that, and she understood that was a problem.

She pulled on a fresh pair of panties and the black lace bra from the day before. She had forgotten to hang up her suit, so it still bore some evidence of lying crumpled on the floor. But it would get wrinkled on the flight anyway, she thought, so she wouldn't worry about it. She pulled on a clean blouse and then added the pants and jacket.

Joe's hoodie still lay at the bottom of her bag. She transferred it to his.

"You can keep that," he said, standing in the doorway of the bathroom with a towel wrapped around his waist.

Sarah went to him, a lawyer already dressed for her day, and ran her hands over his clean skin. She leaned forward and flicked her tongue over the bare nipple of her lover—who was soon to dress in his own lawyer suit and go back to being her opponent.

She pulled his towel away with a single tug and flicked her tongue maddeningly lower.

"Sarah..."

"We have time," she said, too entertained now by the idea of kneeling in front of him in her black wool suit and expensive silk blouse, knowing he'd have to deal with that image and the memory of what she was about to do to him all afternoon long as he sat across from her at the deposition.

She would have to deal with it, too, she realized, as she felt her own body respond.

And that night they were flying home. She wouldn't see him again until Monday.

That might not work out at all.

28

As Sarah packed up her laptop and notes after another long day of travel and deposition, Chapman turned to her and stuck out his hand.

"This is it," he said.

Sarah couldn't bring herself to touch his flesh. Instead she nodded. "This is it."

"Oh, come on, Sarah, you're going to act like that?" Chapman said. He laughed and looked over at Joe. "She's going 'girly' on us," he said, making the finger quotes. "Come on, Henley, this isn't personal—you know that."

"Everything is personal, Chapman," she answered pleasantly. "You know that."

He laughed again, completely missing the look in her eye that should have told him he was marked for destruction. But Sarah had no further need to talk to the man, and instead turned to Marcela.

"Just one more week with us, and then you get a break, huh?" Sarah asked.

"Only sort of a break," Marcela said. "I'll still have to work all the way up through Christmas, but at least I get to stay in town. I'm sorry for you two, though," she said, looking at Sarah and Joe. "You must be sick of it by now."

Sarah shrugged. "All part of the deal."

"Ooh, you're so tough," Chapman chimed in. "Unbreakable Sarah Henley. I told that kid who's taking over for me he'd better watch out for you."

Sarah offered him the thinnest of smiles. "Everyone had better watch out for me. Stop talking, Chapman. We're done here."

She picked up her laptop case, grabbed the handle of her carry-on, and exited the room. She'd barely stepped outside into the cold when a text appeared on her phone:

Balls spontaneously exploding everywhere.

Sarah laughed.

She wished Joe could come out there with her, and they could freely talk. But like she told Marcela, *All part of the deal.*

She looked around outside the small airport to see if there were anywhere reasonable to walk. Since they flew in just for the day, they rented the conference room there at the airport instead of one at a hotel. But now Sarah had no place to escape except to the parking lot, where the temperature was in the low 40s and too cold for what she was wearing.

She paused to pull out her insulated raincoat and the fleece hat and gloves. Those were an improvement, but she thought longingly of the UCLA hoodie currently residing in Joe's bag.

Not that she would have been able to wear it, she realized, even if she had it. She couldn't take the risk that Chapman might see. As self-absorbed as the man was, he still might remember Joe wearing it at their dinner a few nights before, and wonder why Sarah had it now.

So much strategy involved, Sarah thought. All this sneaking around...

It wasn't until her third lap around the parking lot, trying to stretch her legs, that the idea finally dawned on her:

Maybe they were sneaking around in more ways than she knew.

Joe could be involved with someone else.

How would she know? Sarah thought. The only time she'd seen him over the past two months was when they were on the road. It might be the classic case of a man fooling around with his travel buddy, then returning home to the woman who thought he loved her, who had been waiting faithfully for him all week, missing him, ready to throw herself into his arms again the second he walked through the door and rip his clothes off and get reacquainted—

She pulled out her phone, took off her gloves, and typed with chilled fingers.

Are you seeing anyone?

She wondered how long it would take him to answer that. If it was longer than it took to type two letters, she'd know he had to pause, make up a lie—

No, he answered right away. *You?*

No. Would you tell me if you were? she typed back.

Yes. Where are you?

Outside.

Within a minute she watched him exit the building and walk in her direction. Sarah turned to her right, the way she'd just come, and led him toward the end of the terminal furthest away from the passenger area, where she knew it was less likely Marcela or Chapman might see them.

"You shouldn't be out here," Sarah said, looking back toward the entrance.

"Why?" Joe said. "We're two lawyers who just finished a deposition and are discussing our case. I got your text, Henley. You said your client is ready to make us an offer?"

"Ha, ha."

"Three million dollars in exchange for a non-disclosure? Ask me anything, Sarah," he said in a lower voice, meant obviously just for her. "I'll never lie to you."

Ha, ha, she almost said again.

Instead she told him, "I already asked."

"Were you satisfied with the answer?"

She thought about it for a second, then told him, "Yes, I think so." Then she switched back to lawyer mode. "You'll never prove a case against my client, Burke. You should dismiss us now and go duke it out with Atheena. We'd be much more use to your plaintiffs as a friendly than as a defendant."

"All right, I did lie to you once," Joe said. "This morning."

"What?" Sarah forgot all about her performance and instead gave him a hard look. "When?"

"I don't understand your theory of the case," Joe said.

"It's not my job to make you understand," she snapped, "and you'd better tell me, Burke."

He smiled, obviously trying to lighten what had suddenly become a tense conversation. "All right. You asked me why I always stay in a different hotel than the rest of you. It's not because of the firm discount—even though we do get one. It's for the same reason I did it in Illinois." He lowered his voice even more. "I wanted to give us somewhere private to go."

Sarah stared at him in disbelief. "Wait a minute—you think I'm always that much of a sure thing?"

"I've *never* thought you were a sure thing," Joe said. "But if there's anything you and I are good at, it's always planning our moves ten steps ahead of everyone else."

It was true, she couldn't deny it, but it wasn't supposed to apply to her. "So that's what this is?" she asked him. "Your 'moves'?"

"You have moves, too, Sarah. Don't tell me you haven't thought this through."

Not nearly enough, Sarah thought. And that was part of her problem.

The two of them studied each other for a moment in the fading light. Joe blew on his hands, then pushed them back into his pockets. Sarah stood with her arms across her chest, hands tucked under her armpits. She knew they should probably go back inside where it was warm, but she wouldn't leave the conversation now for a million dollars.

"So you think you've been planning this the whole time,"

Sarah said, her voice laced with sarcasm. "You knew we'd end up here."

"That's right," Joe said. "Standing in front of the Pocatello airport, having this exact discussion."

Sarah laughed, despite herself.

"And now you think you know the next ten steps," she said.

"I'm working on it."

"I see." Sarah thought about leaving it there, but Joe must have known her curiosity would win out, because as soon as she asked the question, he smiled.

"So you think you know what happens next?"

"I do," he said.

"Which is?"

"You come home with me tonight or I come home with you."

"That simple," Sarah said.

"That simple," Joe confirmed.

"Why?"

"Because it's what we both want," he said.

And again, she couldn't deny it.

Sarah looked past his shoulder to a couple entering the building. She glanced down at her watch. "We have to board soon. I still have some work to do."

"I meant what I said," Joe told her.

"Which one?"

"You can ask me anything, and I'll always tell you the truth."

"Really, Burke? You sure you want to make me that offer?" She hadn't meant it to come out so hard, but there it was. "Because somehow I don't think so. You obviously haven't thought ten steps ahead on that one."

Because they both knew, Sarah thought, that the only real question in all of this—the only thing she could possibly care about—was *why*: why he left her, why he did it so abruptly and in a way guaranteed to cause her the most pain, why she should ever trust him again, no matter how great he was in bed, no matter how much his strategy might involve being nice to her now, six years too late—

"I have to go," she said.

"You think I don't know?" he asked before she could walk away.

"Know what, Burke? Let's hear it."

"That I blew it?" he said. "That I hurt you? Of course I know that, Sarah."

She hadn't expected him to put it out there like that, to acknowledge it, not to shy away from it, the way she'd been doing every time they wandered too close to the subject. Didn't he realize they weren't supposed to touch that? she thought. Not if he wanted her to be friendly with him and come back to his bed.

"Yeah, you did," she said quietly. Then she left him alone and headed back toward the warmth.

LAST TIME in the Salt Lake City airport, Sarah thought. At least for the foreseeable future—

Foreseeable future? Don't you always plan ten steps ahead, Henley?

—but at least she could always find something to eat

there: Greek salads, hold the feta; bean burros, chips and salsa at the Mexican grill; pasta and marinara sauce at the Italian place; a rice and vegetable bowl at the Chinese.

Tonight she bought a falafel and hummus wrap and carried it to the gate to for the short layover.

Joe sat near one of the windows, eating a sandwich and working on his laptop. Chapman gobbled a double-decker burger while shoveling french fries into his already full mouth. Marcela picked at a salad with her plastic fork and flipped through a magazine.

Sarah sat off by herself, in no more mood than any of them to interact now that they were all off-duty.

She glanced over at Joe again, and found him looking at her. Then he pulled out his phone, and she waited for the inevitable text.

Which didn't come.

She checked the bare screen a few times, then looked up at Joe again.

He smiled.

She narrowed her eyes at him. And shook her head slightly to show she didn't understand.

He sent her a text that said, *E-mail.*

Sarah refreshed the e-mail on her phone.

There were a few new e-mails from lawyers at Mickey's office, responding to a memorandum she had sent them earlier in the day. She could read those later.

What interested her more was the one from Joe. He'd sent her a map.

It showed two different routes from LAX to addresses nearby: one in Santa Monica, another Culver City.

Her specific address in Culver City.

She shouldn't have been surprised, she thought, that he could find it in on the Internet. What couldn't people find?

What did surprise her was the accompanying message:

10 miles or 12 miles. Your choice. I'm not afraid of your questions. Don't be afraid of the answers.

Sarah looked up into his waiting gaze. And realized that was exactly what she felt: afraid.

29

In her second year of law school, Sarah took a night class called Negotiation, taught by an adjunct professor whose day job was as a litigator in one of the bigger law firms in L.A.

It was different from any other class she had taken so far, mainly because it was practical. He didn't assign some textbook in negotiation. Instead he told war stories, gave specific examples from his years on the front lines, and made the students practice their skills in front of him.

So much of what he taught was the psychology of dealing with an opponent: how to assess the other lawyer's personal weaknesses, including pride, fear, and the need to always look good.

One night it was Sarah's turn, along with a classmate of hers named Troy, to practice a negotiation in front of the class. The professor gave them a scenario: Sarah was the defense attorney in a medical malpractice case in which the plaintiffs' child had died during surgery. Troy represented the parents. The professor told them this was their last meeting before the trial began, and they were to try to settle the case.

Beyond that, he let them make up any facts they wanted.

Troy, a very theatrical and demonstrative guy Sarah knew from their Trial Practice class, began right away, really pouring on the pathos, reminding Sarah how devastated the parents were, how sympathetic the jury would be, how the doctor Sarah represented had absolutely no hope of leaving the courtroom room owing less than ten million dollars.

While he ranted and gesticulated, Sarah took her time pulling out a chair from behind the professor's table, then bringing it out to the center of the arena and sitting down. She had a relaxed expression on her face as she listened to Troy and watched him expend every last ounce of energy trying to force her to pay him what he wanted.

When he finally took a breath, Sarah said quietly, "I can only get you two."

"Two million!" Troy shouted at her. "Are you out of your friggin mind? This is a dead kid case. Do you know what those are worth? Your guy's lucky we'll let him walk away for eight."

"I can get you two," Sarah repeated calmly, and Troy went back to his rant.

Finally the professor called time.

And pointed to Sarah.

"She was going to win that negotiation—do you know why?"

Sarah could see from the faces of her classmates that no

one agreed. Troy clearly had the upper hand, they must have thought, with all that power and force behind his argument.

"*Status*," the professor said. "Henley had the higher status."

"She just sat in a chair the whole time," one of her classmates said.

"Right," the professor answered. "She stayed calm and didn't let herself get drawn in. She had her number, and she stuck to it. Collins here could have popped a blood vessel in his brain from arguing so hard, but Henley was never going to give in. Am I right?" he asked her.

"I might have given him a million more," Sarah said. "But that was going to be it."

The professor pointed at her. "She had a plan. She didn't show up wondering what she was going to do, she already *knew*."

"But that's stupid," someone else argued. "The whole point is to negotiate."

"No, the point is to *win* a negotiation," the professor said. "And the way you do that is to make sure you always maintain your higher status. When you shout and loom over people and try to bully them, you're weak. The quieter you are, the less you say, the stronger you look. You want to be the rock the waves crash up against—not the puny wave. No question in my mind: Henley would have won."

It was one of her favorite moments in law school, and one of her favorite classes. The lessons she learned helped mold her into the kind of attorney she was now. The professor taught her to think strategically in ways she never had before.

And she was about to apply one of those lessons now.

"Is it better to go to your opponent's office for a negotiation," the professor asked the class one night, "or make him come to you?"

"Come to you," most of the class answered.

Sarah said nothing. Because she already knew enough of this professor to know he rarely followed conventional wisdom.

"No, you go to them," he said. "For two reasons: first, you can leave. That means you always have the power of walking away if the other side doesn't give you what you want. Second, it displays confidence. Since everyone believes the same thing you do—or did until now, I hope—it means one of two things will happen: they'll either wonder why you're so willing to go to them, which will make them suspicious and off-balance, or they'll think you don't understand such an obvious element of strategy, which will make them overconfident. Either way, you're in the stronger position."

Sarah had sat there listening with a huge smile on her face. It was as if the professor kept handing her all the keys to life.

And it was why she now wrote back to Burke: *Your place.*

SARAH STOOD on the threshold of his front door, studying the room behind him.

It was dark everywhere hers was light: dark hardwood floors, dark rugs, dark furniture, dark cabinets in the kitchen instead of the ones she had painted white.

"Your brooding phase?" she asked, before realizing he might not see anything wrong with it.

Joe glanced behind him. "It came decorated. I don't have the touch, as you know."

She did. His old apartment near UCLA contained a mishmash of furniture he collected from his parents and various other relatives and friends. Joe was never poor the way Sarah was—he had grown up in Palo Alto with parents who both worked for tech companies—but Joe liked to spend money on things that were important to him. A stylish apartment was not one of them.

"Want something to drink?" Joe asked as she followed him inside.

Good question, Sarah thought. Would it be better to stay completely sober and alert, or to ease her nerves with a little lubrication?

"Wine," she said. "Or beer—whatever you have."

"Beer I always have."

He opened the shiny black door of his refrigerator, pulled out two bottles, and set them on the spotless counter.

"Cleaning woman?" Sarah guessed.

"What, you don't think this is all me?"

Considering what a slob he'd been in law school, Sarah doubted it, but maybe he had matured and changed.

"I'm hardly here anymore," he told her, "but she still comes in twice a month, whether I need it or not."

Her mother would love having a client like that, Sarah thought. But she doubted whether any of her mother's customers had Joe's kind of money.

He popped the tops on both beers and handed her one. Then he motioned her toward the living room.

She chose the dark gray couch and let him have the dark leather chair. She kicked off her shoes and pulled her feet up under her.

"Comfortable?" Joe asked.

"Not particularly."

He left the room for a moment and returned with a folded blanket. Sarah took off her suit jacket and wrapped the blanket over her. Then she took a sip of beer.

"Well, I think we know why we're all here," Joe began, and even though he tried to make a joke of it, Sarah could hear the tension in his voice. Was he afraid, despite what he'd said? "Do you want to ask the questions, or do you just want me to tell you?"

"Tell me," she said. She wasn't sure she wanted to be too involved in the conversation. It might be easier just to listen.

"How much do you know?" Joe asked.

"Not much," she said. "Thanksgiving, finals, then that was it." She tried to keep the bitterness out of her voice, but she could hear it just the same.

"First your birthday," Joe said. "You remember that."

Sarah nodded. She looked away and took another drink.

"I meant all of it," Joe said.

She shrugged.

"Sarah..."

"Doesn't matter now," she told him. "Keep going."

He hesitated, but obviously decided not to press it.

But of course she remembered. Everything. She had replayed that night a million times.

Thanksgiving fell during the last week of November that year. Sarah's birthday was the day before. They celebrated before they both went home for the holiday.

That was the night Joe gathered her into his arms after they'd made love, and told her he loved her like crazy. That he could barely stand to be away from her for the four-day weekend. That he loved her so much he wished he hadn't waited so long to come after her. That she was everything he'd ever wanted.

It was how Sarah felt, too. It was how she felt from the very beginning. She had fallen for him so hard, it sometimes hurt just to look at him. She loved him like she never thought possible. He felt like an extension of her mind, her body, her soul.

"I want to marry you," Joe had told her then. "Not now, but after we graduate. I can't imagine spending my life with anyone but you."

She kissed him so hard she was surprised his teeth didn't fall out. She told him yes, and then laughed at the tears spilling down her face. He smudged them away and kissed her, and they went right back to making love as if they had never stopped.

Sarah drank another sip of beer and could feel how much tighter her throat had become. This was why she had never wanted to ask, she thought. Because asking meant remembering, and she had been fighting against that for years.

"So you went home for Thanksgiving," she prompted. "And you found out your mom was sick."

Joe nodded. "She'd been cancer-free for ten years. Maybe

I told you that. We thought it was over. But when I went home, nobody even needed to tell me—I could see it. She'd lost so much weight, she looked like a teenager. And she just looked...bad. My brother walked in about an hour later, and the first thing out of his mouth was, *Shit, not again.* That was when they decided they'd better tell us."

He hadn't given her as many details back then, but she remembered the look of shock and grief on his face when she saw him again that Sunday night after Thanksgiving. He wrapped his arms around her waist and buried his face against her neck. Then he sobbed—so hard, Sarah sobbed right along with him before he could even tell her what was wrong.

Even now, she could see the remnants of grief on his face. She understood that he didn't like reliving this story any more than she did.

"Then we had finals," Joe said.

Sarah remembered vividly the two of them trying to study in between phone conferences with his father and brother. Joe's mother was fading quickly, and every phone call marked the further decline. It finally got to the point where Joe couldn't bear to answer the phone. He let it go to voicemail so he could just listen, and process the information on his own without having to say anything to his dad.

"Advanced Federal Tax Law," Joe said. My last final. December twentieth."

Sarah remembered how nervous he was about it, even though he'd always done well in the class. He planned to take the test, then immediately head home for the winter break. The two of them had kissed goodbye that morning, and Sarah wished him good luck with everything. He promised to call her later.

He never did. And it was the last kiss they shared for six years, until Sarah passed out and woke up in the medical clinic at Snowbird.

"What was so important about that class?" Joe asked her, a new look of pain settling onto his face. "Can you tell me? You were there. Why did I think it was so important to stay? What was wrong with me?"

Sarah shook her head. She was afraid to answer. Because suddenly she remembered something on her own.

When she didn't hear from Joe for days, and then a whole week, she finally did some investigation. She had her suspicions about what had happened, so she searched the public record.

"It wasn't that day was it?" she asked, her voice choking on the question.

He nodded.

"Oh, *Joe...*"

"I was four hours too late," he said. "She died before I got home."

The look of anguish on his face was too much. Sarah got up and went to him. She bent down and wrapped her arms around him and held him hard.

"Why didn't you tell me?" she asked.

"Because of this," he said. "Because of exactly what you're doing right now. You would have tried to comfort me."

"Of course I would!"

"No. You would have said it was okay," Joe told her. "And

it wasn't. I screwed up, Sarah. I wasn't there. I never saw her again."

Sarah couldn't stand it another minute. Couldn't stand hearing him talk like that, knowing he'd carried it with him all alone for all these years. She crawled onto his lap and wrapped her arms around him and held him the way she wished she could have back then, the way she knew he must have wanted, but he hadn't let her, and that hurt her more than she could bear.

"Joe, you should have told me," she said, tears spilling down her cheeks. "I loved you. I would have helped you. You know I would."

"I couldn't think," he said, his voice thick. "It was so.... And then it went on from there: the funeral, her ashes, Nate and dad and I spreading them in her garden—"

A sound escaped his lips, but he covered it with a cough. Sarah could feel his body tighten. He gently pulled away from her, reached for his beer, and drank it to the bottom. Then he patted her on the rear and told her she could go sit down again.

Sarah returned to the couch, but it wasn't where she wanted to be. Joe might not need the comfort right now, but she did. A pain was spreading from the center of her chest outward, and she needed to hold on to him more than he seemed to need her.

But she wrapped herself in the blanket and waited to hear whatever else he wanted to say.

"So then there was you," he said.

Sarah swallowed hard.

"I really did love you," Joe said, looking at her with a

different kind of anguish in his eyes. "But it was too much. I couldn't be happy right then—it would have been wrong. I felt so..." He looked upward as if searching for the word. "...'guilty' doesn't even cover it. I was a total, unmitigated asshole for not being at my mother's side. Why didn't I go home once I knew how close she was? Why did I think any of my finals or my grades were so damn important?"

"Joe, you didn't know..."

"See?" he said, laughing in a way she supposed was meant to disguise his pain. "That's how you would have been. You would have tried to make me feel better. You would have been so *loving* and *supportive*—"

"Of course I would," Sarah said. "I loved you. I wanted to marry you." She hadn't meant to say that last part, but the two truths were tied together. She thought she was part of his life back then—soon to be part of his family. But instead he had kept all of this from her.

"So I did what I had to," he went on, his voice losing its steam. "I came back and I made sure you'd never try to console me. Made sure you'd back away and never try to love me again."

Sarah bowed her head with a grief all her own. It was like reliving her own death, and hearing now how he'd orchestrated it, how he set out to hurt her so much she would never come near him, felt like a blow upon a blow. So cold, so deliberate, while meanwhile her heart had been disintegrating into a thousand minuscule pieces.

Joe's voice sounded dull now, empty. "It's amazing how good it feels to self-destruct. I thought it would be harder, but it was easy once I started. It helped that I stayed drunk most of the time—"

"You did?" She hadn't noticed that. Then again, she avoided him as much as possible that last semester.

"First thing in the morning," Joe said, "some Jack in my coffee. Couple of beers at lunch, then the really serious drinking started in the afternoons."

It explained so much, Sarah thought. The stony, expressionless look on his face whenever she passed him. The reckless way he'd grab some girl and grope her if he knew Sarah was watching. The complete and deliberate destruction of their relationship.

"Joe, all this time, I've..."

"You've hated me," he said. "I know. You should have. It's why I never tried to contact you, even after I sobered up. I know I hurt you, Sarah, and I'm so sorry for that. It's eaten away at me for years. Then for whatever reason, I got the gift of you walking into that deposition in San Diego. It was like you just dropped from the sky. And ever since then... "

"Your strategy is to be nice to me," Sarah said.

Joe nodded.

The two of them sat apart for a long time, while Sarah took it all in.

"Can I tell you now?" she finally asked, getting up from the couch and going over to him again. She climbed onto his lap and wrapped her arms around his neck. "I'm so sorry, Joe. You're a good man. I'm sorry all of that happened to you. It must have been so awful..."

She held his face between her hands and began kissing his cheeks, his jaw, his temple. Treating him tenderly the way she would have back then. Then she brought her lips back to his mouth where they belonged.

Joe deepened the kiss. He shifted her so that she faced him, and she sat astride him on the chair. He threaded his hands through her hair and kissed her with a kind of need different from any he'd shown her so far.

He left her mouth and began kissing a trail down her throat. She undid the top two buttons of her blouse so he could continue following the line down.

There was nothing frantic or playful about how quickly their clothes fell away this time, it was more of a necessity, Sarah thought, one steady, continuous movement from where they had been to where they needed to be. He lifted her and carried her into his bedroom. Then laid her down gently on his bed and continued the slow, steady course toward reminding her why she fell for him in the first place, and how she might find her way back there again.

"Sarah—"

But she silenced him with a kiss. She couldn't hear any more—not tonight. She needed to be in her body now, to feel his, not to think or hear, but just shut out the world and be with him.

She kissed him the way she used to, with a kind of sweetness she had been careful not to show him since they began again on her birthday.

Joe seemed to know the difference, too. He pulled back and looked into her eyes.

"That's it, Red," he said. "That's what I've missed."

30

Sarah's phone rang far too early. She had retrieved it from her jacket some time during the night and plugged into the outlet beside Joe's bed. Now she regretted not letting the battery die.

"What," she answered irritably. She saw who it was on her display.

"Morning, killer. They want a meeting with you as soon as possible. I volunteered to wake you up."

"Mickey..." Sarah batted away Joe's hand, which was already creeping up her torso. "I got in late. I need sleep."

"Then you shouldn't send out e-mails with the tantalizing subject line of 'How We Will Win Our Case.' People get excited."

Sarah pressed the phone closer to her ear. She wasn't sure if Joe could hear Mickey's side of the conversation.

"I'll come in this afternoon," Sarah said. "I'm too beat."

"If by this afternoon you mean nine o'clock this morning, then that should be fine."

"Mickey."

"Sarah. You're doing good work—Calvin's impressed. So tell whoever's there to get off of you so you can come in and show off."

"No one's here," Sarah said, squeezing Joe's fingers to keep them from straying higher. Then she gave him a light elbow in the chest to get him to knock it off.

"See you in two hours," Mickey said.

She groaned. "Yeah."

Then she hung up and burrowed deeper into Joe's arms.

"Mickey, huh?" he asked. "He still after you?"

"Only in the vaguest of ways. But he got me this job, so..." Sarah yawned and spread her hands on top of Joe's. "...if you're enjoying feeling my breasts right now, you have him to thank."

Joe kissed the back of her neck. "I'll send him some champagne."

He got out of bed just when Sarah was looking forward to falling asleep with him again.

"Want some coffee?" he said.

"I don't, but yes. Really strong, please."

Sarah fought reality as long as she could, but had to pry open her eyes once Joe returned with mugs for both of them and climbed back into bed. Sarah propped up her pillow next to him, and draped her leg over his while they drank.

"Now for the legal issue," she said, sighing a little with the effort of it.

It had been easier to push aside when it was just sex. Or just sex and maybe a little more.

But since last night she had no way of rationalizing anymore why it might be all right—an exception to the ethical rule—for her to continue an intimate personal relationship with her opposing counsel.

"Let's lay out the options," Sarah said, trying to sound professional and lawyerly while lounging naked in her opponent's bed. "I tell Calvin, you tell whoever your boss is, we both get fired."

"Option A," Joe said.

"Option B," Sarah continued, "one of us withdraws from the case and frees the other one to continue." She took another sip of blacker than black coffee—Joe really had taken her at her word and made it strong enough that she could feel it searing through her bloodstream—and waited for him to say something.

"Let's...hold off a while longer," he said.

"How much longer? Joe, we could get into serious trouble—"

"We'll be careful," he said. He set down his coffee and looped his arms around her waist. "I don't want to talk shop right now. You and I have plenty of work to do today—we can be lawyers later. Right now we're off duty."

He made a persuasive case, especially since one of his hands was currently threading between her thighs.

"Okay, but we need to talk about it," she insisted as she set her mug on the bedside table and slid back to horizontal. "Tonight, all right?"

"You're the most beautiful woman I've ever seen."

"Joe, focus..."

"I am focusing," he murmured as his hands and lips continued to explore.

They would talk about it that night, Sarah promised herself. Make a decision about what to do.

But for the moment she had to admit that Joe's topic of focus was a lot more enjoyable than hers.

"Welcome back to civilization," Mickey said, leading her toward the conference room. "This is what we call an 'office.' And those are lawyers," he said, pointing to the various people working there on a Saturday morning. "They're not bell hops, so don't try to tip them."

Sarah yawned.

"Come on, now, killer," Mickey said. "Look sharp. Today's a big day for Sarah Henley."

"Why's that?"

He grinned. "You'll see."

He pushed open the heavy door of the conference room and held it for Sarah to pass. There were already four people in there: Calvin and the three other lawyers Sarah had included on her recent e-mail.

Calvin stood up and shook her hand. "Sarah, nice work. We decided we wanted to brainstorm this morning, since you're probably leaving again tomorrow."

"I am," she said.

"Where to?" Calvin asked.

"Portland. Then Seattle, then...somewhere." She wished she felt more alert, and knew she probably should have grabbed another hour of sleep before she came in, but she couldn't say she regretted how she spent her time.

"So, walk us through it," Calvin said. "You noticed a pattern..."

"Right," Sarah said, stifling another yawn. "All the defects are from a particular five-month span of time. Any of the hair irons bought before or after that seem fine, but from September to January two years ago, the products suddenly started catching fire."

"You think it's someone else's parts," Calvin said.

"I do," Sarah said. "If you look at the documents Hector sent me," she said, indicating one of the young associates in the room, "you'll see all the internal memoranda about Mason Manufacturing's labor problems. They finally had to notify their customers—including Atheena—that they wouldn't be able to deliver their orders on time. When you compare all the various timelines, you'll see there's a gap when Mason fell behind by about a hundred thousand units. I'm willing to bet Atheena went somewhere else during that period of time, and found another supplier they're not telling anyone about."

"Why not?" Mickey asked. He wasn't one of the attorneys working on the case, so Sarah wasn't sure why he had been included in the meeting, but she filled him in anyway.

"Atheena makes a big deal about how their hair iron is 'Made in America, with Genuine American Parts,'" she said. "What if they decided they needed to buy parts from say, China, to keep production moving? Not something they'd like to get out—especially if that part is catching people's hair on fire."

"Can we prove it?" Calvin asked.

"I asked Jeffrey," she said, indicating another one of the associates, "to send out requests for production of documents. They're due in a few weeks, so we'll see what's in there."

"Can we prove it otherwise?" Calvin asked. "Just in case the paperwork mysteriously disappears?"

"It's math," Sarah said. "When you look at Mason's shipping schedule, you can see how long it took from the time Atheena received the part, to the time they put the finished product on sale. We can track it from the serial numbers—Mason has those, even if Atheena destroys their records. Then it's just a matter of comparing the timelines, and finding the five-month gap in the schedule. From what I've seen, the numbers match up perfectly. Those aren't our parts."

Calvin sat back in his chair and folded his hands over his stomach. Then he smiled.

"And you did all this while you were on the road," he said.

"Told you," Mickey said, grinning with a kind of pride.

"Sarah, I have good news and even better news," Calvin said. "I didn't just bring you in here to discuss your memo—I already got the gist of it when I read it last night. I brought you here because it's time you joined us."

Sarah told herself to remain calm. To keep her face perfectly expressionless.

"Join you, how?" she asked.

"We're bringing you in," Calvin said. "In from Portland or

wherever you were going next, and into the firm, if you accept."

"Are you...offering me a permanent job?"

"That," Calvin said, "and I'd also like you to take a more active role in this case. If we're going to run with this defense—and I don't see why not—I'd like you to direct it and see it through. Handle all the discovery, the motions, the oral arguments—all of it."

Sarah felt too shocked to be pleased, but she knew the pleasure would come. In the meantime, she glanced at the faces of the three other associates working on the case, trying to gauge their reaction to Calvin's announcement. None of them seemed particularly happy to have been passed over.

"What do you say?" Calvin asked.

"I say yes, of course," Sarah answered, and finally allowed herself a smile. Mickey caught her eye and winked at her. Obviously he knew about Calvin's plan.

"But...what about all the depositions?" Sarah asked. "I still have a full schedule."

"Bingham can take them over," Calvin said, nodding toward the associate Sarah knew was the most junior. "Although I think it's going to be a while before he has to go out."

It took Sarah a moment to process what Calvin just said. But then she asked, "Why would it be a while? We're sched-uled almost until Christmas. Then we start up again in January."

"Nobody's going to care about depositions pretty soon. Tell her, Mickey," Calvin said.

Mickey gave her a look filled with wicked anticipation. "I have a friend who works at the Justice Department," he said. "We were having drinks the other night, and he let slip he's working on a big case involving another dirty L.A. law firm."

Calvin interrupted. "It's because of that guy Fitzgerald in the U.S. Attorney's Office—he's the one who went after your firm, too," he told Sarah. "He has a hard-on for anyone in this town he thinks is making too much money."

"That leaves me out," Mickey said.

Calvin ignored him.

"Anyway," Mickey went on, "they're about to do the perp walk again, parading a bunch of lawyers in handcuffs past the media. It's Fitzgerald's early Christmas present to himself. So I'm guessing your depositions are about to be the last thing on people's minds for a while."

It was too good to be true, Sarah thought. Was Chapman's firm going down? She wondered if Chapman himself would be one of the lawyers hauled off. She disliked the man —sorely—but she wouldn't exactly wish this on him. Mickey and Calvin might think it was entertaining, but Sarah had seen for herself what it was like to be caught up in the turmoil. She almost felt sorry for the man.

"So," Mickey finished triumphantly, "bad news for your old buddy Burke."

Sarah knew she couldn't have heard him right.

"Burke?" she repeated.

"Yes, sirree," Mickey said.

"But...why?" Sarah could feel the blood rushing to her head, could even hear it pounding in her ears. This couldn't be what was happening—not now.

"Seems the lawyers over there have been paying people to be professional plaintiffs in their class action suits," Mickey explained. "Strictly no-no, illegal. Burke's firm fronts the money for them to buy stock in a tech company, then of course the stock prices go up and down the way they always do with the techs, and as soon as they go down, boom, lawsuit. I guess they've filed something like twenty of them in the last three or four years. And finally someone in Fitzgerald's office noticed that a few of the plaintiffs were repeaters."

"But who says Burke's firm is paying them?" Sarah asked. She wasn't going to just buy Mickey's story—especially since he was obviously having such a great time telling it. She needed facts, not just innuendo fueled by some leftover animosity Mickey might feel toward Joe.

"Apparently somebody couldn't keep a secret," Mickey said. "Fitzgerald caught wind of it, and now he's ready to hand down indictments any day. Could even be next week."

"Next week?" Sarah repeated, still feeling like she was two miles behind, struggling to catch up with everything she was hearing. "But...Burke...you don't think he was involved personally, do you?"

Mickey smiled. "Had to be. He was one of the lawyers on the most recent case."

No, Sarah thought. *NO*. It wasn't possible. Burke wouldn't do that—would he? That wasn't the man she knew.

But maybe that was the point. Maybe she didn't know him at all.

"So," Calvin said, moving straight ahead with business while Sarah still reeled from the personal, "what all this means is the plaintiffs will probably be looking for new attorneys before the end of the year. Which buys us some time. I doubt anyone will be worried about taking depositions in Kalamazoo for a while, so Sarah, that's why I want you to hammer this defense now, go out hard against Atheena, and get us dismissed from the case before anyone on the plaintiff's side knows what happened."

Sarah nodded dully. What Calvin said made logical, strategic sense, and she would have loved the discussion if not for the fact that right now her insides felt like glue.

"So go ahead and keep to the schedule for now," Calvin said. "No need to raise any suspicions. But be ready any minute to come home and start working on the case from here. Hell, they might even indict everybody Monday morning—you could be back by the afternoon."

Monday morning...

Calvin stood up and reached out his hand. "Welcome to the firm, Sarah. Glad to have you. Assuming, that is, you accept."

Sarah nodded. Then she remembered she should probably speak. "I accept. Thank you. I appreciate the vote of confidence." She forced her mouth into a semblance of a smile.

"None of these scholars could come up with what you did," Calvin said, indicating the other associates still sitting there. Sarah could feel the resentment wafting off of them. "And you did it while spinning plates and riding a unicycle. Can't wait to see what you do when you get to stay put in one place, with a proper office and a staff. Mickey did right in recommending you."

Sarah smiled again, for Mickey's sake. Even though right at the moment she felt very little affection for the man. Mickey had enjoyed himself far too much. Although if what he said about Joe was true, then maybe he had every right.

Mickey walked her out.

"Buy you lunch?"

"No, thanks," Sarah said, trying to remain neutral toward him, trying not to bolt for the exit and get away from him and everyone else as fast as she could. She needed to think. To process. To sit somewhere alone and let it all hit her again at a pace she might control.

"Amazing, huh?" Mickey asked. "How greedy some people get. I didn't take Joe for one of those, but you never know, huh?"

"Nope, you never do," Sarah said. Her mouth felt dry, but she could feel the sweat still sticky on her skin. "Listen, Mickey, I really appreciate you getting me this job. It's turned out much better than I ever hoped." She wondered if it sounded as false to his ears as it sounded to hers, but from his smile, she guessed not.

He kissed her on the cheek. "Any time, gorgeous. Happy to be of service."

He stood too close to her, too long, until finally Sarah took a step back. "Thanks," she said, aiming now for the door. "I'll see you later."

"You did good, Sarah," Mickey called after her.

She waved without turning around.

Make it to the car, make it to the car...

Then she had to talk herself through keeping it together

while she started up the Saturn and drove out of the parking lot.

Then, and only then—

Sarah pulled off at the first opportunity, shut off the car, and then leaned forward and buried her head inside her arms. Her breath came out in heaves, almost like vomiting again, but this time just pressure and force and nothing but pain and anger behind it.

Joe. You stupid, greedy, idiot, bastard, lying, cheating—WHY? Why now?

But why not now? she thought. He had no idea she was coming back. No idea she might even consider falling in love with him again. No idea he was about to get indicted, lose his law license, probably go to prison—

While Sarah once again had to pick herself up from the ground, wipe off the blood, and force herself to keep moving. Force herself to forget him. Force herself to stop believing they were ever meant to be together.

"Joe," she whispered into the car. "We could have had it this time. Why did you have to ruin everything?"

31

"Ooh," Angie said. "You don't look good."

Sarah's eyes were red and puffy from the effort of not crying. Her sinuses were swollen, too, and her throat felt thick with unspent tears. But she refused to do it, she thought. Not this time, and not over him. Not anymore.

Sarah handed Angie an envelope of cash. "I can't work out today, but I wanted to make sure I brought you this. I just got a job offer this morning, so I should be able to pay back everything by the end of the year."

"Congratulations!" Angie said. "That explains why you look so depressed."

"Yeah, well...it's been a rough day."

"You have an hour," Angie said. "Use it however you want. I was going to make you do squats and lifts, but if you'd rather talk..."

"No, thanks," Sarah said, turning to go. "Let's just reschedule for next Saturday. Or sooner, if things..." She couldn't finish the sentence. She still didn't want to accept what might happen.

She sank onto the bench just inside the door. Three other trainers were in the room, working with their clients. Sarah's shoulders slumped. She felt as feeble as the first time she ever came in there.

"Come on," Angie said. "I'm starving. If you're not working out now, I'm going to eat. Come keep me company."

Angie headed for her office, just off the weight room, and a few moments later Sarah followed. She sat in one of the chairs across from Angie's desk and waited while her trainer microwaved her lunch.

"Want some?" Angie offered.

Sarah shook her head.

"So...work is good," Angie said. "Job offer—that's great. Still traveling all the time?"

"Yeah. Leaving again tomorrow."

"Hm." Angie studied her for a few more seconds, then said, "So. I can keep asking these stupid questions until you get around to telling me what's wrong, or you can just cut to it and tell me."

"I'm not trying to be mysterious," Sarah said. "I just really can't talk about it. It's complicated. And confidential, I'm afraid."

"Okay, so just give me the basic outline," Angie said. "You don't have to worry—we're in the Zone of Silence in here. More sacred than attorney-client privilege. No one can make a trainer talk against our will."

Sarah sighed. "Basic outline. Okay." She lowered her

voice to make sure no one in the other room might hear. "It's about Joe. You remember."

"Of course," Angie said. "Scumbag broke your heart and now you're making him suffer."

"Yeah, well...that didn't exactly work out the way I planned. Things have sort of...progressed."

Angie raised her eyebrows. "I see. So this *is* complicated."

"Right. And then last night he finally told me why he broke up with me before. And even though I don't agree with his reason, I understand it. And I can...forgive it. But then this morning I found out something else that might change everything again. I just don't know."

"Hm. Interesting." Angie unscrewed the lid on her thermos and poured a dark red liquid with flecks of green in it into two cups. She handed one to Sarah.

"No, thanks, really—"

"Drink it," Angie said. "And have a bar, too." She threw Sarah one of the few energy bars Sarah could stand, one made with peanut butter and pretzels. "You're looking too skinny again. Eat up."

Sarah knew there was no use arguing. She also knew Angie might be right. So even though she had no desire to put anything into her belly, she ripped open the package and took a bite, then washed it down with Angie's smoothie. Both tasted surprisingly soothing.

"So let's back up a second," Angie said. She paused to take a bite of her own lunch, a mixture of brown rice and assorted vegetables. "As of last night, good guy, right?"

"Good enough," Sarah said.

"But then this morning," Angie said, "bad guy again."

"Maybe."

"Why maybe?"

"Because I can't be sure," Sarah said. "Not until a certain thing happens. But it could happen very soon."

"So why not ask him?" Angie said, spearing a piece of broccoli.

"I can't."

"Why not?"

"I'm not supposed to know," Sarah said. "It's confidential."

"But you do know," Angie pointed out, "so it can't be that confidential."

"But..." She couldn't finish the sentence. Because maybe Angie was right. If Sarah knew about it—if Mickey and Calvin and the three associates in that room now knew about it—how secret could it be?

It reminded Sarah of one of her mother's favorite sayings: *A secret is something you tell only one person at a time.* Sarah wasn't under any kind of legal restriction. She wasn't a member of a grand jury, sworn to secrecy until the indictments were handed down. She heard about it through office gossip, just like Mickey had heard about it from a gossiping pal of his. Maybe she had as much freedom as Mickey did to talk about it if she wanted to.

If she wanted to.

"I'm just not sure I should confront him about it."

Angie rolled her eyes. "Come on, Sarah. Man up."

"Excuse me?"

"Why are you acting like you're so weak all of the sudden?" Angie asked. "Okay, let me tell you a story."

Sarah settled back into her chair and sipped some more of her smoothie. She always enjoyed Angie's stories. They were usually inspiring vignettes about some burly endurance athlete whose memoir Angie was currently reading.

This time, however, the story was about Sarah.

"When you first came in here," Angie said, "I thought you'd never make it through a whole hour. You were a complete weakling—"

"Thanks a lot."

"This is also the Zone of Truth," Angie said, "so take it. Anyway, you practically crawled out of here that first day, remember?"

"I believe the phrase is '*literally* crawled out of here,'" Sarah said. "I think I was on all fours all the way out to my car."

"I thought you'd never show up again," Angie said. "I've had plenty of new clients just like you, pretending to be all gung-ho at the beginning, then *dying* during their first workout, and never coming back. I thought for sure you'd be one of them."

Sarah shrugged. "What can I say? I obviously love pain."

"No, it's because you *commit*," Angie answered. "You make a decision and you see it through. You get where I'm going with this?"

Sarah bit off another bite of bar. "Is this your 'quitters never win, winners never quit' lecture?"

"Hey, it's what I do," Angie said. "Feel free to tell me something lawyerly later like, 'Always read your contracts before you sign them.'" She smiled and softened her voice.

"Sarah. I've known you a whole year now. And I've seen you go through the absolute worst period in your life, wouldn't you say?"

Sarah nodded.

"You are one of the strongest people I've ever met," Angie said. "And I don't mean physically—I know a lot of people, myself included, who could kick your scrawny butt—but I mean *ferocious*, you know? Never say die. What's that line from Winston Churchill? 'Never give up, never, never, never...' infinity," she said, whirling her wrist, "'give up.' That's you. So why should this situation be any different?"

Sarah sighed deeply. "Because it's *him*. And I've already been through this once before. You have no idea how hard I've been working to stay immune to him these past few months. To make myself Joe-proof. But there's always this...connection, you know? It's more than attraction, it's...a familiarity, I guess. Like we're family."

"That sounds good," Angie said.

"But it's not," Sarah answered. "Not if this new thing is true. I can't ever be with someone like that."

"So it's really that bad?"

"It really is," Sarah said. "Bad for a lot of reasons. Including the fact that it means he's not the kind of man I thought he was."

"But you don't know yet if he did whatever it is you think he might have done."

"Right."

"I don't know what to tell you," Angie said. "Except that the Sarah I know would never be afraid to get right up in somebody's grill and ask them what's going on. I hate it when people try to guess what someone else is thinking or what they might have done. Just get it over with and ask him, and then you'll know once and for all. Come on, Henley, don't be such a wuss."

Sarah couldn't help but laugh. She had come in there prepared to feel as awful as she had for the few hours before that, but now she knew she couldn't sustain it.

Because Angie had a point, Sarah thought. If Joe could finally tell her everything he had last night, he could damn well tell her the truth about this.

And the advantage of confronting him was that she'd get to see his reaction face-to-face, and know for herself whether he was telling the truth.

The downside was that the truth might be something she didn't want to hear.

It was the opposite of *Flourish*, Sarah realized: something she didn't want, but knew she needed nevertheless.

"Thanks, Coach." Sarah stood and threw her wrapper in the trash. "This might turn out to be a total disaster, but I think you're right."

Angie glanced at the clock. "You still have half an hour. Feel like burning up your quads?"

Sarah blew out a breath. "Yeah, I think I do."

"What do you want for dinner?" Joe asked when she returned his call later that afternoon. She had just emerged from a long, hot, therapeutic shower and had at least an hour of hair drying and straightening to look forward to.

"Something light," Sarah said. Even though the snack she

had at Angie's felt good at the time, Sarah doubted she would be able to eat too much for dinner. Not when she knew what subject they were going to discuss.

"Tell you what," Joe said. "I'll even eat something vegan with you tonight. Tell me where you like to go and what to order, and I'll bring it over."

He really was so sweet, Sarah thought. His continuing campaign to be nice to her. She wondered how he'd feel in just a few hours when Sarah laid out her evidence.

She gave him the name of her favorite nearby restaurant, and told him to get the lasagna and bring her the adzuki bean burger. Then she tried not to think too much as she went through the laborious process of taming her hair.

By the time he arrived, takeout containers in hand, Sarah felt she looked calm and put together in her jersey lounge pants, gray cami, and a long gray sweater that tied around the waist. Joe looked far too good in his Levi's and a long-sleeved T-shirt.

He kissed her the moment she shut the door behind him. The arm around her waist lifted her to the tips of her toes. How she'd love for him to put the containers down, Sarah thought, lift her all the way up, and carry her to her bedroom. They could do that first, then talk later.

It was an idea she seriously considered.

But then what? Lie there in the afterglow, and hand him the pleading she had printed out? "Hey, Joe, by the way, I meant to talk to you about this..."

Man up. Sarah knew what she had to do.

"Sit down for a minute," she said, taking the food from him and setting it on her kitchen counter. She could hear the tension in her voice, could feel her heart knocking against her chest. *Please let him have an explanation.*

Joe looked around the room. "This is nice," he said. "It's you. It's just what I expected."

"Nicer than the last place you saw, at least," Sarah said. The guest house where she lived during law school was just one room with a tiny bathroom off to the side.

"No, that was you, too," Joe said. "I never wanted to leave."

He sat on her white couch and reached for her. Sarah took a step back. He wasn't going to make this any easier for her, she realized. She had to get right to it.

She had spent the afternoon on the Internet, searching for what she needed. She finally tracked down the pleadings in the case from the court clerk's website, and printed out the first page of the complaint Joe's law firm had filed. The page showing the names of the parties involved.

She handed the printout to Joe. And waited for his reaction.

He stared at the paper for too long, Sarah thought, before finally looking up at her.

"What do you want to know?"

"Is there something you need to tell me?" she asked.

"How much do you know?" he returned.

"Burke—"

"Uh-oh," he said, "we're back to Burke."

"This isn't funny."

"I don't think it is, either," he said. "In fact, it's worse than you've probably guessed."

Sarah sank onto the couch, keeping to the side away

from him. "Then tell me. Because so far my imagination is doing a pretty good job of freaking me out. You could go to prison, Joe."

"I'm not going to prison," he said. "But first of all, tell me how you heard."

"From Mickey. At that meeting this morning. He heard it from some buddy of his. But Burke, damn it, tell me—are you dirty here?"

"No," he said. "I'm not. But I'm in it. And it's about to get a lot worse."

32

She couldn't keep away from him for long, she realized. She needed physical contact with him, needed whatever reassurance she could gain from tucking her feet under his thighs, from having him reach out and hold her hand.

"Tell me what you know," Joe said, and she did.

When she finished, he said, "That's only part of it."

"Then tell me the whole thing," Sarah said. "Don't make me guess." She understood how Angie felt earlier in the day, trying to drag the information out of Sarah one question at a time.

Joe pulled Sarah's legs over his lap and wrapped his arms around them. Apparently he needed more physical contact for the conversation, too, Sarah thought. It reminded her of how they used to be when they studied together. They sometimes sat just like this, like puppies in a pile, each reading their own books and notes until it was time to take a break and engage in something far less intellectual and much more fun. Then back to the books.

"It started this summer," Joe said. "One of the lawyers in our office quit, and someone needed to take over his cases. I'd just settled a big class action suit, so I had the time.

"I knew Milton," he said, referring to Al Milton, one of the two head partners in the firm, "but I'd never worked with him before. He always worked with a particular set of associates who were more senior than I was. But there was a lot going on in the case at the time—motions, depositions, huge discovery output—and he must have figured he could use someone like me on the periphery without really involving me in the case as a whole. It was a big risk. And now it's about to blow up in his face."

"Too much background," Sarah said impatiently. "Tell me what happened."

"What happened was I had to cover the deposition of one of our plaintiffs," Joe said. "He was this optometrist from San Diego, very aggressive, pugnacious guy, and as soon as the deposition was over he took me aside and asked me where his money was."

"What money?"

"He said he was late on his car payment. I told him that was unfortunate, but what did he want me to do about it? He said I'd better pull out my phone and call Milton and tell him to send the goddamn money today. It was the third month in a row he was late."

"Wait a minute," Sarah said. "So your firm was making this guy's car payment? You can't do that, can you?"

"No. We're not supposed to have any financial dealings

with a client, other than giving him the recovery from a case," Joe said. "But it wasn't just the car. The firm was also covering a lot of his other expenses, and the guy was tired of waiting for his money."

"So what did you tell him?"

"I pretended I knew all about it," Joe said. "I asked him for a list of everything he was owed, I wrote it down, and said I'd call Milton that night. Then I told him how sorry I was for any inconvenience, especially since Milton said this guy was our top client and I was supposed to treat him like a king and give him whatever he wanted."

"Did the guy buy it?"

"You bet," Joe said. "Probably because it was exactly what he wanted to hear. So then I took him out for a very expensive meal and lots of liquor, and I was the best listener you've ever seen. The guy never stopped talking.

"Speaking of food," Joe said, patting her leg, "I need some. I worked through lunch. Can we take a five-minute break here?"

"Sure." Sarah swung her legs off his lap and moved toward the kitchen to reheat their dinner.

She felt easier now—so much easier she realized she was actually hungry herself. Even though Joe's story made her feel anxious, she could tell from the way he was telling it that she didn't need to worry about him—not the way she had. He was clean, she felt sure of it. And that mattered more to her than anything.

Joe joined her in the kitchen and wrapped his arms around her from behind while she transferred food into microwavable dishes.

"This seems familiar," he said, kissing the back of her neck.

Sarah had had the same thought. She started the microwave, then twisted around to face him. They were both expert at making the most of a five-minute break. It was something they practiced often as they studied for finals.

Joe untied her sweater and immediately slipped a hand underneath her cami.

"No bra," he murmured. "Thank you." He teased his thumb over her already erect nipple and let his other hand drift down her back and inside the waistband of her pants. "Nothing here, either," he observed. "Very thoughtful." Then he pushed her pants past her hips.

Sarah had dressed for her own comfort, not his—especially since the last thing on her mind when she dressed for her confrontation with him was that they might end up in her kitchen just like this—but now she was happy for the convenience. She had just widened her legs so he could explore further, when the microwave dinged.

"Hold," she said breathily as she dragged her mouth away from his, hating that she had to trade out the dishes and hit start again before she could let Joe resume, too. But the pause only lasted seconds.

She undid his belt and pulled open the buttons on his jeans. Then she glanced at the timer on the microwave. "Two more minutes."

"Go for it," Joe growled, and Sarah reached in to stroke him at the same time his fingers worked their charms on her. When the microwave dinged again, Sarah pulled away from him, feeling completely disheveled and keyed up, and smiled as she tugged her shirt down and her pants back up.

Joe groaned, but he knew the rules. He left his jeans unbuttoned and pulled his T-shirt over the top. Sarah assumed it was the best he could do at the moment.

She made him sit at the table rather than risk lasagna sauce on her white couch. They were both still breathing hard, but that was part of the game. She pulled her chair up close to Joe's so she could still drape one leg over his. He rested his hand on her shin, and the two of them ate while he continued his story.

"Turns out we employed his whole family," Joe said.

"What do you mean?"

"His mother, brother, sister-in-law, a few cousins—all of them on the firm payroll, all of them repeat plaintiffs in a whole variety of class action suits. He told me Milton would call them up, tell them which stocks to buy in which tech companies, then the firm would send them out the money to cover the cost of the investment."

"Totally illegal," Sarah said.

"Completely," Joe confirmed. "Then once the stock went down, the firm would file a lawsuit immediately, and start paying for these people's monthly expenses to keep them happy while they went through the whole process of litigation."

"Why?" Sarah asked. "Your firm seems like it has plenty of work. Why would Milton gamble like that?"

"Because there's huge money in it," Joe said. "With these class action suits, if you're the first to file, you usually end up as the lead attorney, which means you get the bulk of the fees. So Milton created a stable of plaintiffs, always ready to go. It brought him in millions every year."

Sarah shook her head. "It still doesn't seem worth it."

"To you," Joe pointed out. "But some of these guys...they just don't know when to stop. They need *five* beach houses, not just four, they need two yachts, two private jets—it gets crazy."

Sarah thought of her own bank account at one time, with its balance of $4.32. All she had ever wanted was security— to have enough. Even her *Flourish* list was laughably modest, compared to the kinds of things Joe was talking about. She just didn't understand the mentality of someone like Milton, who would risk prison and the loss of his law license just to buy himself another jet.

"So now you had all that information," Sarah said. "Now what?"

Joe took his time scraping up the last of his lasagna before leaning back and looking at her.

"Well, that's where you come in."

"Me?"

"You have to know I followed everything that happened to you last April."

Sarah set down her fork. "Oh." She'd suddenly lost her appetite. She had the feeling she wasn't going to like what she was about to hear next.

She slid her leg off Joe's lap and then took him by the hand, leading him back into the living room. She pulled the faux-fur blanket off the back of the couch and laid it over both of them as she curled up next to him again.

"Okay," she said, "go."

"I know it was a nightmare for you," Joe said. "You don't know how many times I thought about contacting you, saying something..."

"I wouldn't have wanted you to," Sarah said, knowing it was true. She would have felt even more humiliated—and more of a failure—than she already did if Joe had suddenly reappeared. It would have compounded her misery a hundredfold.

"I figured," Joe said. "That's why I didn't. But Sarah, I thought about you all the time. Not just then, but in all the years since law school. You know that, don't you?"

Sarah looked down. She felt a hardness in her throat. But she wrapped her fingers around Joe's and forced herself to look up again. She kissed him softly on the lips, the same way he'd kissed her that afternoon in the mountain medical clinic. Then she smiled. "Go on. Don't distract me."

He wrapped his arm around her waist and pulled her closer. "I didn't want to go through that," he said. "The feds rushing in, the whole firm collapsing around me. So I took steps."

"Steps," Sarah said. "Such as?"

"I wrote a memo. A long one. To Milton and the other partners. I laid out in detail everything the optometrist had told me, and everything I found once I started investigating on my own. Now that I knew the names of all his family members, I could find them in the firm's files. They'd been on the payroll for years. So I put that in the memo, too. Then I sent it."

"Why did you do it that way?" Sarah asked. "What did you think it would get you?"

"Some protection, for one thing," Joe said, "in case anyone wanted to accuse me of being involved. But I also had at least a slim hope that none of the other partners knew what Milton was up to, and they'd crack down on him and do something about it."

"But they didn't, I assume."

"No, they cracked down on me instead."

"What happened?" Sarah asked.

"Purgatory."

Sarah drew back and looked into his face. "Wait a minute—that's why you were on the road?"

"Yep."

"I remember I asked you if they were trying to make you quit."

"Right," Joe said. "And they were. They were afraid to fire me, but if they gave me the world's crappiest assignment—"

"Traveling from city to city with Paul Chapman—"

Joe smiled. "And then you showed up. From then on, it was perfect."

"Somehow I doubt you felt that way at first," Sarah said. "Not with the way I was treating you."

"I didn't care," he answered. "You could be as hostile as you wanted. I was just so happy to be with you again."

Sarah shook her head. And thought of what she'd said to Angie about returning after that first, excruciating workout: *What can I say? I obviously love pain.*

No, Angie had corrected her, *it's because you commit.*

Was that what this was? Sarah wondered, looking at Joe. Had he really been so happy to see her he was willing to put up with two months of her anger before finally breaking through it only the week before? Or was it just the natural outcome of the two of them being thrown together again, day after day, week after week, until finally Sarah's defenses wore down?

She didn't like to think of it that way, but she also didn't want to blindly romanticize the situation. The truth was, if she had never taken that job with Mickey's firm, she and Joe would have continued along their separate paths and probably never seen each other again.

"Red?"

"What?"

"You have that look. What's going on in that clever brain of yours?"

"You don't want to know," she said.

"I always do." He loosened his grip on her waist so she could turn to face him. "Tell me. I'm done with all these secrets."

"Then why did you keep this one?" she asked quietly. "Why didn't you tell me yourself? You think I liked hearing about it from Mickey today?"

"I couldn't say anything," Joe answered. "I'm a witness now—a star witness, they tell me."

"Who tells you?"

"The U.S. Attorney's office. One of the paralegals at my firm saw the memo and turned it over to a friend of hers who works there. Next thing I knew, I got a call, then had a meeting, then more phone calls...and now I'm at the top of their list to testify. Which should keep me in the news for a little while."

"Is that what you meant when you said it's about to get worse?"

"That's part of it," Joe said. "It's also about trying to time everything perfectly so I get out before the indictments, but land a new job before I'm branded a snitch. It's tricky times, Red."

"Don't make a joke out of this."

"I'm not," he said. "I'm just stating the facts."

"Well explain this fact to me, then," she said. "Why haven't you quit yet? What are you doing still hanging around that place? Is the U.S. Attorney making you stay?"

"No, I can leave anytime."

"Then, why haven't you? Do you not understand what's at stake here?"

"No, what's at stake?" he asked calmly.

"Your career. Your reputation. You can't go down with that ship, Joe. You saw what happened with me—I didn't work again for six months."

"I'm not worried about it," he said.

"Well, you should be."

"Something will come along."

Sarah groaned in frustration. "How can you say that? You don't know."

"I've already had one offer."

"Well, then you should take it!"

"I can't," Joe said. "The offer expired last month."

Sarah stared at him, confused. "But why? How could you let it go?"

Joe tilted his head and gave her a look she knew too well.

It was a look that said, *You know the answer here, Red. Think about it.*

"No," she said. "You didn't.... You didn't let it go because of me."

"I told you I have a strategy," he said. "Why do you think I've spent the last two months traveling with you almost every day? Why do you think I stayed behind at Thanksgiving? Why have I been handing over all my cases to other people in the firm, but holding on to this one?"

Her throat felt dry, but she forced herself to answer. "Because you're crazy."

"No," Joe said, "it's because I'm not stupid. And I know a second chance when I see one. I'm not quitting this case or leaving the firm until I know: are you with me, Sarah? Have I done enough to convince you that I still love you and I wish I'd never let you go?"

33

Sarah stared at him, too overcome to answer.

Joe lifted her hand to his lips. "That's all this is, Sarah. One long, two-month argument for why you should give me another chance. I know how you are—you're going to want to be stubborn here. It's always your first reaction. So I don't expect any kind of answer right now—in fact, I don't want one."

"That really pisses me off," she said. The words were out before she could stop them. Maybe he was right about her first reactions.

"Why?" he asked. "Because I know you?"

"No, because you *think* you know me. You don't. You used to."

"Then tell me the truth," Joe said. "Are you feeling all mushy toward me right now? Ready to throw yourself into my arms and tell me, 'Yes, Joe. I'm with you. Let's run away together tonight'?"

"Of course not," Sarah said.

"Then tell me what's on your mind."

Sarah narrowed her eyes. Because what was on her mind could very well be interpreted as stubbornness, and she didn't want to give him the satisfaction of proving his point.

"It's like I've said before," she answered. "You take a lot for granted. You always seem to think I'm a sure thing."

"Sarah," he said, "have you not been listening? You're the opposite of a sure thing. A sure thing would have smiled the first time she saw me in six years. She would have been friendly. Happy to be around me. You've been like a junk yard dog I've had to sing to and feed scraps of meat night after night until you finally trust me enough to let me climb over the gate."

She couldn't help it—she had to laugh. Even though she knew she should be annoyed at the comparison. But she also knew he was fairly close to right.

"See?" Joe said, pointing to her smiling face. "*That.* Do you know how long it's taken me to get that?"

Sarah closed her eyes and dropped backward onto the red velvet pillows. She never imagined when she bought them that one day she'd be sitting on her catalog couch, resting her head on her catalog pillows, while Joe-freakin-Burke sat there with her, telling her he had made an absolutely horrendous career move just for the chance of flying with her to Missoula and Billings and Pocatello so he could carry out his campaign to woo her.

"I'm not stubborn," she said from her prone position. "I'm just practical. And you realize a part of me wants to tell you whatever you want to hear so you'll quit that damn law firm tomorrow—tonight, even—and get out before it's too late. You know that, right?"

"But I also know you're a woman of your word," Joe said, "and so you would never lie to me like that."

Sarah sighed. And aimed one frustrated but mild kick at his thigh.

Joe caught her foot and held it. "Red?"

"Yes?"

"It could be like this again."

"I know." She knew she sounded serious, not soft. Like a lawyer conceding a point.

"Do you have a good reason not to?" Joe asked. "Tell me the truth. I'm willing to listen if you've got one."

"So easily deterred, huh?" she asked, poking him with her free foot. He held on to that one, too.

"No, but I've thought it through and I'm ready for you. So make whatever kind of case you want for why you and I shouldn't be together."

"We're opponents," she said. "Or have you forgotten?"

"Easily fixed, and you know it. I'll hand it over to someone else this week. Next?"

Sarah scowled. She wanted to give him other reasons: that the way he'd treated her before was unforgivable, that they had only been together again for less than a week, and that was hardly proof that they could sustain it, that, that...

But he had narrowed her arguments by telling her they had to be true. And she knew those weren't.

The truth was, she could forgive him—and last night she had. Any anger she felt was gone. Maybe it had already left her before that, she thought, maybe at the ski area above Salt

Lake City, maybe outside the airport in Pocatello, maybe in one hotel room or another. The moments had begun to blend, and she knew her heart had been changing all along. She couldn't point to one single event and say, *Yes, that one. That's where I gave up being angry and started falling in love with him again.*

And the truth was that even though they had only been "together," in that sense, for the past week, they'd been together for two months. And for seven weeks before that. And in the same way she knew by the end of a weekend in Illinois that Joe was a man she could love, she knew that now, and didn't feel right lying about it.

"You're right," she said, her body going limp. "I've got nothing."

"Wait a minute," he said, "no argument?"

"No, I'm too tired."

"Not good enough," Joe said. "I'm not winning this by default. You can't give in because you're tired."

"Yes, I can. You win."

In one swift move, Joe yanked Sarah toward him by the feet until her legs lay over his lap. Sarah laughed. "Look at me," he told her. "Sarah, I'm serious."

"What? You got what you wanted, didn't you? You can quit, I'll be your girl..."

"This is not satisfying," he said.

"Well, too bad. You wore me down. You're like water on a rock—drip, drip, drip..."

But then she sprang to life again, straddling him, pinning him to her couch. "Is this what you want, Burke? More of a fight? You want me feisty?"

"A little feist is good," he said. "But I want to hear the words, too—can you give me that, Henley? Or are you going to leave me here hanging?"

"I will not leave you hanging," she said, pressing her groin against his. "By no means. I'm feeling a second wind. And yes, Burke," she said, resting her hands gently on the sides of his face and gazing into his eyes, "I'll give you the words: I'm with you, Joe. Whatever this whole thing brings, I'm with you. Satisfied?"

"Getting there," he said, standing up and lifting her with him. She wrapped her legs around his waist as he carried her in the only possible direction.

"You still haven't said the other thing I want to hear," Joe said.

"You'll have to earn that, too," Sarah answered. "Keep working on it."

34

The flight to Portland left at 5:40 Sunday night. It was later than Sarah liked to fly, since it meant she would have to find dinner in the airport, but it was one of the few nonstops, and she was tired of changing planes. Joe's office had made the same reservation. She knew she'd be seeing him at the airport.

It was strange, she thought, knowing this would be their last trip together. When he left her apartment that morning, he promised to start working right away on finding his replacement. Sarah wanted him out of that firm as soon as possible. She could feel the hot breath of Fitzgerald and the U.S. Attorney's office on her neck, even if Joe didn't seem as concerned as she did.

It was only because he hadn't been through it yet, she thought. If he had been there April 6, he would have seen the panic, the misery, the chaos and confusion as the feds raided her firm. He would have wished as ardently as she had that someone had whispered in her ear, *"Hey, you might want to quit by April 5. Just a suggestion."*

She finished going through airport security, then searched for something decent to eat. She settled for her old standby, a rice and vegetable bowl from the Chinese fast food place. It didn't look nearly as appetizing as the one Angie had been eating the day before—probably because Angie made it herself.

Sarah looked forward to the time when she would be home long enough to cook for herself again: winter soups like gumbo and corn chowder; pastas with zucchini or asparagus tossed in olive oil and garlic; Mexican and Indian dishes; fresh baked bread.

But to be home that long meant Joe's firm would have to implode first, and she was in no hurry for that.

She settled into the gate area with a view of the approaching passengers. Marcela wasn't there yet, she noticed, so either the court reporter was running late or had taken another flight.

Then finally Sarah was rewarded with a long-range view of her lover. Wearing jeans and a sweater, carrying the raincoat he had needed outside in the cold drizzle, smiling as soon as he caught sight of her. Sarah returned the smile. Even after only a few hours apart, she missed him.

He took the seat next to hers and leaned over to whisper. "Are you wearing anything under that?"

She had on a pair of jersey pants similar to the ones he stripped off her the night before. On top she wore a comfortable knit shirt under a soft jersey hoodie.

"Sorry to disappoint you," she said.

"It's all right," Joe said. "Shouldn't slow me down too much. I can probably find us a place if you want to spare five minutes."

Her skin warmed at the suggestion. She had a hard time keeping a straight face. "Sorry, Burke, we're back on duty. Did you find your replacement?"

"His name's Felix," Joe said, shifting back to professional mode just like she had. "I think he'll do all right. It was hard to find someone on such short notice. He'll take over on Wednesday."

"Did you hand in your resignation?"

"Not yet. I'll do that on Wednesday, too."

"Joe..."

"It's not fair to the clients," he said. "We already have depositions scheduled. I want to make sure they're covered before I leave."

She understood his reason, and couldn't object to it. Even though she hated to think of even two more days going by before he was free of the firm. A lot could happen in two days. She'd seen for herself how quickly a firm could go from viable and working, to crumbling and in disarray once the feds showed up at the door.

"Felix is pretty new," Joe said, "so take it easy on him."

"No promises," Sarah said.

But the truth was, she doubted she would spend very much time with Joe's replacement. She agreed with Calvin's assessment of what would happen once the indictments hit the news: the firm's clients would scramble to find new lawyers. There would be chaos for a few months while everyone sorted themselves out. And meanwhile Sarah and her team would be working at full speed to make sure Mason Manufacturing was dismissed from the case.

"I need to grab some dinner," Joe said. "I'll be right back." He leaned over once again to whisper, "I want my hands on you, Henley. As soon as possible. Do you think that can be arranged?"

"Fairly certain," she answered, once again trying to keep her face completely neutral. For her sake and for Joe's. They didn't need to work each other up right before a two-and-a-half hour flight. There would be time enough after that.

Just two more nights with him, Sarah thought, then she'd have to wait again until the weekend. She almost wished she had taken better advantage of all their weeks together.

But things had turned out the way they had for a reason, she remembered. Joe had only been waiting to win her back before quitting the case. So if he had convinced her sooner, he would have left sooner. What she should really be wishing, she thought, was that she hadn't been so stubborn, just like he said. If she'd softened a little earlier, bent a little instead of so rigidly clutching on to her anger, she could have bought him a larger window of time in which to maneuver.

But whatever happened now, they would just have to deal with it—together. *I'm with you, Joe.* She meant that.

What that meant for their future at large, she couldn't say. But she did know that for now, at least, she had tied herself to his fate.

She thought about how different she would have felt back in April if she'd had someone like Joe on her side. Someone to come home to that day, to pour out her heart to, to reassure her, to hold her. She knew Joe's situation wouldn't be that dramatic—he already knew what was coming, he just didn't know when—but still, she was happy she could offer him the kind of support she wished she'd had herself.

She had no idea what his finances were. She had been caught in the middle of an upward climb, at a time when she'd been spending money—including sending some to her parents every month—instead of saving. If Joe had this much warning, maybe he had been able to set some aside. Or maybe he wouldn't have to wait as long as she did before finding another job. The fact that he'd already been offered one was excellent news. Maybe the whole situation would be much easier for him.

Although she still wished he hadn't turned the job down, whatever it was. Just one more consequence of her staying hostile to him for so long.

She could drive herself crazy with what-ifs.

"Where are you sitting?" Joe asked her when he returned. He bought a deli sandwich and a bag of chips he opened up and propped between their seats for her to share.

"Eleven-F. You?"

"Nineteen-B. Maybe we can find someone to switch."

"No," Sarah said, "just in case." She glanced around the boarding area. She still didn't see Marcela, but she wanted to be careful. They weren't completely free yet.

"Are you checking into your hotel tonight?" Joe asked.

She had thought about that. In a way, she was wasting client money by checking into a hotel for whatever short period she'd be there, knowing she would spend the night with Joe.

"Maybe not," she said. "I'm not sure yet."

He turned and gave her a look. "I don't want to act like you're a sure thing, since I know how much you hate that, but...come on, Sarah." The smile he gave her was far too seductive. Then she watched his eyes shift to her mouth.

She wanted the same thing: to drag his mouth to hers, to feel his hands underneath her shirt, grasping her bare breasts, to climb on top of him, right there in the metal seats of the boarding area so the two of them could take their five minutes of tease.

She forced herself to look away. Her breathing felt rapid and shallow. She laughed in a husky, self-conscious way, knowing how easy it must have been for Joe to read her mind just then.

"Later?" he asked.

"Later," she promised. And then she intended to make all the waiting worth it.

SHE'D RESERVED A RENTAL CAR, but it didn't make much sense to pick it up. Just another unnecessary expense, she told herself, since Joe was renting a car anyway, and she could ride with him to his hotel. Then take a cab back in the morning before the deposition, and another cab to the airport that afternoon.

She waited while he filled out the paperwork. It reminded her of the beginning of their whole relationship, back in the rental car area of the small Illinois airport. How she stood off to the side while that bossy third-year completed the transaction. How she had been so cold, and Joe noticed. The way he silently brought her hands into his pocket and held them there. The way his touch had felt, even then: right. Natural. And nearly irresistible.

"Ready?"

Sarah nodded. Joe laid his hand against the small of her back as the two of them walked toward the doors outside.

They walked all the way to the garage, down the rows to where his car was, loaded their luggage into the trunk, then waited until they were safely in their seats.

Then as if someone had shot a starter's pistol, they were immediately at each other, lips parting, hands reaching, bodies stealing just a few minutes of release after too long in such careful close contact.

Sarah pulled her mouth away, panting. "The sooner you get there—"

Joe started the car. Sarah buckled in and closed her eyes.

God, she needed this man. How had she ever thought she could do without him? No one—*no one*—had ever excited her more, understood her better, or, she freely reminded herself, *loved her* the way Joe had. And she had never loved anyone else. No one before him, no one after. It was Joe for her, or no one.

She almost said it. Almost told him. But it was her one remaining gift. If she just threw it out to him now, what value did it have? He'd said it to her in a way that mattered: *"Have I done enough to convince you that I still love you and I wish I'd never let you go?"* Words she would never forget. Just like the simpler words of a younger Joe telling her, *"I love you like crazy, Sarah."*

Words mattered. Context mattered. She would wait for the right time.

For now, she reached across the seat and squeezed his hand. He lifted her hand to his lips and kissed the knuckles.

"No," she said, laughing at the instant heat and moisture his gesture had brought on. She reluctantly pulled her hand away. "Just get me to the hotel. Then we'll take care of all of this."

"No belt," Sarah murmured appreciatively as she began stripping Joe of his jeans.

He was right: her undergarments barely slowed him down. He unhooked her bra and divested her of her panties before his own clothes hit the floor.

This time, instead of carrying her to the bed, he took a detour toward the bathroom.

He set her on the floor and turned on the hot water.

"No, my hair—"

He had a three-word response to that, ending in *your hair*, then he pulled her naked into the shower.

They were both so different now, Sarah thought. She continued to marvel at that. How much broader and more muscular he'd gotten, how much tighter and stronger she had. It was a pleasure, just in a pure aesthetic sense, to run her hands over his body, to feel what it was like pressing herself against him now, to know that they were both older and better versions of what they had been the last time they were in love.

Joe soaped up his hands and went to work. Sarah let him. She braced her hands against the tile walls and let him touch her however he liked. She would take her own turn with him later, she knew, but for now she had absolutely no problem with Joe exploring her first.

He slicked his hands slowly over her breasts. She leaned back against him, feeling the hardness, savoring it, knowing how it would feel inside her, in no hurry to get there. She was tired of rushing with this man. She wanted long hours with him, the languorous kind of sex they had experienced the past two nights in the privacy of their own apartments. No more furtive lovemaking on the run. She was tired of hiding. She couldn't wait for him to be free of the case so they could be together in the open.

Her carefully styled hair was already in uncontrollable coils, but she didn't care. He had seen her that way plenty of times when they were younger. What she cared about were his hands, now venturing lower, coaxing her thighs apart, one strong arm bracing her against him while the fingers on his other hand did their delicate work.

Sarah sighed with the force of a body finally letting go: letting go of the tension, the anger, the resentment, the fears that held her back. She thought she had already given it all away, but here was the last of it, the marrow of it, working its way up to the surface and washing away in the steam. If she was with him, she was with him all the way now. He could have her in every configuration: her body, her desire, her passion, her heart, her mind, her love.

She turned to him, and if it wasn't the right time, not important or special enough, then she couldn't help it: it had to be said.

"I love you, Joe. I've always loved you."

He covered her mouth with his and pulled her tightly against him. Then he shut off the water, lifted her from the shower, and set her dripping on the floor. They dried each other as hurriedly as they could in between kissing and caressing, and then Sarah knew there would be no slowness this time, no long, languid build-up, because it had to be now, they needed each other too much, and Joe barely got her to the bed before sheathing himself and entering her in almost the same motion.

She lay wet and loose against the sheets, her legs wrapped around him, her hands gripping his shoulders as he kissed her deep and long, her body absorbing every thrust of his hips, wanting this part to go on and on, because it was the best expression she could think of for how close she felt to him now, how much she needed him, how much she trusted and loved him and wanted him to feel the same from her, how she was with him now, and would be, how much better it could be now that they knew what they'd had and knew too well what they had lost.

Sarah could feel the power mounting, the force of her desire pushing its way to the surface, the release that her body craved even if her heart never wanted this part to end.

She exploded with a cry, her hips bucking against him, her back arching, her fingers digging into his shoulders as Joe drove into her harder now, more urgently, and then he was with her, too, shuddering with the release, his face and body slick with sweat, his mouth still hungry for hers.

Sarah held him against her for a long time, captive in the double bind of her arms and legs. Then finally the two of them realized she couldn't breathe with his full weight on her, and she let him shift to the side.

She heard him say something, but the curtain was already lowering in her brain, and she was almost asleep. Joe pulled the covers over both of them and that was the last she remembered before his watch alarm woke them in the morning.

Joe kissed her awake and told her that he loved her.

"I love you, too," she said.

Such a sweet beginning, Sarah thought later, to one of the hardest days of her life.

"Hi, Ms. Henley. Ryan Sollers. Very nice to meet you." Chapman's replacement shook Sarah's hand.

"'Sarah' is fine," she said, taking in the upgrade in both manners and appearance of the new attorney. He looked more like a California surfer than a litigator, with his blond hair and a tan that looked like he earned it honestly out in the sun, rather than at a salon.

A court reporter Sarah had never seen was setting up. "I thought Marcela was with us this week."

"She lost a crown over the weekend," the woman said. "She had to get it fixed today. I'm Wendy. I'll be here and in Seattle tomorrow."

Sarah shook her hand. "Thanks for filling in."

Joe entered the conference room along with his client, a young woman who looked like she was in her early 20s. Ryan stood up and introduced himself to both of them. He even shook the plaintiff's hand, which Sarah had never seen Chapman do.

"Before we get started, Ms. Townsend," Ryan said to the woman, "is there anything we can get you? Water, coffee?"

"No," she answered nervously. "Thanks." She looked at Joe as if seeking some reassurance that she'd given the right answer: *We don't take food or comfort from the enemy.*

Joe smiled encouragingly. "Just speak up if you need anything," he said, "all right?"

The young woman nodded.

"Well, let's get started then, shall we?" Ryan said. "I promise I won't take too much of your time today, Ms. Townsend. Just a few questions, then we'll have you on your way."

Sarah caught Joe's eye and gave him a look that said, *Not bad.* So far this new lawyer was a vast improvement over Chapman.

While Ryan began his preliminary questions—"Please state your name, your date of birth, address," etc.—Sarah booted up her laptop. Then she entered a search for "Ryan Sollers."

Bachelor's in Political Science from University of California, Berkeley, then law school at Stanford. Member of the law review. Twenty-eight years old, had been practicing law for three years.

Sarah looked over and noticed Joe reading something on his phone. She wondered if he was checking up on Sollers, too.

"Now," Ryan said, "if you wouldn't mind, Ms. Townsend—do you mind if I call you Amanda?"

"No," she said, still sounding slightly nervous, "that's fine."

"Great, thanks. All right, Amanda, if you would, I'd like you to take me through a typical routine of straightening your hair. From wet to beautiful, just like it is right now. Can you do that for me?"

Sarah admired Ryan's way with the plaintiff. He phrased everything as a request, not a demand. A "would you," "can I," "could you?" Lawyers like Paul Chapman were so heavy-handed, they ended up making people say as little as possible just to try to get by. But someone like Ryan Sollers could coax a lot more information from a witness by coming across as polite and curious, with a few humble and sincere-sounding apologies thrown in here and there.

The guy was good, Sarah thought. Especially for someone who'd only been at it for a few years.

She continued her search, looking for any information about cases he might have been involved in before. When she didn't find anything right away, she realized she should stop focusing on her screen and instead listen to the testimony.

"So in between," Ryan was saying, "when you're unclipping the next section of hair and getting ready to straighten it, where do you usually put the hair iron?"

"You know, on the counter right next to me," Amanda Townsend said.

"Give me a picture," Ryan said, "if you don't mind. What's your bathroom counter made out of? Tile, or maybe a laminate of some kind—do you know?"

"Um…you know, it's just this blue counter. It's whatever came with my apartment."

"Okay," Ryan said, writing something down, "got it. Now, what do you usually have on your counter? Probably some makeup, your toothbrush—give me a picture, please."

The young woman described the clutter of items on her counter.

"Great," Ryan said. "Thank you. It sounds like there might not be much room there. Do you ever have a hand towel nearby? Or a washcloth?"

"Sometimes."

The two of them went back and forth discussing in minute detail everything that might be on her counter on a typical day. It was starting to sound as boring as Chapman's questions about a plaintiff's educational history or where her parents were born.

But then one of Ryan's questions had Sarah turning to her Internet search engine once again.

"Do you ever let the hair iron rest on a towel?"

"I don't know, sometimes."

"Do you remember if you did that the day it caught on fire?"

Sarah brought up the Atheena instruction manual. She quickly paged through to the warnings, and found the one she was looking for:

Never allow appliance to touch any fabric or other flammable materials.

She continued searching through the instructions for other clues about what Ryan was asking.

Do not place heated appliance directly on any surface while it is hot or plugged in.

Do not operate appliance where aerosol spray products are being used.

Keep away from cosmetics and hair products, as these may be flammable.

A whole list of warnings, and Ryan Sollers was covering them one by one, while pretending to have a conversation.

The guy was smooth.

By the time Ryan thanked Ms. Townsend again for her time and her patience, Sarah realized he'd already asked many of the questions she normally did. The only area left to cover was the frequency of use and the period of time the young woman had owned the product before it caught on fire.

It was only quarter to eleven when the deposition ended. They wouldn't have another one until the afternoon.

"Pretty fast," Sarah complimented Sollers while Joe and his client were out of the room.

"Well, there's not that much to this, is there?" Ryan answered. "Shouldn't take too long. I've been meaning to talk to you and Joe about that. I think we might want to revise the deposition schedule, now that I'm taking over."

Joe came back into the room.

"I was just telling Sarah," Ryan continued, "that I'd like to make some changes to the schedule. Mr. Chapman was..."

Ryan turned to the court reporter. "Actually, Wendy, would you mind leaving us alone in here for a little while?"

"Oh," she said, looking a little flustered. "Sure."

"It's nothing against you," Ryan assured her. "I just have a few boring details to discuss with the other lawyers here, and I'm sure you'd rather take an early lunch break than be stuck in here with us."

Wendy smiled. "Okay, sure. Thanks. I'll be back at one."

Ryan waited for her to leave before resuming. "Paul Chapman has a different philosophy about this case than I do," he said. "I assume I can speak frankly?"

Sarah and Joe both nodded. Sarah resisted shooting Burke a look. What was Sollers up to?

"Let's just say his case load isn't as heavy as mine. Paul...well, he might be more in need of the billable hours than I am."

Now Sarah and Joe did exchange a look. Normally lawyers didn't talk about their colleagues to their opponents in a case.

"I'm not interested in spending five days a week flying to every podunk airport on the map," Ryan said. "I have better things to do with my time, as I'm sure you do, too. So I'm prepared to cancel the current schedule and propose a new one where we only fly to cities with major airports, and only places where there are at least four plaintiffs in the area. I'm talking about Dallas, Atlanta, New York City. No more flying for six hours just to take one or two depositions in a small town. What a waste of time and money."

"I agree," Sarah said, relieved to find someone sane on the other side. "I don't know if Chapman told you, but I was going to add some cities myself—"

"He did," Ryan said. "That's why I wanted to discuss it

with you first, Sarah, before I did anything. And you, too, of course, Joe. I think we can make this a lot simpler for all of us."

Sarah glanced at Joe again, and saw him regarding Ryan with an odd expression on his face. Was it suspicion? Wariness? She couldn't quite read it.

"Let's take a break now," Ryan said, "and I'll have my office e-mail me the proposed schedule over lunch. Does that sound all right?"

He smiled at both of them. Sarah noticed Joe did not return the smile.

"Now," Ryan said, standing, "Sarah, can I buy you lunch? Sorry, Joe, defense side only."

"Sure," Joe said, "no problem." But something about his tone didn't sound right to Sarah. Something was up.

"Sarah, I understand you're a vegetarian?" Ryan asked, moving now toward the door. He held it open for her while she took her time putting her laptop away. She continued wondering if Joe was trying to send her a signal of some kind, or if he just didn't particularly like Sollers.

"I am," she said. "Where'd you hear that?"

Ryan smiled. "I always do my homework. We'll see you at one," he told Joe as they finally left the room.

"Sushi all right?" Ryan asked. "I noticed there's a place nearby. I used to date a vegetarian girl. Sushi was always our compromise, since we could both get what we wanted."

"Sure," Sarah said. "Fine."

But she was still distracted by Joe's reaction. Did he think Ryan was hitting on her—was that it? He had to know Ryan was no threat. But men could get strange ideas sometimes, Sarah thought, and maybe Joe still wasn't feeling secure enough about where she stood. She'd have to make herself crystal clear next time they were alone together. Just the thought of it made her have to hide a smile.

They had been so domestic that morning, both of them getting ready for the workday, Joe shaving next to her at the sink while Sarah went through the process of straightening her hair once again, since he had showered it back to kinky the night before.

"I don't know how you can still use that," he'd said, shaking his head at the Atheena in her hand.

"I bought mine three years ago," Sarah said. "There's no danger."

But then she realized she'd already said too much. Granted, he was leaving the case in just two days, and even his replacement would find out about her strategy eventually, but Sarah knew better than to tip her hand this early. The man standing next to her in the bathroom wasn't her lover at that moment, he was still her opponent. And Sarah had no desire to violate the rules of the game.

In fact, in a way, it made it more fun to know that months would go by before he would ever hear about what she came up with. She relished the idea of springing it on him one night after work, announcing that she'd gotten Mason Manufacturing dismissed from the case. That would be worth a celebration or two.

"This place look all right?" Ryan asked her as they approached the small restaurant.

"Sure," she said. "Fine."

She checked off her selections on the order card, choosing an avocado roll and another with fried tofu. Ryan handed both cards to the server, then motioned toward the tables.

"You choose," he said, then he rested his hand lightly against Sarah's back as she passed him.

She took a longer stride to move out of range of his touch. Maybe Joe's suspicions were right.

"So," she said, adopting her most professional tone as Ryan slipped into the booth across from her. "How'd you end up with this assignment? I can't imagine you volunteered."

"Oh, you know," he said modestly, "low man on the pole. I do what I'm told."

Sarah took in the confident posture and smooth easiness of the man across from her. "Somehow I doubt that," she said.

Ryan shrugged. "Never say no when another lawyer asks you for a favor. There'll always come a time when they have to pay you back."

That sounded more like it, Sarah thought. A young lawyer with a clear vision of what he needed to do to get ahead. She could certainly understand that.

"So, I assume you did your homework, too," Ryan said.

"What do you mean?"

"I saw you typing away. I assume it wasn't a letter home. What did you find out?"

Sarah saw no reason to lie. She gave him the brief history she'd uncovered.

"Did you get to the track scholarship?" Ryan asked.

"No."

Ryan nodded. "Ran my way into UC Berkeley. But once the coaches and I agreed I probably wasn't the next great 800-meter Olympian, I started looking around for something less competitive."

"So of course you chose law," Sarah said.

"Naturally. How about you? Graduated from high school in only three years, got your insurance agent's license at eighteen, so I'm guessing you worked your way through college, probably a combination of savings and maybe academic scholarship to pay for law school—what am I missing?"

Sarah laughed. "Well, you really did do your homework. The insurance agent thing—that had to be hard to find. I don't think anybody knows about that anymore."

"Just have to know where to look," Ryan said.

Their lunches arrived, and both spent some time mixing wasabi and soy sauce and otherwise tending to their plates. But finally when they had both downed a few rolls, Ryan looked across the booth at her again.

"You're very pretty. That must be a hazard."

"How so?" Sarah asked, her voice decidedly chillier than before.

Ryan smiled. "It's still a man's game, isn't it? Even though I heard law schools are admitting about fifty-fifty, you still don't see that many females in the top spots. Why do you think that is?"

"I don't know, Ryan, why do you think it is?" Sarah hated discussions like this—as if she were expected to account for the success, or lack thereof, of every other woman lawyer.

"It'll happen," Ryan said. "Old institutions are slow. Look at politics—it's taken forever for the women to catch up. And it's not because they're not capable—obviously they are."

Saying what people want to hear? Sarah thought. *Check.* Clearly the guy was skilled at reading his audience and feeding it all the right lines. He was no amateur at manipulation.

Which made Sarah wonder what was behind this lunch in the first place.

"So," she said, "is this just a friendly get-to-know-you, or is there something else I should know?"

"Sarah," Ryan answered, clicking his tongue. "So suspicious. What if I'm just the new kid in school, trying to make friends on the playground?"

"We may both be on the defense side," Sarah said, "but we're opponents. I'm afraid friendship won't take you very far."

"Really? Too bad." He smiled in an easy, casual way, and there was nothing about it that should have made her uncomfortable, but it did. She felt the same way she thought Joe might: wary.

When the bill came, Ryan snatched it up before Sarah could lay a fingerprint on it. "I offered," Ryan reminded her. "You can get the next one."

"I think it's best if we all pay for our own," she said. "Keeps things cleaner."

"Just this once, then," he said. "Don't worry, I'm not going to tell."

They walked back the few blocks to the hotel. The day was cloudy and cold. Sarah was grateful she'd dressed warmly.

"Which flight are you on tonight?" Ryan asked as he held the lobby door open for her.

"The five-forty."

"Too bad," he said. "I'm on the six-fifteen. Oh, well, we all end up in the same place. Maybe I can buy you dinner."

"I don't think so," she answered.

"Let me know if you change your mind."

Sarah stopped walking and faced him. "Look, Ryan," she said, keeping her voice low. "I don't want to make any assumptions here, but just in case you thought there might be any kind of...personal interaction between us..."

"I'd never think that," Ryan answered. "I'm sorry—I didn't mean to—" He laughed. "Sarah, I meant what I said: I think you're a beautiful woman. There's nothing wrong with being friendly. But I'd never pursue you while this case is going on—we both know that's wrong. And I assume you wouldn't try anything with me. But we also both know that these cases don't last forever. There's always an afterward."

Sarah patted his chest. "Thanks, Sollers, but I'm afraid the answer's always going to be no."

Ryan shrugged good-naturedly. "Like I said, just being friendly. See you in there, Sarah."

"Right." She made a detour toward the bathroom before heading for the conference room again. She needed a few minutes alone.

The guy unnerved her—she couldn't exactly say why.

She'd been hit on plenty of times, but there was something about how he did it, the things he said.

Sollers seemed smart. She doubted he said or did anything without thinking it through first.

So what was his game?

36

The afternoon deposition followed the same basic course of the morning's, with Sollers gently charming and then leading Joe's client through the elements of the defense he obviously felt he could build: these plaintiffs were at fault. They created their own fire hazards by not handling the iron properly. Atheena had done everything it should by printing out warnings in an instruction manual that came with every product. It wasn't Atheena's fault if the customer chose not to read it.

It was only around three o'clock when Sarah finished her questions. Ryan thanked Joe's client again for coming in.

"I hope that wasn't too bad, Mrs. McKinley."

"No," she said, smiling in a motherly way, "it wasn't too bad."

"You have a good evening now," Ryan said.

"You, too," she answered. Then she let Joe lead her out.

Sarah turned to Ryan and shook her head. "Wow. You could charm the pearls right off that lady."

"Like I said," Ryan answered. "Nothing wrong with being friendly."

When Joe returned, Ryan once again asked the court reporter to leave. "We have some scheduling matters to go over, Wendy. I hope you understand."

"Of course," she said, smiling at him this time. "I'll see all of you tomorrow. I might try to catch an earlier flight now and actually see some of Seattle."

"Sounds good," Ryan said. "Maybe we'll get out of here soon, too. See you tomorrow, Wendy."

The court reporter waved to him and carried her equipment case from the room.

Looking at the woman's face, the way she smiled at Ryan and shyly dipped her head down, Sarah had no doubt Ryan could charm more than the pearls off of that one. He was a good-looking, confident man—no question about it. And Sarah had no trouble believing that those qualities worked for him more often than not.

Ryan handed one sheet of paper to Joe and another to Sarah. "Here's my proposed schedule. You can look it over and give me your thoughts later."

He had been sitting next to Sarah, but now Ryan got up and moved to the chair at the end of the table where the court reporter had been sitting, so that he had an equal view of Sarah and Joe.

"Now. There's something else I'd like to discuss with you two." He gazed from one of them to the other, his posture still as relaxed as ever, but there was something in his eyes, Sarah noticed. A look of excitement. Pleasure.

"I find I'm in an interesting position," Ryan said. "As Sarah knows, I like to do my homework. Your law firms' websites—even your old one, Sarah—had very nice photos of both of you. So I knew who I might be looking for. Which means that as of last night, I knew who you two were, but you didn't know me. So you didn't realize I was on your flight."

Sarah's heart thudded in her chest. Her skin went cold. Every nerve in her body felt on high alert. Had she seen him last night? He was right, she wouldn't have known what he looked like—she didn't even know who he was until he showed up at the deposition that morning. He could have been sitting right next to them in the airport, and she might not have noticed.

Had he overheard something? Seen something? She remembered letting her guard down when she saw that Marcela wasn't there. For all she knew, Wendy the replacement court reporter had been on the flight as well, but Sarah had been too wrapped up in Joe to notice.

She wanted so badly to look over at Joe then, to see his reaction. But she forced herself to keep her eyes on Sollers instead. She needed to play this whole situation as coolly as possible.

"I thought it was interesting that you both graduated from UCLA Law the same year," Ryan went on. "I wondered if you two knew each other back then. You did, didn't you?" he asked Sarah.

She didn't say a word, but sat frozen, watchful.

"Doesn't matter," Ryan said. "That part's history. I'm more interested in the present."

He pulled out his phone. "I didn't realize there'd be anything to see," he said, swiping his finger across the screen, "but that's the nice thing about modern technology—you always have a camera with you."

Now Sarah did lock eyes with Joe. He subtly shook his head, as if warning her not to say anything. She already had the same instinct.

"Nothing too incriminating at first," Ryan said, looking through his pictures. "Just a few smiles, some laughter—the same sort of thing someone would have seen at our lunch today, Sarah. Ah, but then," he said, smiling, "we get to the rental car counter."

Sarah tried to swallow, but there was no moisture left in her mouth. Her eyes burned into Joe's.

"A nice photo here," Ryan said, still not showing any of them to either Sarah or Joe. "The two of you standing so close. But I can see how someone might still interpret that as two old law school friends catching up. So we'll let that go. Even this one, Joe, where you have your hand so nicely against her back as the two of you head for the garage. Very nice. But maybe you were just being a gentleman—I can understand that."

Sarah thought of Sollers making that same gesture as the two of them walked to their table in the restaurant. She hadn't mistaken it for the touch of a gentleman.

Ryan swept his finger across the screen again, then sat back with a satisfied grin. "And then...oh, yes, these really are the best ones. The lighting in the garage wasn't great, but still…" He looked up at Sarah and Joe. "You know, you two really should be more careful."

Sarah's skin felt cold and sweaty. Her heart pelted against her chest. She didn't dare look at Joe now, for fear that the panic would show in her eyes.

"This is all very interesting," Joe said calmly, "but what do you want?"

"Wait," Ryan answered, holding up a finger, "there's more. I thought I should at least introduce myself to you last night, Sarah, since we were both defending this case, so I tried to call your room several times. All the way up until midnight, in fact, but the desk clerk said you still hadn't checked in. Then I tried again this morning, but still, no sign of you."

She had been so *stupid*, Sarah realized. So *reckless*. Thinking that just because Joe was leaving the case soon— just because they had settled things between the two of them —there was no danger anymore. Forgetting that there might be other eyes watching them. Other people anxious to make the most of their misdeeds.

"What do you want?" Joe asked again.

"Well, you can see my dilemma," Sollers answered, giving them both a benevolent smile. "I'm in a very difficult position."

"How so?" Joe asked, his voice still calm—calmer, Sarah knew, than she could have possibly managed at that moment.

"Obviously I'm an officer of the court, just like you two," Sollers said. "I have an ethical obligation to report any violations to the Bar. I imagine if they decided to investigate, they'd ask for all sorts of information—maybe e-mails between the two of you, texts—nothing in this world is secret anymore, boys and girls."

It was his smugness, Sarah thought, his assurance, that finally made her blood grow hot again until she could feel the pressure rise inside her chest. She understood now exactly what that lunch had been about: Ryan was someone who liked to play with his food. He had been toying with her, drawing out the pleasure of the hunt before finally going in for the kill.

Sarah found her voice again. "So, Ryan, how did you see this playing out today? I'm sure you had a plan."

"Oh, I did," he agreed. "But there are so many variables."

"Such as?" she asked.

"Sarah, don't say anything more," Joe warned.

But she felt calm now, clearer. And she needed information. She wouldn't allow herself to feel trapped and at this man's mercy. She needed to hear from him what he thought he stood to gain.

"It's all right," she told Joe. "Ryan and I understand each other, don't we?"

"I think maybe we do," he said cheerfully, and it took everything she had not to leap across the table and punch that smug smile from his face.

"So," she said, keeping her voice low and deliberately slow to hold her pulse in check. "Tell me what your scenario looked like: you'd spring this trap on us, and then...what? One of us would quit?"

"'Trap' is too strong," Sollers said. "Remember, I didn't force you to do anything. I was just in the happy position of observer. But yes, quitting would be one solution—and certainly an honorable way for the gentleman to handle it." He turned to Joe. "Or what do you think?"

"I think you're a pr—"

"It doesn't matter," Sarah said, cutting him off. She was in full-on lawyer mode now, heading deeper into the negotiation. She had gone past it feeling personal anymore. "So, Ryan, what are your terms?"

Because she felt certain he had them.

Ryan shrugged. "I keep this whole tale to myself—action photos included—and you two figure out between you who goes. It doesn't matter to me, although Sarah, you provide much better scenery."

Sarah could see Joe's jaw tighten. But she knew him well enough to know he wouldn't do anything stupid.

"What's in it for you?" Sarah asked, although she already knew. She just wanted to hear him confirm it.

"Never say no when another lawyer asks you for a favor," he had told her at lunch. *"There'll always come a time when they have to pay you back."*

That was exactly his game, Sarah thought. Make both of them owe him. Then at some point during the case, when Sollers saw the greatest advantage to himself, collect on it.

"What's in it for me?" Ryan repeated. "Oh, I don't know. I'm sure we can figure something out. We're all smart, civilized people."

Sarah nodded. Then she pushed back her chair and stood. "Okay. I think we're done here." She slipped her laptop back into its bag and turned to retrieve her luggage from the corner of the room.

Just one more piece of evidence, she suddenly realized, that she'd spent the night somewhere other than at that hotel. If she had checked in the night before, she probably would have left her luggage in the room. Instead she walked into the deposition first thing that morning wheeling her bag.

"Maybe I'll see you tonight," Sollers said to her. "I think we're both registered at the same hotel—that is, if you check in this time. We can talk about it more over dinner. I'll even let you buy."

Sarah didn't answer. Instead she headed for the door.

Joe remained in his seat.

"Burke?" she said, hoping to shake him loose. She didn't know what he might say or do, but she doubted it would help. And it might make matters worse, although at that moment she couldn't imagine how.

What she really needed was to talk to him privately, to process everything that had just happened. But Joe didn't budge.

So Sarah kept on going. Out of the room, out of the hotel, into a taxi, and bound for the airport.

It would catch up to her, she knew. The knowledge that what had just happened in there, in the space of however many minutes, had irrevocably changed her life. Because Sollers was right: it wasn't his fault. He hadn't tricked them or trapped them. Sarah and Joe had done this to themselves, gotten sloppy and careless, had given an outsider the chance to destroy their careers.

Would she go to prison for it? No. What they'd done wasn't criminal—they hadn't swindled anyone, laundered money, violated any federal laws the way the partners in both Joe's and Sarah's firms had.

But an ethical violation like this could get them both disbarred. At a minimum, suspended. And Sarah couldn't afford a suspension any more than she could afford quitting this case or losing the job Calvin had only recently offered her.

Sarah leaned forward in the cab and dropped her head into her hands. What a complete and utter mess. And she had no one to blame but herself.

She would have to figure out a way to dig out of it, but she knew it wouldn't be easy—no part of it would be easy. And she knew Joe wouldn't agree with what she was already thinking she had to do. But she couldn't worry about that. He had his own career to think of, and she had hers.

I'm with you, Joe.

That was before, Sarah thought, when it was Joe alone who seemed in danger of going down with the ship.

Now it was Sarah's turn—again—but this time she knew she had a choice. She could stay on deck and wait for the water to lap up over her feet, or she could take the leap now, plunging into the roiling seas.

37

Sarah found an earlier flight, and she took it. She wanted to get away from Portland as soon as possible. She had no idea what Joe was thinking or doing, but she knew they would find each other eventually.

She needed time on her own first.

She checked into her hotel, found her room, and immediately undressed and stepped into a hot shower. She needed to wash the day away. Stand there in the steam and accept the emotional earthquake she had been holding off for the last several hours.

Sarah tried not to allow herself to cry too often. It never felt as cleansing as people said it would. In fact, it made her feel weaker, more vulnerable, more open to attack. It had nothing to do with anyone seeing her that way. It had everything to do with feeling herself lose control.

When Joe left her that December six years ago, when he wouldn't return her phone calls or talk to her about what had happened with his mother, when she watched him deliberately take up with woman after woman without any explanation of what went wrong, Sarah fell apart in a way she never had in her entire life.

She cried then—plenty. She felt raw, turned inside out, unable to think in logical, rational ways anymore about what she should do next, how she should behave, whether she should study for this class or that one, whether she should confront Joe or leave him alone and keep hoping one day he would explain.

If she had clung to that last hope, she knew now she would have waited a long time. In fact, she might never have learned the truth if she never had this case against Joe. She would have gone on with her life just as before, hating him, resenting him, wishing she had never fallen in love with him in the first place. It left a wound that never quite healed. And made her never want to put herself in that position again.

So there had been other lovers after him, but not love. She always stopped herself short. And the men she was with didn't seem to mind. Maybe, Sarah thought now, it was because she chose them so carefully: men just like Ryan Sollers, with a certain charm and confidence, but whose primary interests lay in advancing their own careers. Men who wouldn't hesitate to take care of themselves first in any situation, and Sarah second, if it was convenient.

Sarah always told herself she felt the same way. She had worked hard all her life to get where she was, and even after April 6 she knew she would keep fighting hard to keep it. Her law degree wasn't just a piece of paper in a frame. It meant as much to her as the first paycheck she ever earned as a secretary at the insurance agency. As much as the first commission she earned as the youngest insurance agent in her region. Her mother and father had brought her up to believe that her own efforts could take her far. And Sarah still believed that.

But she also knew she had to take responsibility for her own mistakes. No matter how much better it would feel to blame them on someone else.

And who were the contenders for blame here, anyway? she thought. Not Joe. She was glad he'd made a project out of her, glad he came up with a strategy of treating her well and trying to win her back. She didn't regret a single aspect of their short time together, except maybe how long it had taken them both to find each other again.

Ryan Sollers? Maybe she could blame him for taking such obvious pleasure in laying out every new piece of evidence against them in that slow, methodical style. But another part of her—the lawyer part—had to admire how he'd gone about it. She had to make sure the team at Mickey's office understood that Chapman's replacement was not to be underestimated.

But not yet. There was a time for work, and a time for grieving. And Sarah felt she had earned herself a few minutes of grief. She turned her face into the water and let the hot tears stream down her cheeks.

Nobody to blame but yourself. Nobody to blame but yourself. The refrain continued ping-ponging in her brain until finally she had to accept that her few moments of peaceful self-pity were over.

It had been the same after April 6. She wanted to hide in a hole. Live in the darkness, never come out again.

But Angie had badgered her so hard, in texts and phone messages, Sarah finally dragged herself back for a workout just to make the relentless woman leave her alone.

She had gone in that morning sullen and weak and broken, and emerged an hour and a half later—after running and lifting and kicking and sweating—a different person. One who had reclaimed her clear, logical mind.

No, she'd acknowledged back then, none of what happened was fair. She hadn't done anything to bring it on herself. But it didn't change the fact that this was her life now, reality wasn't going away, and so she had better pull herself up and figure out what to do.

And that was why, Sarah realized now as she climbed out of the shower and toweled off, *Nobody to blame but yourself* was actually a very powerful statement. It meant that she had created the situation herself, and now she could find some way to manage it herself, too. Maybe not fix it—not entirely—but at least do something besides curling up in a little ball and letting other people decide her fate.

She had already been considering her next move ever since she left the conference room that afternoon. But now she knew for certain.

Sarah pulled on a robe, set up her laptop on the desk, and prepared to do what had to be done.

Where are you? the text from Joe asked.

My hotel.

Want me to come get you?

Yes.

She thought about what Sollers had said about the Bar wanting to see any texts or e-mails between Sarah and Joe. *Hardly anything is secret anymore, boys and girls.* But she didn't think a few more would matter. The damage was already done.

Joe texted her again from the parking lot. Sarah wondered if she would see Sollers on her way through the lobby, but she really didn't care anymore. She found Joe's car, opened the door and slid onto the seat, then leaned over and cupped her hand behind his neck and gave him a long, lingering kiss.

Joe seemed surprised.

"You're all right?" he asked once she let him go.

"I'm fine," Sarah said. "Except I'm starving. Come on, let's find something to eat."

He still wore his suit, whereas Sarah had changed into the jersey pants and hoodie she wore to the airport the night before. She had also straightened her hair again after the shower, treating the process like a meditation as she reflected on the e-mail she composed.

Her finger had hesitated just a little too long, she thought, before finally hitting Send. But once the message was gone, she could relax. And wait for the storm to brew.

"So," Joe said as he drove away from the hotel, "almost makes you miss Paul, doesn't it?"

"Let's not talk about it yet," Sarah said. "I want to have a nice dinner with you. We can talk later."

She reached out for his hand, and he lifted hers to his lips and kissed it. "I just want you to know it's going to be all right," Joe said.

"I know. But feed me first."

They found a decent-looking Italian restaurant not far from the hotel. As the two of them walked to the entrance, their hands intertwined, Sarah said, "I think this might count as a date."

Joe paused to take her into his arms. He kissed her with a kind of possessiveness no one would mistake as appropriate for a first date. Sarah laughed when he let her go. "Pace yourself," she said.

"Why are you in such a good mood?" he asked.

"Because you're here, and I'm with you, and we're actually out in public together for once."

"We were in public on your birthday," Joe pointed out.

"Not for very long."

The hostess seated them at a table small enough that their knees touched underneath. Joe kept a hold on Sarah's hand. It was sweet, she thought, just being out with him like this. And exactly the kind of thing she needed after the rough day they'd had.

Although the way he was stroking his thumb across her knuckles reminded her that being alone with him in his hotel room, eating room service or takeout, also would have had its merits. Sarah's eyes met his, and from the subtle way his mouth curved up, she could tell he'd been thinking the same thing.

"You're buying me dinner first, Burke."

His chuckle was low and suggestive. "Who said I wasn't?"

She reached over and stroked the dark stubble on his

cheek. "You look tired." He covered her hand with his and brought her palm to her lips. Sarah smiled at the seductive feel of his kiss against her sensitive flesh.

Hardly anything is secret, boys and girls. She had quick flash of how they might look if someone took a picture of them just then. But she managed to shake it off. *It doesn't matter,* she reminded herself. *It's over.*

When the food arrived, Sarah attacked hers like a wrestler. She remembered feeling this hungry after her first week of training with Angie. Her body seemed to realize that Sarah was about to put more and more demands on it, and for the next several weeks her stomach felt like a bottomless pit. She could eat every two to three hours without ever feeling full.

Maybe her body understood what was happening now, Sarah thought. It knew it needed its strength because it was about to go to war.

"You about done?" Sarah asked once she'd eaten every morsel of her spaghetti in marinara.

Joe leaned back and surveyed what was left on his plate. "Are you making me a better offer?"

"Only one way to find out," Sarah said.

As they walked out to his car, Joe's arm around her waist, Sarah couldn't help wondering how long their happy, romantic mood would last. She guessed it would evaporate within the next half hour. But she didn't regret what she had done. Wished she didn't have to do it, yes. But regret how she'd handled it, no.

She just hoped that Joe would see it that way.

38

It was different this time when Joe opened the door to his room. Instead of the two of them rushing into each other's arms, Sarah moved to the bed alone. She kicked off her shoes, then pulled out the pillows from beneath the bedspread and fluffed them against the headboard. She propped herself up on one of them and waited while Joe removed his own shoes, his coat and tie, then joined her on the bed.

Sarah draped her closest leg over Joe's. "Okay, go," she told him. "Don't leave anything out."

"I let him gloat for a while," Joe said. "That seemed important. He wanted to make sure I understood how clever he was."

"Good," Sarah said. Letting an opponent bask in some momentary triumph was always a good foundation for then chipping away at his victory.

"He wanted information from me," Joe continued. "How

long it had been going on, whether I thought Chapman suspected, but you know me."

"You didn't say a thing."

"Nope. Then after a while, once he'd talked enough, I finally told him he'd convinced me—I'd have to leave the case."

Sarah had been expecting that. It made strategic sense.

"I told him it might take me a day or two to find a replacement," Joe said, "but that I'd be gone sometime this week."

"So Felix shows up day after tomorrow," Sarah said, "you're gone, and Sollers thinks he won."

"Yep."

"Then you quit the firm at the same time and hope you're out of there before the indictments get served."

"That's the plan," Joe said.

Sarah nodded. "Good. I think you handled it right." And she meant it. He'd done the right thing—for him.

But now came the hard part.

"I quit, too."

Joe rounded on her. "You what?"

"I sent an e-mail to Calvin. I told him I have to leave the case."

"Why?" Joe roared. "Sarah, are you crazy? Why would you do that? Why didn't you at least wait to talk to me?"

"Because I knew you'd try to talk me out of it."

"Damn right I would have!" Joe ran a hand over his tired face. "Sarah, you didn't have to do that. All it takes is for one of us to quit—you know that. Sollers got what he wanted. So why would you throw away your job, too?"

"Because it's already over," Sarah said. "You understand that guy as well as I do. He'd always keep this hanging over my head—*our little secret.* Then one day he'd use it against me when he thought he could get some advantage in the case."

She looked him intensely in the eyes, willing him to understand. "Joe, I actually have a viable defense in this case. Something I came up with that nobody else has. Do you think I'm going to jeopardize that for the client just so I can hide something about my personal life?"

Joe groaned. "There has to be some other solution."

"There isn't," Sarah said. "Believe me, I thought it through for hours and hours this afternoon. But I kept coming back to the same thing: I'm not going to be one of those people who pretends the law doesn't apply to me. Look what happened to the partners in our firm—is that the kind of lawyers we want to be?"

"This is a hell of a lot different, Sarah, and you know it."

"You're right, it is different. But the fact is, Joe, we got caught. We've been doing something that is technically, ethically wrong, and now there's a price to pay for that. And I'm willing to pay it."

"Tell me how this is different from what I did after my mother died," Joe said.

"What?" The comparison made no sense.

"Me punishing myself for not being there. And look how I did it—by pushing you away. Do you think that was smart?"

"No," she said carefully, "I think it was dumbest thing you've ever done in your life. But I'm not punishing myself

335

by pushing you away. I want to pull you toward me, Joe. A night like tonight? I want that all the time. No more of this sneaking around, waiting for someone like Ryan Sollers to snap a few pictures of us and hold them over our heads. I want what we had before. I want a redo. I think I'm entitled."

Joe shook his head, but she could see a light glimmering somewhere in his eyes. She was getting through to him—she knew it.

"Do you remember that Negotiation class I took?"

Now it was Joe's turn to seem confused. "Yes, but what—"

"It has everything to do with this," she answered before he could finish. "The professor—that guy Shefter—told us the most important thing in any negotiation is to understand our bottom line. Then to pile on a whole basket of terms we don't actually care about, so we can start giving them away, one by one.

"So I asked myself that this afternoon," Sarah continued. "What is my bottom line? What can I absolutely not give away? And I came up with two things."

She shifted position now, kneeling on either side of his thighs. "One of them is the interests of my client—I'm never going to sacrifice that. And the other one is you, Joe. You have to know that now."

He shook his head. "Henley..."

"That's right," Sarah said. "It is Henley to you. Because right now I'm thinking like your opponent. But in a few minutes, I'm going to start acting like your lover again, so if you have anything else of a lawyer-like nature to say to me, you'd better say it right now."

"So it's already done," Joe said. "You've already sent the e-mail, there's no room for interpretation."

"No. I think the phrase, 'have to remove myself from this case due to a personal conflict of interest' is going to be pretty clear once Calvin discusses it with Mickey."

"You're sure about this," Joe said.

"I'm sure this is how it is," Sarah answered, "and now we'll just have to see what happens."

"I had a plan, you know," Joe said.

"I'm sure you did." She shifted one knee, then another, crawling higher up toward his hips. "Anything else, Burke?"

"I think you're beautiful. And smart. And sexy as hell. And I agree you're entitled to a redo. But Sarah, if we're in this together, then we're in this together. I still wish you'd talked to me about it first."

"I couldn't," Sarah said. "It wasn't in my client's interests. And I was still their attorney as of this evening, which meant it wasn't any of your business what I did. Now that's all I'm saying about it for the rest of the night. Off-duty. Do you want me or not?"

Joe moved so quickly it shocked the breath from her lungs. He flipped her over onto her back and had her beneath him in a second, his knees pinning her hips instead.

"So I'm part of your bottom line?" he asked.

"Yes."

"That could be the nicest thing you've ever said to me."

"Then I must be a very cold woman."

"Far from it," Joe said, then he set about to prove it.

. . .

JOE DROPPED her back at her hotel around five o'clock in the morning. He grumbled about the two of them having to leave his warm bed, but Sarah convinced him fairly quickly that she was already back to business mode and it might be dangerous to stand in her way.

He parked at side of the hotel closest to her room, and left the car idling while he gave her a proper kiss.

"You'll be all right today?"

Sarah nodded. Already her stomach was twisting at the thought of what messages awaited her. She had deliberately left her phone off the night before. But now it was time to hear everyone's reactions to the e-mail she'd sent out.

"Are you flying home tonight?" Joe asked.

"I don't know yet." She kissed him one more time, then got out and prepared to go to work.

Back in her room, she booted up her laptop and turned on her phone.

Mickey had called her four times.

"You'd better be joking, Sarah."

"Sarah, call me back right away."

"Where are you—with him? Call me back, damn it."

"Do you understand I did you a favor? *How do you think this makes me look? You can't keep your legs together for five min—"*

She stopped listening after that.

There was a series of e-mails from the associates on her team. Questions about what was going on, what they were supposed to do now, what the status of the case was, who should take over which of her assignments...

A short e-mail from Calvin stating simply, *"I'll expect you to meet with me immediately upon your return. Please notify my secretary of the time."*

Sarah felt tired already. She hadn't gotten much sleep the night before, but she was used to that by now. What she needed, she decided, was coffee—and strong, not just what she could brew up on the hotel coffee maker.

So she donned her warmest layers, including the hat and gloves she bought with Joe what seemed like months ago instead of weeks, and took off in the pre-dawn for the two-block walk to a Starbucks. She wanted to feel the cold air on her face and the long stretch of her limbs on a brisk walk as much as she wanted the caffeine.

The first few sips of the dark roast hit her like a mallet and alerted her mind that it had better shift into a higher gear for what Sarah expected of it that day. She walked back, sipping along the way, warming her hands on the cup, and by the time she returned to her room felt better ready to face the onslaught.

She had learned over the years not to give people options or to ask for permission when she'd already made up her mind. Not to say, "Would it be okay...?" when what she really meant was, "I'm doing X." Letting people think they still had a chance to change her mind only led to fruitless, frustrating conversations. It was one of the reasons she hadn't consulted Joe before sending out her e-mail. She had already decided it was the right thing to do.

So instead of writing back to her team, "Would one of you be able to take over for me immediately, and fly to Spokane tonight for tomorrow's deposition?" she wrote, *"One of you needs to fly to Spokane tonight. Please make this arrangement among yourselves and book the plane ticket immedi-ately. I will not be attending Wednesday's deposition."*

Sarah sat back and looked at the e-mail before sending it off. She knew she had to be very careful with her words from now on. Every one of them would be scrutinized by someone—maybe even by the ethics committee of the Bar at some point. She was willing to face the consequences of her behavior, but she saw no reason to make her situation worse.

With that in mind, she deleted the last line, and changed it to, *"Let me know as soon as possible who will be attending Wednesday's deposition."* Joe had had the right attitude about not leaving the case or his firm until his colleague Felix could take over. Sarah couldn't abandon the client, no matter what. She would have to wait until she knew for certain some other lawyer had taken her place.

She pressed Send, then checked the clock. The morning was already flying. She still needed to eat, shower, and dress for the morning's deposition.

A text popped onto her phone.

Are you there?

It looked like Mickey was awake.

Sarah thought about what she might say: *Thanks for everything; thanks for getting me that opportunity; I'm sorry it didn't work out; I'm sorry.*

A text wasn't going to do it. A phone call probably wouldn't, either.

Sarah left the phone on the desk and went to take a shower.

. . .

"Good morning." Ryan Sollers seemed especially cheerful. "So nice to see you today, Sarah."

"Oh, you, too, Ryan," Sarah said just as cheerfully. She greeted the court reporter more sincerely, then sat and unpacked her laptop.

"Sleep all right?" Ryan asked.

"It's so nice of you to be concerned," Sarah said.

Ryan grinned. He seemed to think there was no reason to hide how much he was enjoying himself.

Joe entered a few minutes later with a woman around Sarah's mother's age. She had short wiry hair that looked like it had never met a brush.

While Ryan began his seduction—"Can I get you anything, Ms. O'Connor? Coffee? Water? Are you comfortable? How's the temperature in here?"—Sarah refreshed her e-mail. There were already several from the associates.

The one named Bingham—the one Calvin had already mentioned would take over for Sarah if and when there were more depositions in the new year—had arranged a flight to Spokane that would arrive that night.

So Sarah was off the hook.

Or, put another way, she thought, she was now officially out of work.

She only half-listened while Sollers quizzed Joe's client about every aspect of her hair routine. About every single flammable item near where she set her hair iron down. One by one, methodically going through the instruction manual, all while pretending to have a pleasant conversation.

Sarah had harder things to think about. She had been

putting it off until just this moment, when the final piece was in place, but now she knew she had face the next step:

She was about to be poor again.

She had negotiated a good salary with Calvin. And had been frugal with it, not spending wildly just because she had money again, but instead dutifully paying down her debts.

But now she would be back to the bare bones again. Trying to budget for her rent, car expenses, groceries, utilities. Forget any of the *Flourish* like workouts with Angie or sending money to her parents. Sarah would have to draw in tightly now, defend her borders, and not let a single cent out of her fortress unless it was absolutely necessary and she could justify it.

She mentally reviewed her bank accounts. How much did she still have in savings? She had depleted the fund substantially over the six months she was out of work, and had only put back a little in these past two months. How much longer would it last? And if the money ran out before she found another job—then what?

If she could find another job. What were the chances now? It wasn't as if Calvin would send her off with a glowing letter of recommendation...

"Ms. Henley?"

Sarah didn't realize how far she'd drifted away until she heard Joe say her name. "Do you have any questions?" he asked.

She startled back into action. Smiled at Joe's client, went through the motions of asking her a few handfuls of questions.

Once again, they were finished much earlier than if

Chapman had been running the deposition. Sarah had at least three hours before she had to return for the one in the afternoon.

She repacked her laptop, then left the room without saying anything to anyone. She needed to make lists. Plan. Think through how she was going to live now, from the moment her plane touched down at LAX tonight.

Change her flight, too—she needed to do that. She wouldn't be going on to Spokane tonight. A whole list of actions she could tick off one by one.

She unlocked the door to her room and stood just inside for a few moments, wondering which task she should tackle first. But a lethargy had already begun seeping into her bones, and the tiredness overwhelmed her.

Sarah pulled back the covers on the bed, pried off her shoes, then slipped between the sheets still wearing her expensive wool suit. It had been easy to be brave and principled last night when she explained all her motives to Joe. But now that she was alone again, she had to wonder whether she had done the right thing—for her.

"I'm not going to be one of those people who pretends the law doesn't apply to me," she'd told Joe. *"Look what happened to the partners in our firm—is that the kind of lawyers we want to be?"*

She knew what kind of lawyer she wanted to be—what she'd wanted from the moment she ever decided to become a lawyer in the first place. Back then she had an image of her future self wearing fancy clothes just like these, feeling strong and smart and capable, feeling confident and in charge of her life, unafraid and in total control.

And she had experienced moments just like that, Sarah

thought—enough that the young dreamer inside her felt proud of all she had been able to accomplish.

But that young woman hadn't factored in Joe Burke. Hadn't factored in love. Hadn't realized that at some point Sarah might have to make a choice between her personal life and her professional one.

Well, now she'd made the choice. And her dream of being a happy, successful lawyer might have disappeared in the bargain.

Sarah indulged in that melodramatic, self-pitying thought for one whole, luxurious minute before groaning and making herself sit up. She got out of the bed and went to her laptop case to retrieve a legal pad from the side. Then she sat back against the pillows, pulled the sheets over her cold legs, and began to make her list.

Change plane reservation.

Schedule meeting with Calvin.

Prepare final report and case analysis.

Sarah heard the dings of two text messages in quick succession.

The first was from Mickey:

I assume you warned him?

The second from Joe:

It's happened.

39

Sarah quickly checked one of the law blogs she always read. There it was, the featured story:

AL MILTON, KENNETH FEINBERG, OTHERS INDICTED

The United States Attorney's Office for the Central District of California announced this morning the indictments of Albert Milton, Kenneth Feinberg, and other lawyers within the Milton Feinberg law firm for charges including racketeering, mail fraud, and bribery, stemming from alleged illegal payoffs to clients. Attorneys for Mr. Milton and Mr. Feinberg deny the charges, but indicate their clients will cooperate with authorities by surrendering to law enforcement within the next 24 hours.

The indictments follow several months of investigation...

Sarah quickly texted Joe her room number. Within minutes there was a knock on her door.

He strode into the room, a curse on his lips.

"How bad is it?" Sarah asked.

"Bad. A buddy of mine from the firm called, said it's World War III over there, everybody pointing fingers, people cleaning out their desks, calling clients, trying to take as much business with them as they can before the whole place folds."

"What are they saying about you?" Sarah asked.

"As far as anyone knows, I'm off here in the wild blue yonder and don't know anything. Luke—that's who called—asked me if I wanted him to box up my desk, too, and send me a list of all my clients' phone numbers so I can start siphoning off the business."

"Joe...maybe that isn't so stupid. Have you thought about it?"

"Taking clients with me?" Joe sat down hard in the upholstered chair in her room and ran a hand over his short hair. "I told you, I already transferred my cases over to other lawyers. This is the only one I've kept."

"Well?" Sarah pressed. "I've seen you with your plaintiffs. I'm sure a lot of them would rather go with you than have to find someone else and start all over."

"Maybe," Joe said. "But do you know how much it costs to run a class action suit?"

Sarah shook her head.

"It's expensive as hell, and the firm has to front all the costs—expert witnesses, travel expense, all of it. I have money, but not like that. And it takes more than one lawyer to work it. Maybe if I joined another firm I could convince some of the plaintiffs to come with me there—"

"Well, wouldn't that make you more attractive as a hire?"

Sarah asked. "Tell some other firm you can bring, I don't know, thirty or forty plaintiffs with you? How many could you get?"

"I don't know, Sarah." He gave her a tense, tired look. "I thought I was prepared for this, but from what Luke was saying, the firm is going to split apart much faster than I guessed."

"Well, maybe that's good," Sarah said. "If everyone is scrambling to get out of there, you'll look like you're just one more of them. The other firms in town are going to be watching for people like you they can snatch up, don't you think?"

"Is that how it worked with your firm?" Joe asked with just a hint of sarcasm.

"Not exactly," Sarah admitted. She wasn't the only attorney from her firm who had to wait several months before finding a job. "So what are you going to do?"

"Go back tonight," Joe said, "get into the office if no one has changed the locks yet—"

"I hadn't thought of that." Once she left her office on April 6, she never tried to return.

"Yeah, well somebody probably will," Joe said. "But assuming I can get in, I'll clear out all my stuff, then hole up for a while and figure out the next step."

"I'm going home tonight, too," Sarah said. "They found my replacement."

"You might want to tell whoever it is to hold off," Joe said. "I talked to Felix, and I doubt he's coming up here—he doesn't even know if he has a job anymore."

"But *you're* not—"

"No, I'm not staying on the case," Joe said, reading her mind. "No matter what. I can't—not after yesterday. But I think I should ask Sollers to postpone any more depos until we sort out who the lawyers on this case are anymore."

"My guy's going to be getting on a plane soon," Sarah told him.

"I think you'd better call him."

SARAH DIALED the law firm and asked for Bingham.

But someone else picked up his line.

"Sarah? What the hell are you doing up there?"

Mickey, Sarah mouthed to Joe.

"I need to get a message to Bingham," she said. "Tell him we're going to postpone any more depositions—"

"No one's taking orders from you anymore," Mickey interrupted. "Do you not get that you're fired? Calvin tore my head off this morning—wanted to know how much I knew about you before I recommended you, what I thought was going on. I stuck my neck out for you, Sarah. And this is how you repay me?"

"I'm sorry," Sarah said, and she meant it.

"Tell your boyfriend he's finished, too," Mickey said. "His law firm is officially in the toilet. That place looks like it's been hit by looters. Couldn't happen to a nicer guy, as far as I'm concerned."

She didn't know if he meant Al Milton, or Joe. Probably Joe, she guessed.

"Mickey, I have to go. We still have one more deposition."

"For who, Sarah?" He laughed grimly. "Do you not get it?

You're *gone.* Finished. You don't represent Mason anymore. Stop playing lawyer and go ball your boyfriend. The two of you will never work in this town again."

Mickey hung up the phone.

Sarah stood where she was for a moment, trying to steady her nerves. She could deal with confrontation, but fury like Mickey's required an advanced level of self-control.

Joe was still studying her face. "What did he say?"

Sarah attempted a smile. "They love us in L.A."

"YOU'RE NOT HAVING A VERY good week, are you, Joe?" Sollers said.

Sarah would have gladly paid for the privilege of ripping the grin right off his perfect beach-boy face.

But Joe was calm, as usual. "On the record," he told the court reporter. "Due to circumstances involving my law firm, there is currently a question about who will be working on this case in the future. I ask counsel for both defendants to stipulate to a postponement of any further discovery."

"Not all discovery," Sarah said. Mickey might be right about her not representing Mason anymore, but she still had to protect the company as well as she could. "Mason Manufacturing reserves the right to continue any discovery as it sees fit. We're only agreeing to postpone depositions of the plaintiffs."

Ryan raised his eyebrows as he looked from Sarah to Joe, as if he were watching some sort of lovers' spat. But Sarah wasn't angry, just firm. She wanted to make sure Calvin and the rest of the team could still request whatever documents they needed to prove her theory about the counterfeit parts.

"Ryan?" Joe asked, waiting for Sollers to agree to the postponement on the record.

"What about this afternoon's depo?" Sollers asked.

"I'd like to postpone that, too," Sarah said before Joe could answer. She knew his client was already waiting outside, but she also knew she shouldn't be the one taking the deposition anymore.

Sollers shrugged. "So stipulated. All the currently-scheduled depositions are hereby postponed. Guess we can all pack up and go home. Off the record." He waited for Wendy to stop typing before adding, "Actually, this might be a lucky break for you after all, huh, Joe? You get to leave tonight and no one knows why. No one except a few of us, of course."

Sarah glanced at the court reporter. Wendy was clearly curious about Ryan's comment. Which was just what Sollers wanted, Sarah thought: to remind both Sarah and Joe that he held all the power and could expose them at any minute.

Further proof that she'd made the right decision.

"Sarah, I'm sorry I won't see you for a while," Sollers said. "I was looking forward to working with you."

"Oh, me, too, Ryan. It's a shame." She knew he would find out soon enough that she had been fired, but she felt no need to fill him in.

Besides, Sarah thought as she left the conference room, if the work she had already done in the case resulted in Mason Manufacturing being dismissed some time in the future, she would at least have the private satisfaction of knowing her fingerprints were all over that weapon. She would have beaten both Paul Chapman and Ryan Sollers in the most honorable way: by working harder and ultimately outsmarting them.

Now if only she could translate that private victory into some sort of career for herself in the future, Sarah thought. From what Mickey had said, it wasn't looking good.

For either her or for Joe.

40

Everybody loves a parade, Sarah thought, scrolling through the photos on the Web. Lawyers in their fancy suits, hands cuffed behind their backs, beefy law enforcement officers holding them by the elbows as they endured the gauntlet of media and sneering bystanders.

The head partners, Milton and Feinberg, had been first, but now there were more lawyers from the firm indicted every day, it seemed. More white-collar criminals for the perp walk. The news outlets loved it.

The optometrist, his family, and a whole collection of other professional plaintiffs had been arrested, too. Mickey was right: Mr. Fitzgerald of the U.S. Attorney's Office was giving himself a very large early Christmas present indeed.

"Anything new?" Joe asked, joining Sarah in her kitchen. His hair was still wet from the shower.

"Not really." She handed him a cup of coffee. He had brought his own brewer over when it became clear they both liked spending the night at her apartment more than his.

Joe set the coffee down and gathered Sarah into his arms.

"Mm, you smell good," she said.

"You, too. What time's your interview?"

"Nine."

Joe checked the clock. "Too bad."

Sarah smiled. It was so much nicer being unemployed with Joe around this time. Even though she knew either of them would have been happy to trade their current hours of leisure for the stress of a billable workweek again.

"I might have something later today," Joe said.

"Oh, yeah?"

He shrugged. "We'll see."

She'd gotten used to Joe's reluctance to talk about any of his prospects ahead of time. Maybe he was superstitious, Sarah thought. Or maybe he didn't want to get her hopes up.

It had only been two and a half weeks since their return. That wasn't much time, she reminded herself. Plus Christmas was just a few days away now, and then it was the end of the year, so people weren't really hiring...

She could make excuses all day. And sometimes she did. Anything to keep the panic at bay.

They hadn't really talked about money, and she didn't intend to yet. She had already set aside her rent payment for January, and she had enough, if she kept her expenses close to the bone, to last her through at least March. Probably.

She knew Joe wouldn't hesitate to pitch in. All she had to do was ask. Or maybe he might offer once the idea occurred to him. But Sarah still had hopes it wouldn't come to that.

She had never asked for help before, and she didn't intend to start now.

"I have to get dressed," she said, heading for the bedroom.

"Great. I'll come watch."

THE MORNING after her return from Seattle, Sarah had done as Calvin asked and made an appointment to see him.

He was brief and to the point.

"How much damage have you done?"

"In what way?" Sarah asked him. She could feel his tightly-controlled anger, but she had some of it herself. Mickey was in the room.

"He means how much did you give away while Burke was going down on you?"

Calvin shot him a glare. "Get out of here, Hughes. I'll talk to her myself."

Mickey got up with a smirk, as if he'd been expecting that. As if all he wanted was just to get a jab or two in, then he would happily walk away.

"See you, Sarah. Hope it's the last time."

Then he stalked out the door.

Sarah took a breath and tried to seem calm. She turned back to Calvin. "I never told him anything. I've always been very careful to protect the interests of our client."

"Except when you decided to fuck the other attorney." Calvin held up his hand before she could answer. "It's done. What I need to know is whether I have to tell Mason about this, or whether it gets to stay our dirty secret."

Sarah hated agreeing with the way he put it, but there was no use arguing. "I think it can stay our secret." Calvin might not believe her, but she knew she'd done absolutely nothing to harm their client's case.

Other than put herself in the position of having to resign. But she hoped the lengthy, detailed exit memo she sent Calvin and the associates gave them all enough information to see the defense through to the end.

"You might not want this," Sarah said, "but I'm still willing to consult on the case. For free."

"You're right," Calvin said. "I don't want that. And by the way, your last two weeks are for free. I'm not paying you for your little sexcapade."

Sarah nodded stiffly. She hadn't expected that, but there was nothing she could do. Or more accurately, nothing she would do. She understood the need to punish people and exact some revenge. She wouldn't be hypocritical about it now.

Calvin dismissed her with a flick of his hand. It was humiliating, especially since the last time she had been with him, he offered her such high praise—not to mention a job. But Sarah understood that all of this was the price she had to pay.

And she still thought she'd gotten the better side of the bargain.

When she returned home that afternoon, Joe was waiting for her, sitting on her couch wearing sweats and a T-shirt, working on his laptop. He looked up as she came in, then shifted over and held out an inviting arm. She plopped down next to him, laid her head on his shoulder, and let out a big sigh.

"So it went well," he guessed.

"Fantastic." Sarah filled him in on the details.

"He probably can't do that about your pay," Joe said.

"Yes, he can. He can do whatever he wants. It's over."

She kicked off her pumps and curled her legs up next to Joe. She wanted to change out of her suit into something more comfortable, but Joe's arm was too comfortable to leave.

Sarah glanced at the laptop open on the table next to the couch. "What are you working on?"

"Fitzgerald had some questions," Joe said. "Other people in the firm are turning already, and he wants to verify their stories."

Sarah kept forgetting that in the midst of their other troubles, Joe still had responsibilities as Fitzgerald's star witness.

"Does anyone know about you yet?"

"Seems so," Joe said. "There was some teaser about it on one of the law blogs—'Which insider blew the whistle?' They described me as a five-year associate on the partner track, who worked directly with Milton on the most recent case. I'd say that narrows the field."

"And then what?" Sarah asked.

"Then people either think I'm a hero or a trouble-maker. And since we both know no firm is completely clean, I'm guessing trouble-maker is what's going to stick. Not really expecting many job interviews once the news hits."

Sarah groaned, then snuggled deeper against him.

"But we're okay, right?" she asked.

He gave her a squeeze. "Yep."

"And we don't' regret any of it, right?"

"I don't," Joe said, "do you?"

Sarah angled her face toward him so she could press a kiss to his warm lips. "Just you and me against the world, Burke."

"Then I'd say our odds are good."

Sarah waited in the law firm lobby for her nine o'clock interview, taking in her surroundings. The office was nice, but not plush. The receptionist behind the counter was dressed professionally, not cheaply. That mattered to Sarah.

Whenever she went to another attorney's office for a negotiation, she always took note of the receptionist first. If it was a man, she assumed the lawyers in the firm were open-minded and flexible, and would be willing to make a deal that was advantageous to both sides.

If the receptionist was a woman, Sarah looked at her outfit. She knew it was probably a stereotype, but she always assumed if she could see too much cleavage, the attorneys in the firm didn't respect women. If they did, someone would have taken the employee aside long ago and given her the same kind of speech Sarah gave women at her previous firm.

"You might be the smartest person in the room," she told one new associate who had come into work for the second day in a row flashing a considerable amount of boob, "but if you dress like that, everyone's going to assume you're stupid. I know," she said before the blushing associate could answer, "it's not fair, it's not true, but I'm just telling you, based on my experience, that's how people are."

"But..." The young woman cleared her throat. Sarah worried she might cry. But instead the associate drew herself up as if ready to take Sarah on, and answered in a steady voice. "I like to dress this way. I think women can be both feminine and strong. I disagree that I won't be taken seriously."

"Okay," Sarah said cordially. "I just wanted to give you the benefit of my experience. Good luck."

It took a full month before the young woman appeared in her office again one day and closed the door behind her.

"Okay," she said, slumping into the chair on the other side of Sarah's desk. "I think you're right."

"What happened?"

The associate grimaced and rolled her eyes. "Judge Walters."

"Oh," Sarah said, understanding everything. "Right."

The associate folded her arms across her still overexposed chest. "He called me back in chambers this morning after my hearing."

"And said..." Sarah prompted.

The associate looked behind her to make sure the door was really closed. Then she repeated a line Sarah had heard before. "'I can't wait to get into your pants.'"

"Yep. Old Walters."

The associate shook her head in disgust. "This was *after* he ruled against me, you understand."

"Of course," Sarah said. "He thinks you're stupid. He

thinks I am, too," she hastened to say. "All women. But you know what I always tell myself when I'm in his courtroom? 'At least the creep doesn't get to look at my breasts while he's thinking that.'"

The associate nodded. "Got it." She stood up to go.

"Sorry," Sarah said. "I agree with you: women can be both sexy and smart."

"I think I said 'feminine and strong.'"

"Those, too."

"Sorry if I was rude before," the young woman said.

"You weren't, and it's fine," Sarah answered. "Always happy to help a colleague."

And after that, the associate started dressing almost exactly like Sarah. Showing a little leg, fine. Cleavage, no.

"Miss Henley?" the receptionist said. "I'll show you back now."

She stood up from the desk, and Sarah could see more of her outfit: skirt barely covering the booty. Breasts spilling out of her low-cut top.

"How long have you worked here?" Sarah asked conversationally.

"Little over a year," the receptionist answered.

Sarah could already tell the interviewers weren't going to like her.

"I've never seen you in these before," Joe said, holding up a pair of modest-looking cotton underwear. "Sexy."

Sarah grabbed them from him and added them to her suitcase. "They're part of my special 'going home' collection."

"What else do you have in there?" he asked, craning his neck to see.

"Long dresses, pinafores—we're very *Little House on the Prairie*." She zipped up her bag before he could snoop anymore. All she really had in there were jeans and T-shirts and sweats.

She shifted the luggage from her bed onto the floor, then took its place. Joe stretched out next to her on the bed and wrapped her up in his arms.

"What time do you have to leave?" Sarah asked him.

"About an hour."

"Nate's picking you up at the airport?"

"If he feels like it," Joe said of his older brother. "No guarantee. Otherwise I'll take a cab."

Both of them would be spending the long weekend with their families. Sarah wished she could be with Joe on Christmas, but they would have to create their own holiday later. She had plans with her parents, and Joe needed to be with his father.

"He gets pretty down around Christmas," Joe told her, which was understandable. Sarah had noticed Joe's own quiet mood throughout the day on the anniversary of his mother's death. It must be hard for them all, she thought, seeing all the trappings of Christmas in the stores as early as Halloween some places, knowing it meant something completely different to them than to most people.

Sarah snuggled up closer and threaded her hand under Joe's shirt so she could feel the warm skin of his chest.

"Good idea," Joe said, tugging her own shirt up her torso.

"No," Sarah said, laughing and angling away. "I have to go."

"Come on, Red..."

"Seriously," she said, forcing herself off the bed. "I told them I'd be there this afternoon, and I still have to stop by Angie's."

Joe groaned. "Four days is a long time."

"We'll survive," Sarah said. "Think of me in my granny panties. That ought to cool you off."

"Not possible," Joe said.

As Sarah bent over to tie her sneakers, she cast a sideways glance at Burke.

"I'm going to have to tell my mother about us, you know."

Joe propped himself up on one elbow. "Why does that sound like a bad thing?"

"Because she doesn't like you," Sarah said. "She thinks you broke my heart. Actually, she knows you did, but she thinks it's still broken."

A look of—what? Concern? Guilt?—crossed Joe's face, and Sarah realized he didn't like her making light of what had happened.

She dove back onto the bed and pinned Joe beneath her.

"But you'd never do that again, right?" she said.

"Not in this lifetime." He tried to flip her over, but for once Sarah had better leverage.

"And you're very, very sorry you were such a stupid ass and ever left me, right?"

"You don't know how sorry," Joe said much more sincerely than her playfulness called for.

"So it's fine," Sarah said, giving him a deep and tempting kiss before finally releasing him and sliding back to the floor. "I'll explain it all to my mother, and one day she might forgive you. Eventually."

"Should I send her something for Christmas?"

"Chocolate is always nice," Sarah said. "And a happy daughter—what mother can resist that?"

"WHAT'S THIS?" Angie asked.

Sarah set out five tall containers on Angie's desk.

"Crack?" Angie said, her pupils dilating. "Oh, my God, you're the *best*."

Sarah was glad she thought so, since it was all the holiday bonus she could afford.

Angie glanced at the clock. "I don't have anyone for fifteen minutes. Mind if I heat some up?"

"Go ahead. But you know there's always a three-bowl minimum."

"One will have to do."

Angie poured into a microwave dish a huge portion of the vegetable soup she'd renamed Crack Soup. Sarah couldn't disagree with the title—the soup was positively addictive. She had perfected the recipe, figuring out how many vegetables she could throw in, in what combinations, and which spices to use. She had also gotten over thinking of parsley as just a garnish, since she added a whole head of it, chopped fine. The result was a soup so delicious it tasted almost like dessert at the same time as dinner. Both she and Angie were notorious for eating through half a pot of it before finally retiring their spoons.

"You'd better be here to give me a report," Angie said, cutting right to the point.

"I think you deserve that," Sarah agreed. She waited while Angie removed the soup from the microwave even before the timer buzzed. Sarah could understand that, too. She could never wait for it, either.

"So," Angie said, "did I give you good advice or bad?"

"Good. Some people might not think so if they saw where we are right now, but I'm telling you: good."

She filled Angie in on everything that had happened

since the last time they sat together in that office. Meanwhile Angie powered through her bowl and quickly heated another.

The door to the gym opened, and Angie's next client came in. He was a tall, gangly man with bright red hair and an immediate smile for Sarah.

"Hello, fellow ginger."

She laughed. "Hello." She started to stand, but Angie motioned her down.

"Go ahead and warm up," Angie told the client. "I'll be out in five."

The man nodded and left the two of them alone.

Angie lowered her voice. "So. You're both without jobs, but you're deeply in love, and you have me to thank for both."

Sarah smiled. "Something like that."

"When are you coming back to workout?"

"I'm not sure. Depends on..." Sarah rubbed her thumb and her third finger together, in the universal sign for money.

"You can always go on credit," Angie said.

"Not this time, but thank you. I know you have a business to run. I'm not going to be one of those dead-beat clients who keeps using you but never pays."

"Sarah, you know I don't think that about you."

"I know. And I appreciate that. But I'd feel better if I could pay as I go." Sarah stood and stepped toward the door. "And it'll happen—I know it will. Then I'll be back and you can kick my butt again."

Angie walked her to the front door. Then she gave Sarah

a hug. "I have a couple's discount, you know. Get your man in here, too. I'll be happy to boss you both around."

"I'll call you in the new year," Sarah promised. Then she waved to the tall redhead. He kept jumping rope, but gave her a nod.

"Thanks for the Crack," Angie said.

"Any time. Thanks for calling me a wuss. I needed it."

"Hey," Angie said with a smile, "whatever it takes."

"Hi, sweetheart." Her mother greeted her at the door wearing her traditional Christmas apron, the same one she had put on for holiday cooking for as long as Sarah could remember. The snowman on the front was looking a little tattered, but otherwise as cheerful as ever.

Sarah interrupted her father's football watching long enough to give him a hug, then carried her bag to her old bedroom. The room was still pink and white, the way she'd kept it since she was a little girl and even later in college. She still had her old canopy bed, too: her first experience in *Flourish* back when her parents could barely afford it. It had been a big deal then, and it still was to her. Even though she knew any other adult woman would look at her room and snicker.

Sarah set her bag on the floor, then lay on her bed for a few minutes, just soaking in the place. This was where she had studied her brains out night after night. Where she made lists and plans for her future.

Where she had tried again and again to call Joe on Christmas six years ago to find out what was going on.

That's when she finally took matters into her own hands and searched the public records. And when she had cried on Joe's behalf when she saw the notice about his mother.

A long time ago, Sarah thought. A long way to finally come around full circle.

Her mother knocked on the open door. She smiled at the sight of Sarah stretched out on the frilly bed.

"You still don't want something more modern?" her mother asked. "Something more grown up?"

"Absolutely not," Sarah answered.

She wondered if little boys ever felt that way about the race car beds they finally outgrew. She could think of a few men she had met who probably wouldn't mind sleeping in a bed frame shaped like a Ferrari.

"Dinner'll be ready in about an hour," her mother said. She came in and sat on the edge of Sarah's bed. "How's work been? How's *Joe*?" she added in an icy tone.

"Good...fine..." Sarah wondered if her mother could hear the falseness in her voice. She had meant to tell her about Joe right away, but somehow now didn't seem like the right moment.

Wuss, she could hear Angie say.

"Well, come out and talk to us. Your father'll turn off the game. We want to hear what you've been doing."

Sleeping with opposing counsel, declaring my love to opposing counsel, resigning from my case, losing my job, bombing out at interviews...

"Great," Sarah said. "Sounds great."

· · ·

"How's business, Dad?" Sarah wasn't just deflecting the attention from herself, she honestly wanted to know. Her parents had always included her in their money and work discussions, even when she was still too young to understand all the details. She grew up feeling like a partner in both of her parents' businesses.

"Oh, you know," her dad said, "always slow this time of year. But it'll pick up again in January—always does."

"How's all the equipment holding up?" Sarah asked.

"Mostly good. I'll probably have to upgrade some of it next year. I'll work it out."

Sarah could hear the worry in his voice, but there was no point in pressing it. She couldn't help him right now anyway.

"How's Grady been?" she asked.

"Meaner than ever," her father answered with a laugh.

Grady was his oldest employee. He'd been with Sarah's father almost as long as her mother.

"How about you, Mom?" Sarah asked. "Busy this month?"

Mrs. Henley gave a weary laugh. "Just like every year. Relatives come to town, holiday parties, so everybody needs their houses to look perfect ahead of time. Then all those cleanups from office parties—I've been working double-time for the past three weeks. But the money's good, so who's complaining? It's nice to be busy when your dad's work is slower."

That's how it had always been, Sarah thought: the two of them taking turns supporting the family, riding the highs and lows of the economy, always treating each other like equal partners in keeping the family afloat. It was why Sarah had always looked forward to playing her own part in it, helping her parents out with whatever money she could.

"But we want to hear about you!" her mother said. "You know everything about us. Come on, tell us what you've been doing."

Here it was, Sarah thought, her chance to tell them everything.

"Work's been...good," she began, testing the words on her tongue. "It's, you know, challenging..."

"Especially with that Joe Burke there, I'm sure," her mother added.

Now there's an understatement, Sarah thought. "Right..."

"Any word yet on the job turning into something more permanent?" her dad asked.

"Um, well, that's kind of interesting," Sarah said, again seeing her opening. "I think—" She paused to clear her throat. "There's some stuff going on with the case right now. I think my part of it might actually end a little earlier than I expected..."

She hated to lie to her parents, but it wasn't technically a lie, she told herself. Except for the word *might*.

"How much earlier?" her father wanted to know. "I thought you had at least five months guaranteed."

"Yeah, well, not exactly."

"So you'll be out of work again?" he asked, making no effort to hide his concern.

"Just until I find something else," Sarah said. "It's fine. I've already started interviewing."

"Well, that's smart," her mother said. "Better to be ready than sorry."

Sarah nodded. She hadn't exactly been living by that motto for the past few weeks.

On the other hand, she hadn't exactly been this happy in her personal life for the past several years.

"I bet that Joe Burke will be sorry to see you go," Sarah's mother said. "He should have been nicer to you in the first place."

"He's been nice lately, Mom," Sarah said. She couldn't bear to just sit there and hear Joe maligned, even though she still didn't feel ready to confess everything. She dreaded seeing the disappointment on her parents' faces when she explained that she lost her job because she had been doing something unethical. Not just *doing* something unethical, but been *caught* doing it.

Sarah's mother patted her hand. "Like I always said, you were too good for that man. I'm sure he always sees you as the one who got away."

"So," Sarah said, blatantly changing the subject, "what's our cookie schedule tomorrow? How many batches are we making?"

"I think at least seven this time," her mother said. "I have some new clients, so I want to make sure there's enough for everybody."

It was her holiday gift to her clients, which used to drive Sarah crazy. She argued for years that the clients should be giving their cleaning lady a year-end bonus, not the other way around. But her mother continued to think it was good business to bake treats for her customers, so Sarah had finally given in and simply offered to help. She had been her mother's chief cookie decorator for the past several Christmas Eves.

"Sarah, you going to be okay?" her dad asked. "With that job situation?"

"Yeah, Dad, I'm sure I'll be fine. The law business is the same as yours—really slow this time of year, but then people will start hiring again in January."

She tried to say it like she believed it. She had already lied to her parents enough.

42

Cookie baking was in full swing around noon when the doorbell rang.

"Want to get that, honey?" Sarah's mother asked. Her hands were currently buried deep in cookie dough. "I'll bet it's Nancy. I told her she could borrow my big cake pan."

"Sure," Sarah said, wiping her hands on her own traditional Christmas apron, the one with the sassy girl elf on the front, winking as she placed a huge star on the top of a tiny tree.

Sarah passed her father sitting in the living room, apparently too mesmerized by the football game to have heard the doorbell.

Sarah opened the door.

"Joe! Wh-what are you doing here?"

Within what seemed like seconds, Sarah's mother appeared behind her. Joined surprisingly quickly by her father. The best Sarah could do was give Joe a tentative smile and widen her eyes in warning.

Joe smiled easily and stuck out his hand. "Hi, Mrs. Henley. I'm Joe Burke."

If he hadn't gotten it from Sarah's expression before, the look of shock on her mother's face should have said it all. Joe glanced at Sarah for a quick confirmation, and she subtly shook her head.

"Mr. Henley, nice to meet you, sir."

Sarah's father had a sturdy handshake, but it looked like Joe could take it. Then all four of them stood around the doorway looking at each other.

"Merry Christmas," Joe said, handing Sarah's mother a box of chocolates.

"Merry..." But that was as far as Mrs. Henley got. She looked from Sarah to Joe, then asked him, "Did you...need to come in or something?"

"No, thank you," Joe said. "Actually, I was hoping to borrow your daughter for a little while, if that's all right."

"Something about the case?" Sarah's dad asked. "Seems unusual on Christmas Eve."

"No...not that," Joe said, again looking to Sarah. Once again she gave him a subtle shake of her head.

"I'll be back in a while," Sarah said, stripping off her apron and handing it to her mother. She grabbed a coat from the rack by the door. "I won't be gone too long. Just...some things we need to discuss."

"Are we supposed to ask him to dinner?" Sarah's mother asked her, as if Joe weren't standing right there.

"Um...sure," Sarah said. "Joe?"

"Sounds nice," he said. "Thank you."

Sarah gave him a look that she hoped conveyed how surrealistic the whole situation felt. Joe simply smiled back.

"So...shall we go?" she asked. She didn't wait for his answer, but already headed for his car parked at the curb.

Joe waited until they were out of earshot before muttering, "I take it you haven't mentioned me yet?"

"No, I was going to get to that."

"Or the fact that we're not working on that case anymore?"

"That, too," Sarah said.

"Liked your apron, by the way."

"Watch it, Burke."

"How's that Audi?" Sarah's father called from the door.

"Generally all right," Joe said, turning around to face him. "Tail lights keep going out, though."

"Probably the electrical," Sarah's father said.

"Probably so."

"You should get that looked at."

"Yes, sir," Joe answered. "I will."

He opened Sarah's door for her, no doubt feeling her parents' eyes still boring into his back, then he came around and got in and started the car. Sarah waved to her parents and Joe gave them a friendly nod.

"Your dad's not going back in the house to get his shotgun now, is he?"

"Nah, he's more of a bare-knuckle fighter."

"Good," Joe said. "Then I have a chance."

She suppressed her laughter until they drove away.

"Joe, what are you doing here?"

"Hold that thought." He cruised one more block before parking and shutting off the motor. Then he unbuckled his seatbelt, popped the release on Sarah's, and pulled her toward him for a proper greeting.

It had only been a little more than twenty-four hours since they last saw each other, but she didn't mind showing she missed him. And there was something wickedly appealing about steaming up his windows on a street in her old neighborhood.

"Are you here to steal me away from my parents and seduce me?" Sarah asked.

"Would you like me to?"

"Obviously." The Audi wasn't made for full makeout maneuvers, but they did their best.

When finally Sarah realized he probably shouldn't have his hand up her sweatshirt and inside her now unclasped bra while little kids skateboarded by, she slid away from him and readjusted her clothes.

"Seriously," she said, breathing a little too hard, "do you have a hotel room? Because I can probably be gone for an hour."

Joe started up the car.

SHE HAD GOTTEN SO USED to checking into hotels, she almost gave the clerk her name before Joe stepped up and asked for a room.

"How many nights, sir?" the clerk said.

Joe looked at Sarah. "Two, I think."

Sarah lifted her eyebrows. "So this isn't a quick drive-by, huh? You're actually here to spend Christmas with me?"

"Do you mind?"

"Yeah, Burke, I mind." She slipped her hand into his and leaned against him.

She felt almost giddy on their way to his room. It was like their first date out in public, back at that Italian restaurant in Seattle. Eons ago.

"You know, I meant to ask you something," Sarah said as they walked up the single flight of stairs. "Remember how you said you always booked a hotel room someplace else from me? But you didn't. I know you stayed at my hotel when I was sick—you said something about it."

"I moved over there," Joe said. "To take care of you."

Sarah shook her head. "Why was I still mad at you after that?"

"Probably because you have a good memory," Joe said.

He was just about to sweep his key card when Sarah remembered something else.

"I don't have a gift for you here. It's back in my apartment."

"No, it's not," Joe answered as he opened his door and pulled her into the room.

A laugh barely escaped her lips before Joe's mouth overtook them. Sarah liked him like this: hungry for her, happy, his hands already searching for bare skin and ridding her of her clothes. She'd made love to him in so many moods and under so many circumstances, but so far this was her recurring favorite: joyful and guilt-free. She didn't miss sneaking around at all.

Unless, she thought for a brief moment, that counted keeping Joe a secret from her parents.

She pressed her palms flat against his chest and made him stop what he was doing. Even though what he was doing was so unbelievably good.

"I have to tell them tonight."

"Okay."

"We both have to tell them."

"Right." Then he hoisted her over his shoulder and carried her laughing to the bed.

They lay sprawled and sweaty, limbs tangled and relaxed, while Sarah rehearsed what they should say.

"Mom, Dad, Joe and I have something to tell you—"

"No."

"Why not?"

"They don't know me. They don't want to hear anything from me. It's all got to come from you."

She groaned, but she knew he was right.

"Mom, Dad, I have some…pretty interesting news."

"No."

"Why not?" Sarah said. "Okay, fine. You come up with something and I'll criticize it."

"Mom, Dad," he began, "Joe's the greatest man I've ever met in my life, and I've agreed to marry him."

"Ha, ha. Try again."

"Mom, Dad, Joe flew back from his father's house and then drove all the way out here so he could propose to me today, and I said yes, because I love him more than anything and want to spend the rest of my life with him."

Sarah turned her head just enough to give Joe a single arched eyebrow. "Mothers don't appreciate it when you joke about that."

"Mr. and Mrs. Henley," Joe tried again, "I love your daughter more than anyone on this earth, and I would be honored if you would accept me as her husband."

Sarah rolled halfway up on top of him so she could look him in both eyes. She drilled a finger into his chest. "Burke, I'm not kidding. This isn't funny. You don't joke about stuff like that. My parents will have you on a skewer."

"If I'm joking, or if I'm telling the truth?"

"If you're joking," Sarah said, "then *I'll* have your head on a skewer."

Joe gently wrapped his hand around the finger sticking into his chest. "Sarah, I'm not joking."

She stared at him with steely eyes, then rolled all the way on top of him. She pinned his thighs beneath her knees and pushed her palms against his shoulders. Hovering over him now on all fours, like a dog who had flattened an intruder, she dipped her face down just an inch from his. All that was missing was the growl.

"*This* is your proposal?" she demanded.

"Yep."

"*This* is what you came up with while you drove to Fontana?"

"No, it sounded a lot better in the car."

A laugh erupted from her chest. "Well, let's hear that one!"

Now Joe was laughing, too. "Come on, Red, don't make me beg."

"Beg? I just want a decent proposal, man! Give it to me!"

"Sarah Henley, love of my life, will you please consent to marry me?"

"I'll think about it!"

She rolled off of him and pulled him with her. He covered her slim body with his.

"Sarah Henley," he said, smoothing the hair away from her temple and planting a soft kiss on her cheek, "please marry me. I love you."

"Much better," she said. She wrapped her arms around his waist and made sure as much of him was against as much of her. "I love you, Joe. Yes, I will marry you. I love you. Let's get married."

"I don't have a ring."

"Oh!" she cried, throwing up her hands in mock exasperation. "What happened to Mr. Strategy? Mr. I-Always-Plan-Ten-Moves-Ahead?"

"Yeah, well I need to discuss that with you," Joe answered, suddenly more serious than she expected. "That's the other reason I'm here. Something's come up."

43

Once she realized the discussion was going to need more than a few minutes, Sarah made a quick phone call to her mother.

"Hi. I just didn't want you to worry. Joe and I still have some things to go over. Sorry I left you with the cookies."

"It's fine," her mother said. "I'm almost done. Everything okay?"

"Everything's great," Sarah said, giving her new fiancé a gentle nudge with her knee. "We'll be back soon."

"So he really is coming to dinner."

"Yeah, Mom. But it'll be okay—I promise. Joe's a nice guy. I think you and Dad will really like him."

Sarah's mother scoffed. Sarah twisted away with her phone, hoping Joe hadn't heard that. But by the amused look he gave her, she knew he had.

"So the chocolates weren't enough?" he asked when she hung up.

"Good start, though. Truffles make a good impression. Okay, so back to it. You got the call."

"Yesterday. Message when I landed."

"Offering you a job."

She would have sounded more excited, but from Joe's attitude, she knew there had to be a catch.

"More than a job," Joe said. "A 'business opportunity.'"

Sarah lifted herself higher on Joe's chest so she could look him in the eye. "What kind of opportunity?"

Joe pulled up the blanket to cover her shoulders again. "It's the Rawlins firm. They're expanding. They have enough business in a few other states now, so they want to start opening up satellite offices. They're offering me the one in Texas."

"Texas?" She didn't have anything against the state, but it wasn't California.

"Build everything from the ground up," Joe said. "Find space to rent, hire the staff, bring in any attorneys I want. They'd feed me some files to begin with, but then I'd grow the firm on my own. With you, Sarah—I'd want you to be my partner."

She took a moment to let that sink in. "And they're okay with that?"

"We were all talking theoretically—you know how it is, nobody wants to act like it's a done deal. But I told them you're the best attorney I know, and I'd want you right there with me."

"And they...know about us?"

"Theoretically," Joe said. "I couldn't tell them you were

going to be my wife—I know how much you hate it when I act like you're a sure thing."

This time Sarah wasn't so gentle with the knee into his thigh.

"Husbands and wives work together in law firms all the time," Joe pointed out. "Boyfriends and girlfriends, boyfriends and boyfriends, girlfriends and girlfriends—"

"I get it."

"And we'd always be on the same side," he reminded her, "so no conflict of interest."

"But really, Joe? Texas?"

"It would be ours," he said. "A fresh start. Get out of this place and go build something new."

Sarah drummed her fingers against his chest. "When do you have to let them know?"

"End of the year."

"That's next week."

"I know," Joe said. "They were already considering someone else. I'm a late entry. But they said it's mine now, if I want it. That's why I came out here today instead of waiting till you got home. I wanted to give you as much time as possible to think about it."

Sarah blew out a breath. "I don't know..."

"Think it over," Joe said. "Obviously I'm not making a move without you."

Sarah lifted her head and looked at him. "Were you going to propose to me anyway?"

Joe smiled and wrapped his arms around her more tightly. "What do you think?"

"So what was your original strategy?" Sarah asked. "Flash mob? Proposal on the score board at halftime?"

"Get you a ring, for one thing," he said. "Probably take you with me to pick it out."

"Oh, yeah? Where?"

"Our place," Joe said.

Sarah studied him for a moment before cracking a smile. "Walmart?"

"Of course," Joe said. "Where else?"

SARAH HELD TIGHTLY to Joe's hand as the two of them walked back into her parents' house.

That got a raised eyebrow from her father, but no other comment. Then Sarah's mother came into the living room.

She stared at their clasped hands for a moment, then lifted her gaze to her daughter's face. And then much to Sarah's surprise, she smiled. "You don't say."

Sarah tilted her head and squinted at her, not really sure her mother understood.

But when Mrs. Henley set her hands on her hips and turned to her husband and said, "What do you think about that, Gene?" Sarah knew her mother hadn't missed a thing.

Although her father still needed to catch up.

"You kids together now or something?" he asked.

"It's a long story," Sarah said on a sigh. "But yes. In fact, Joe's just asked me to marry him."

Sarah's mother let out a yelp of glee or surprise, Sarah wasn't sure which. Then she hurried across the room to fold Joe in her sturdy embrace.

"You were a stupid, stupid man," she scolded him, holding his face now between her hands and looking him in the eye. "But I'm glad to see you came to your senses. Our Sarah's a prize, isn't she?"

"Yes, ma'am, I was," Joe said, "and yes, ma'am, she is."

Sarah offered him a sly smile to let him know he was doing well.

Sarah's father rose from the couch and shook Joe's hand. Then got to the most important issue. "You a football fan?"

Sarah and her mother rolled their eyes at each other.

"You bet," Joe said.

"Then if we're done here for now..." Sarah's father said.

"Go right ahead, Dad." Sarah whispered to Joe, "He likes the Jets."

"That game's already over," Sarah's father said. "Don't worry, Joe and I'll get along fine."

Sarah followed her mother back into the kitchen. Where she had a feeling she knew what was coming.

Her mother pointed a stern finger at the kitchen table. "You sit right down there, young lady, and don't you leave out a thing."

arah spent a restless night staring up at the pink canopy above her bed. Joe had left around eleven, and Sarah still lay awake two hours later.

Texas.

A clean slate.

Jobs, for heaven's sake. Something neither of them could be guaranteed otherwise.

But the more she thought about it, the more she analyzed the pros and the cons and every little nuance her brain could manufacture, the more one single fact continued to nag at her:

She felt like she would be running away.

Running away from her problems, running away from what she'd done—even running away from the regular day-to-day life she and Joe had established over the past few weeks. Texas would feel exotic and exciting and stressful for a while. They'd both have to study for and take the Texas bar exam, while also attending to every detail of starting a new law firm. She knew she and Joe were up to the challenge, but she wasn't sure it was the *right* challenge. That was bothering her, too.

Finally as the clock pushed closer to two, Sarah gave up trying to sleep. She got out of bed and dressed, then quietly left the house.

She hated to wake anyone else along that hallway, but Joe didn't answer her first soft knock. She knocked again, harder. She thought about trying to convince the desk clerk she was the occupant's fiancée and he had just forgotten to give her a key, when finally the door opened.

Joe squinted out at her. Then he smiled and motioned her inside.

Sarah followed him to the bed, kicked off her shoes, and climbed in next to him wearing her Utah sweats. She snuggled down under the covers and Joe drew her in closer until their faces were an inch apart.

"Let's hear it, Red," he said sleepily.

"I don't like it."

"Which part?"

"The Texas part," she said. "The building something for someone else part. Why should we do that? If we're going to put in all the effort to start a law firm, let's do it for us. Here in California. Make something for you and me."

Joe held her at the small of her back. He laid a kiss on her lips, then pulled her hips into his and angled her knee over his leg. It was how they liked to sleep sometimes, and Sarah realized that was exactly what was happening: Joe was falling back asleep.

She poked him. "Joe."

"Hm?"

"So what do you think?"

"I think you're right."

"You do?"

"Sure."

She poked him again.

He peeked open one eye and smiled. "What?"

"Are you just yessing me so I'll let you go back to sleep?"

"No. I'm with you, Sarah. Here, there, anywhere."

"But you think it's a good idea, right? That we should start our own firm?"

"I think it's a great idea. Now shhh. I'm with my girlfriend."

Sarah waited a minute more, then poked him again.

This time Joe yanked her underneath him and straddled her from above as he smothered her laughter with a kiss.

"What is it, Henley?" he growled.

"I want to marry you."

"Okay."

"I want to be your business partner."

"Okay."

"So we have a deal?" She held out her hand.

"The law firm and marriage of Burke and Henley," he said, shaking her hand. "Deal."

"Henley and Burke," she corrected him.

"Burke is first alphabetically," Joe pointed out. "It'll show up sooner on lists."

"Really, Eight? Because I think Henley and Burke sounds better."

"Oh, Seven, that's a low blow."

Sarah laughed again. "All right, tell you what—why don't we flip for it? One coin, and we go with whatever it says. No arguments from either of us."

Joe leaned over and kissed her. "You're a tough one, Henley."

"I know."

"Tough and sexy and beautiful."

"Why, thank you."

"And smart," Joe added. "Let's not forget that."

"Thank you. Same to you." Sarah wrapped her legs around his waist and made him kiss her some more.

Then she let him go and leapt out of bed and went in search of a coin.

Sarah and Joe's story continues in the short story RIGHT ON TIME, available now in ebook. You can download it for free from my website at: https://robinbrande.com/products/right-on-time-love-proof-sequel. At checkout, use the discount code LOVEPROOF2.

And as another bonus, read on for the Crack Soup recipe. Enjoy!

- 1/4 cup olive oil
- 2 onions, peeled and chopped
- 2 carrots, peeled and chopped
- 2 celery stalks (I always use those tender ones from the very middle of a celery bunch—the ones with leaves still on the top. They're the most flavorful. Don't feel shy or bad about throwing the rest of the celery stalks away. Think of them as just the packaging.)
- A little salt & pepper (or a lot, depending on what you like)
- 1 bunch parsley, washed and chopped, thick stems discarded (I know you think parsley is just a garnish, but it's NOT. I never understood that until I made this soup. Parsley is essential and worthy, so please take me seriously when I say use the whole bunch.)
- 3 green cabbage leaves, chopped
- 1 bunch chard, washed and chopped (I like rainbow chard because it has that pretty red, but Swiss or green chard will do)
- ¼ cup tomato paste
- 2 cans cannellini or other white beans (but I like cannellini best)

Heat about half of the olive oil in a deep pot over medium heat. Add half each of the chopped onions, carrots, and celery, and cook, stirring occasionally, until they soften (about 10 minutes). Add the remaining oil and repeat the process, seasoning with salt and pepper as you go. Once those ingredients have softened, add the parsley, cabbage, and chard, and cook, stirring occasionally, until everything is softened but not browned.

Add the tomato paste and stir. Add one can of beans as-is, then partially mash the other can of beans before adding (you can do this by draining the can into a colander, then mashing the beans against the mesh with a spoon). Once all the beans are in, add just enough water to make the whole mixture thick like a stew, and not too watery.

Keep cooking, tasting, and seasoning as necessary, until all the vegetables are very tender and the soup is hot. I've cooked it anywhere from half an hour to an hour. It just sits there, and you stir it every now and then until you can't stand it anymore and MUST eat it.

Serve with some nice crusty bread. You won't need a salad— the soup IS the salad. It's also dessert. You'll understand once you taste it.

ABOUT THE AUTHOR

Robin Brande is an award-winning author, former trial attorney, black belt in martial arts, Reiki Master, and wilderness medic. Her outdoor adventures range from the Rocky Mountains to the Alps to Iceland.

She writes in multiple genres, including mystery, adventure, fantasy, science fiction, young adult, romance, and self-help.

For more information:
https://robinbrande.com/

For information about new releases, along with special discounts on books and merchandise, subscribe to the Robin Brande newsletter: https://robinbrande.com/ pages/subscribe.